Tiers of Joy

LG CAMPBELL

Acknowledgements

This book is very close to my heart and I think it may be close to a lot of people's hearts.

I poured my heart and soul into this book; it's something I have wanted to write for a really long time. I hope you love it just as much as I enjoyed writing it. I hope this story makes you laugh, cry, and hits you with all of the emotion I poured into writing it.

To Robyn Greenwood, my PA, my friend, and my ball buster: I could not have written this book without your help. I could not have written it without you cracking the whip, without you organising practically everything for me. I would have crumbled and most certainly had a meltdown. You are an absolute godsend. Thank you my lovely.

To each and every one of you that buys and reads any of my books, it goes without saying that I owe you all a huge thank you from the bottom of my heart. I just, well, there are no words. Without you, authors would just be weirdos who write fucked up stories because the voices tell them too.

Thank you to all of my family, friends, readers, and bloggers who have supported me from the start and who continue to do so with each book.

To my long suffering husband: you are my world, my number one supporter, and I love you.

Prologue

"What about this one?" I ask, pointing to the computer screen.

"Yeah, I like it. You know we need another twenty thousand pounds until we can actually move out there and buy a place like that." Jay reminds me.

"I know, I know, but there's no harm in looking. I wish we could move there now. I wish we could get away from this place, so you can finally leave the job you hate so much it's making you ill." I state, resting my head on his shoulder.

Jay kisses my head as I cuddle in further, sitting on his lap on his office chair.

We've been dreaming for so long about selling up and moving to Nova Scotia for a quieter life. I will open up my own little bakery and Jay will start his boat restoration company. He wants to make the hobby he loves into his dream job.

He currently works in the city for his dad's insurance company and he hates it. His father never gave him a chance to do what he wanted; he was expected to work for his father's company. He was told that his dream job was beneath him and a hobby and it was to stay that way.

Jay and I have been together since high school but I was never good enough for his parents. I didn't want a high powered stressful job. I've always done what I love, and that's baking. I currently work in the kitchen at a nursery; it isn't great pay, but I love baking treats for the kids and whenever there's a birthday I make a birthday cake. I even bake at home in my spare time for friends and family. I never really make any extra money though because I don't like charging people. I just love to bake.

We eloped when we were eighteen and got married in Gretna Green without telling his parents. Jay always fought his parents when it came to me. He said he could handle working a job he hates if it meant coming home to me every night.

Now the stress of the job is becoming too much. He's constantly exhausted, losing weight, and losing his appetite. I've told him to go to the doctor but he insists that he will feel a thousand times better when we go away on our holiday.

"Have you eaten today?" I ask.

He sighs.

"I tried eating some toast this morning but it just made me feel worse. I binned it." He yawns.

I sit up and cup his face in my hands.

"Jay, I'm ringing the doctor. This is getting silly now. You need to see a doctor. Please, for me." I beg.

Jay gives me a nod and I smile and kiss him softly.

"Thank you. I quite like having you around and I'm not ready to be a widow at twenty-three. We have so many more years of me nagging you ahead of us." I tease.

"I can't wait." Jay rolls his eyes.

"I'm sure it's nothing. It's probably low iron or at the very worst a stomach ulcer, but I need you fit and healthy if we're going to live out our dreams. I don't think I could live out my dream without you." I kiss him softly.

He cups my face and whispers across my lips.

"I will be with you forever until we are old and grey. I'll be tripping over my saggy balls and you'll be tripping over your saggy tits." He jokes.

I slap his chest and laugh.

"Oh you're such a romantic!"

"I'm joking! I will love you always, saggy tits and all."

We're sitting in the doctors' waiting area, waiting for Jay to be seen. They've done some tests and a full body scan. Thankfully his job comes with private health care so the tests have been done quickly. The doctor got the results back and asked him to come in. I'm hoping it's nothing too serious because I can tell Jay is secretly worried. He hasn't let go of my hand the entire time. The last time he did this was when we told his father we were married.

"Mr Tucker?" The doctor calls.

I give Jay a small smile and walk with him into the doctor's office.

"Please take a seat." He gestures.

We sit, Jay still holding my hand in his.

"We have your results back." He pauses while looking over the file in his hand.

"I'm dreadfully sorry Mr Tucker, you have cancer." He says sympathetically.

I stop breathing. Cancer. He has cancer. I feel my body start to shake.

"When can I start treatment?" Jay asks, his

voice gravelly.

His grip on my hand tightens. We both look at the doctor, waiting for a response.

"I'm sorry Mr Tucker, it's terminal. We suspect that it started in your liver, but it has spread to your stomach and other organs."

"No. You've made a mistake, he's only twenty-three. You must have picked up someone else's file. He has his whole life ahead of him. We're moving to Nova Scotia to live our dream. No, this isn't right. There's been a mix up, check your files!" I demand.

"I'm sorry Mrs Tucker. I have the correct file, there has been no mix up. Now Mr Tucker, while we can't give you treatment to prolong your life, we can give you medication so you can live as comfortably as possible." He states.

I sob, the pain in my chest makes it hard to breath.

"How long do I have?" Jay asks.

The doctor sighs.

"I'm afraid maybe a few months at most."

Jay lets go of my hand and puts his face in his hands. I jump up and wrap my arms around him, holding him tight.

Chapter One

It has been nine weeks since we were told the news that Jay has cancer. It's been nine weeks of helplessly watching the man I love, my world, slowly and painfully dying. Jay insisted on going into a hospice. He said I shouldn't have to take care of him and see him this way. I refused. I wanted him here at home with me; I wasn't losing a minute with him. I'm his wife. I will never leave his side, I will be the one to care for him.

I'm sitting downstairs in our little house, staring out of the patio doors. The community nurse is upstairs with him. She's giving him his pain medication and checking him over.

Our old school friend Sally brings me a cup of tea.

"Thanks." I mutter.

I've lost count of how many cups of tea people have made me. It's like they think it's going to magically make this all okay. This will never be okay.

"I'm going to the supermarket; do you need me to get you anything?" She ask softly.

"No, I'm good." I answer numbly.

"You need to eat Esme. Your cupboards and fridge are bare. When was the last time you ate something?" She asks.

I don't answer, I just shrug.

She sighs.

"I will get you some food at the shop." She squeezes my shoulder and then leaves.

I wait for the nurse to leave, anxious that I'm not with Jay. I'm scared every moment I'm not with him. I don't want him to die without me there. He can't be alone, he needs to hold my hand. I don't want him to be scared.

"Mrs Tucker?" The nurse calls as she reaches the bottom of the stairs, I snap out of my thoughts and wipe away the tears that were falling.

"Yes, sorry." I apologise and force a smile.

"He's comfortable now. His blood pressure has dropped and his breathing has slowed. I'm sorry, I don't think he has long left. Do you want me to stay? I'm technically off shift from now, but this part can be distressing and I'd understand if you didn't want to watch." She says softly.

I shake my head.

"No, I want to be with him."

"Okay, do you need me to call his family or your family for support?" She asks kindly.

"No. His parents are abroad and I have no family." I inform her.

She nods.

"Okay. Well I'm going to leave you my personal number. If you need anything, call me." She squeezes my arm and leaves.

I look up the stairs and take a deep breath. I wipe away my tears and walk upstairs to Jay.

I lay down on the bed with him, holding his hand in mine.

"You know this is a very dramatic way to get a few days off of work." I try and joke.

Jay's eyes come to mine. His arm shakes as he lifts my hand to his mouth. He places a kiss on my hand.

"You always said that job would be the death of me." He rasps, struggling for breath.

I let out a small laugh and sob. I can no longer hold back my tears,

Jays eyes close.

"I'm scared." He whispers.

Holding his hand in mine I lean in and whisper in his ear.

"Don't be scared, I'm here. I will always be here holding your hand. I promise I will never let go. I love you Jay, always and forever." I sob.

"Always and forever." Jay breathes.

He doesn't say anything after that. I lay with him, never letting his hand go. I watch as his breathing happens less and less. I watch until it stops altogether.

"Jay?" I whisper.

"Jay." I whisper again.

I lean forward and place a soft kiss on his lips.

"Forever and always." I whisper.

I make the call to the nurse. She arrives and makes the necessary calls.

I call the hotel his parents are staying at and take a deep breath, waiting for the call to be connected.

"Hello?" His father answers.

"Hello Frank. It's Esme...I...I...he's gone." I sob.

There's silence on the phone. I hear Wendy, Jay's mother, take the phone.

"Hello? What's going on?" She asks.

"Wendy," I sniff, "he's gone." I whisper.

"Thank you for contacting us Esme. We will fly back immediately." She rushes out, trying to hold it together. I hear her voice waiver with emotion.

"Speak soon." I say before disconnecting.

His parents never showed emotion; they saw it as weak and improper to cause a scene.

I sit here sobbing and holding my chest. I feel like someone has come and ripped my heart apart.

I watch as the men came to take Jay away. I want to stop them, to scream at them for taking him away. Sally comes back with the shopping. Her face pales and she drops the bags of shopping and runs straight to me, tears running down her face.

"Oh god Esme, why didn't you call me?" She sobs, hugging me tight.

I don't say anything. My eyes are fixed on Jay's body as it's placed in the back of the black ambulance.

As the ambulance pulls off I crumble, unable to hold myself up any longer. My body wracks with tears at the pain, the loss. It's just too much. I've lost my world, my soul mate. Life is nothing without him in it.

The days that followed Sally stayed with me, refusing to leave my side. I just stayed in bed, hugging Jay's pillow and wearing his football shirt. I refused to eat, I refused to leave the bed. I was staying there with him. I could still smell him.

Every time I woke, I woke crying, the memory hitting me that I'd lost him.

There's a knock at the bedroom door and in walks in Jay's father.

I don't say anything, I just look at him. He gives me a brief smile and perches himself on the edge of the bed.

"You know, Jay always used to use humour to lighten the darker times. I wish I could do that for you now." He sighs. "I know I failed as a father, I know I made him unhappy. You were the only thing in his life that brought him happiness. I know you may not see it this way, but I thought what I was doing was the best for him. I know I was wrong. I was too damn stubborn to believe it." He looks at me. I don't say anything, I just stare blankly.

"I'm sorry Esme. I'm sorry; I should have listened to my son. Now, well, now it's too late. I should've never gone on that business trip. I should've never left him. I will forever live with that guilt. I owe you a lifetime of gratitude for making my son's life, one full of love and happiness." He pats my hand and then stands to leave.

"Frank." I call out. He stops and turns to face me.

"He never hated you, despite it all. You were his father, he loved you." I state.

He nods.

"Thank you Esme. However true that may be, you were his world, and he would never want to see you suffering like this." He states before walking out and closing the door behind him.

I stayed in bed until the day of the funeral. I left the arrangements to his parents.

Sally hangs my black dress on the wardrobe door for me. I stand in the shower, the tears silently falling. I wash with Jay's bodywash and shampoo, needing him, missing him. I stand in the bathroom wrapped in a towel, looking in the bathroom cabinet and seeing his aftershave. I grab it and smell it. I close my eyes and let out a sob.

"Jay." I whisper.

I walk into the bedroom. Sally is waiting for me. She helps me get dressed and does my hair for me. I just sit numbly, staring out of the window.

"There, all done. Here, drink this. You're going to need it today." She hands me a glass of scotch.

She has one too.

"To Jay," She mumbles before downing the scotch.

I down it too, the liquid burning my throat. I cough.

We both look out of the window and see the hearse pull up. Sally takes a deep breath.

"You ready?" She asks.

I don't say anything. I stand and walk downstairs and out of the front door. Sally locks up behind me.

White roses cover his coffin. A flowered reef saying son lays alongside it. I rest my forehead and press my palm against the glass.

"Forever and always Jay." I whisper.

Sally places her arms around me and guides me to the car.

"Come on sweetie." She soothes.

I don't speak or look at anyone at the funeral. My eyes never leave the coffin. As the curtains go around the coffin, panic sets in.

"No! No!" I cry. Jumping up out of my chair I go to the coffin: to Jay.

I drape myself over the coffin. Sally tries to pull me from him.

"Come on sweetie."

"No! I'm not ready, I can't say goodbye. He was supposed to be my forever and always! He lied. He promised me." I cry.

"He promised" I whisper.

Sally, with tears streaming down her face, envelopes me in her arms and cries with me.

Everyone else leaves, we are completely alone. Sally leans back and wipes her tears.

"You have to say goodbye Esme. I'm sorry but you do. He's gone, but his memory will live with you forever and always." She squeezes my hand.

"Give me a minute?" I ask.

She nods and leaves me alone.

I place my hand on the coffin and wipe my tears.

"I wish I could hold you. I wish this were all a horrible nightmare. I don't know what to do without you. My entire life is you. I'm not sure who I am without you. I will love you forever and always. Sleep tight Jay."

Chapter Two

The months that followed I was like a robot; I wasn't living, I merely existed. I didn't know how to live without Jay. Sally helped me as much as she could, but I wasn't myself. I'd lost the other part of me and all I felt was emptiness.

It's a Sunday afternoon and I'm still in my pyjamas, watching Jay's favourite films. The curtains are closed and empty takeaway cartons and wine bottles fill the coffee table.

The doorbell rings and I shuffle towards the door, expecting it to be Sally. I open the door and am surprised to see Frank, Jay's father, standing in front of me.

"Esme, can I come in?" He asks.

I stand to the side and let him in. He walks into the lounge and I don't miss the shock on his face at the state of the place.

I sit down, not caring, and press play to continue watching the movie.

"Esme, can I talk to you for a moment?" He presses pause on the TV.

I turn to him as he takes a seat.

"I know you're hurting. Believe me, I know... but Jay wouldn't want this for you. He would want you to live your life, not mourn him." He says gently.

"What would you know about your son? You barely spoke to him unless it was to do with the business. You hated him and I being together, so why would you give a shit?!" I snap.

"I deserve that, I know I do. Jay came to see me after he was diagnosed."

That news has me sitting up straight.

"What?" I ask in disbelief.

"He came to the office. He told me about the diagnosis. We talked, cleared up a lot of things. We even hugged." He smiles.

My eyes are wide. I don't think Frank has ever hugged Jay in his entire life.

"Anyway, he asked me to give you this." He pulls out a white envelope.

I take it and run my fingers over Jay's handwriting.

"He asked me to give it to you a few months

after the funeral. He wanted to give you some time. He said to tell you that he knows you're sad and angry, but you need to stop wallowing. You are to read that letter and do as it says." He states with a smile.

"I am not wallowing." I defend.

"He said you would say that too. He said to tell you that if you don't read the letter he will haunt you for eternity and...I apologise for this, but he insisted I say it. He will haunt you for eternity and laugh every time you trip over your saggy tits." Frank blushes.

I smile a genuine smile for the first time in months.

"Don't worry yourself about saying that, Frank. We always said we would grow old together, that he'd be tripping over his saggy balls and me...my...well...you know." I say, feeling warm in my chest at the memory.

"Yes, well, you two always did have an odd sense of humour." He smiles.

He pauses for a moment and then turns serious.

"There's something else you should know, I'm divorcing Wendy. For too long I stayed quiet with her, but when Jay became ill it was the final straw. She didn't even shed a tear. I will forever pay for my mistakes with Jay, but I have learnt from my own son that life is far too precious and short to be unhappy. For Jay's sake I wish I had grown the balls sooner." He sighs.

Shocked by his statement I reach out and squeeze his hand. He gives me a warm smile.

"It's sad that it takes losing someone you love to realise what's important." He says patting my hand.

"Now I must go. If you need anything Esme, call me. I made a promise to Jay that I would look out for you and while I let him down all of those other times, I will not do it now." He says while standing to leave.

"I will see myself out." He leaves me staring at the letter from Jay.

My hands shake as I open it. I unfold the letter and take a deep breath and large sip of wine.

My Esme,

I know you're hurting and I know you miss me. I'm a loveable guy, of course you would. God, believe me when I say that even beyond the grave I know I will miss you.

You're surprised about my dad right? Yeah, me too. See, I came from some good after all.

Anyway, I know you. I know that you'll be sitting there now in your teddy bear pyjamas, probably surviving off of takeaways and wine. I'm right, aren't I?

I would be doing the same if I lost you. I'd be wearing your teddy bear pyjamas too.

I laugh and wipe away the tears that are falling.

I am asking you, no, I'm begging you to go and live your life. Go and live your dream; own that bakery in Nova Scotia. Go meet the second man of your dreams, because let's face there ain't no one that can compete with me; I'm in a league of my own.

You'll notice on the back of this letter there are some bank account details. I had them put the account in you your name. There's enough money for you to go live your dream, our dream. I had an insurance policy with the company and I had Dad make sure it got paid into this account for you. So go live our dream for me, but most importantly, live it for you. Go and open your bakery. Share your love of baking with the people of Nova Scotia.

So stop crying those sad tears. Go, be happy, build a new life, and cry tiers of joy! (See what I did there?) I love you more than I can ever express. Promise me you'll go and live your life and be happy?

We didn't get the forever we had planned, but I will never stop loving you.

Forever and Always.

Jay

Xxxxx

I wipe the tears that are falling and turn the letter over to see the bank information. I fire up my laptop and log in using the details given.

Then the balance appears.

"Holy fuck Jay." I whisper,

Staring at me is a balance of seven hundred and fifty thousand pounds. I grab my phone and text Sally to come over immediately.

I sit staring at the screen, blinking and wondering if it's a mistake, if I am seeing it wrong.

The doorbell goes and I answer the door to a panting Sally, holding her side.

"What…huh…is…huh…the…matter?" She puffs out.

"Shit, did you run here?" I ask.

"You text me saying there was an emergency! Of course I ran here!"

She follows me into the lounge and scrunches her nose up in disgust.

"Jesus Esme! It's like walking into a teenage boy's bedroom, just without the wank tissues." She says brushing down the sofa like it's covered in dirt.

"Shhhh okay. Just look." I point to the screen.

Sally's eyes squint. As soon as she sees the balance they go wide.

"What the fuck is this?!" She screeches.

I hand her the letter and watch the tears fill her eyes.

"Oh my god Esme." She sniffles.

"I know. His dad came over and gave me it." I state.

I down some more wine from the bottle. Sally snatches it from me and drinks some herself.

"Well, I'm going to miss you like crazy. You know that, right?" She says and then drinks more wine.

I snatch the bottle back and drink some more.

"I can't go to Nova Scotia." I point out.

"Jay wanted you too. You've wanted to ever since I can remember. Now you actually have the chance to go! Do it. You have to go." Sally points out.

"It's not the same dream without Jay living it with me." I say, drinking more wine.

"So make it your new dream. I mean, this clearly isn't working for you. Jay has been gone nearly six months. You need to start living your life again. Eating takeout, not washing your hair for days, drinking your body weight in wine, and sitting in complete darkness, is not living. I already watched one of my best friends fade away, don't make me watch you fade away too." Sally pleads.

I bite my thumb nail anxiously. I look at the

balance again. I close my eyes and take a deep breath and nod.

"Let's just see what property there is for now. I doubt there will be anything like I dreamt. There's no harm in looking though, right?" I ask. Opening my eyes I see Sally already has my laptop and is searching.

"Esme, look." She says, turning the laptop to face me.

On the screen is a cute wooden shop painted lemon yellow with white features. A cute little sign hangs outside. Sally scrolls through the pictures; it's perfect.

"The interior needs updating but you can get someone in to do that. Oh and it has a two bedroom apartment above it. The price is $240,000 CAD. Get your phone out and google the exchange rate." She orders.

I type it into my phone and search.

"140,400 pounds." I state.

"Oh Esme, you have to do it! You have to go for it. You have more than enough money to get you started. You have plenty of money to refurbish it."

My heart is racing. I know I could do it; I have the money. I just don't know if I have the strength. It's not even being on my own that scares me; I had no parents or family growing up,

I can survive on my own. It's that I was done surviving on my own. I was no longer just surviving, I was living my life with Jay. I don't know how to live my life without him. I hated my life before him and I never want to go back to that.

Sally holds my hand in hers and gives it a gentle squeeze.

"Let me ring the estate agent and see what the situation is. You need to look into the visa thing as well and laws on buying a property over there. This isn't an instant decision Esme. Don't panic, okay? We will take it one step at a time." She comforts.

I nod and breathe a sigh of relief. I can do one step at a time.

Sally checks the time difference and calls the estate agent. I sit holding Jays letter, tracing his writing with my fingers. God, I miss him so much it hurts.

Sally comes back in after being on the phone. Her eyes are alight with excitement.

"So it's been empty a while; the family moved states. The estate agent said it's in a prime high street location! There is no other bakery in town apart from the counter in the large supermarket which is two towns over. She said she will email you the paperwork, and also all of the contacts you need to get in touch with for your visa." Sally says, bringing up my email inbox. There is the email from the estate agent.

"She said it could take a few months to go through but you can place an offer now if you'd like?" Sally asks.

I shake my head.

"No, I need to think some more. Bookmark it for me and I will look later. I'm going to bed. Do you mind seeing yourself out?" I ask as I pick up the laptop, the letter, and the wine.

"It's 6pm Esme." Sally points to the clock.

"I know but I'm tired." I say as I walk upstairs. I just want to be alone and shut everything and everyone out.

Sally doesn't say anymore. I hear her leave and curl up in bed and cry myself to sleep.

I awake to the room covered in darkness. I switch on the lamp and see it's 1am. I read through Jay's letter again and again.

"How am I supposed to be happy without you?" I ask the empty room.

I sigh and open my laptop. There on the screen is the bakery. I lay staring at it for I don't know how long.

"Fine Jay, you win. I will try but I'm not making any promises." I say before picking up my phone.

I call the estate agent and bite my thumbnail

nervously, waiting for her to pick up.

"Hello?" She answers cautiously.

"Umm hi, I'm Esme. My friend rang earlier about the shop." I state.

"Oh yes, I'm Cassie. It's good to speak with you. Sorry, it's late here. I don't normally get calls after eight." She says. I hear her moving around.

"Oh god, I am so sorry! I didn't even think about what time it is there. Have I woken you?" I apologise.

"No, no. You caught me just before I was taking myself off to bed. Did you want some more information? I can ask my son to help me do a virtual tour of the place tomorrow if you'd like?" She offers kindly.

"The video would be great, but the reason I'm calling is because, well, I'd like to take the place. I'm happy to pay the asking price too." I breathe out. My heart feels like it's about to beat out of my chest.

"Oh yes. Yes of course, that will be fine. Let me email you the forms you need to fill in. If there's anything else you need help with please just give me a ring. I will be in touch soon." She says excitedly.

"Speak soon. Thank you Cassie." I say before disconnecting,

"Well I did it, are you happy now?" I sigh.

The laptop pings with the email. I click it open and fill in the form. I watch the mouse hovering over the send button.

"Fuck it." I breathe out and click send.

I just lay in the dark, unable to sleep. I can't stop thinking about the bakery, about Jay, and wondering how the hell I'm going to do this on my own without him by my side.

Over the next few days I contact the people on the list to get the ball rolling. Our house is rented so I have no worries about having to sell it. I start by selling lots of my furniture. I'm left with a chair and the bed. I know it's going to take a few months to all go through, but I figured I may as well start.

Now there is just Jay's things to go through. I can't do it on my own so I call Sally.

She doesn't let me down. She turns up with two bottles of wine, a box of tissues, and a bag full of chocolate.

I'm sitting on my bed as Sally pulls Jay's clothes from the wardrobe.

"No not that. It was his favourite hoodie." I yell, jumping off of the bed and snatching it out of her hands and putting it on.

"You don't have to wear it. It's August and

it's twenty-nine degrees! I'm not about to rugby tackle it from you." She states.

I take it off and fold it, placing in the keep pile.

Sally keeps pulling out items of clothing and I keep taking them. Come the end and the keep pile is bigger than the donations pile.

"Esme, the only thing in the donation pile is Jay's hideous Christmas jumper from his aunt, and his 'Where's Wally' costume from Halloween. You need to give some of that away." She says pointing the pile of clothes.

I look to the pile and look back at her.

"I can wear his t-shirts and hoodies." I state.

She sighs and shakes her head.

"You can. However you can't wear his jeans and trousers." She points out.

Sulking I hand her the jeans and trousers.

"Now pass me his trainers and shoes." She holds out her hand.

"But." I start to protest but Sally just shakes her head.

"You're not going to be wearing them! He was five shoes sizes bigger than you." She laughs.

I nibble on my thumb and shrug, refusing to admit that she's right.

"Now pick two t-shirts and two hoodies

that you want to keep. The rest will go to the charity shop. I will not let you take more than that. I can't have my best friend moving to a new country wearing men's clothes." She holds out her hand, waiting for them.

I pick the ones I want, Jay's favourites, and hand her the rest. I stare at the bare space in the wardrobe and sniffle, trying to hold back my tears. Sally moves towards me and holds me in her arms.

"It feels like we're erasing him from my life." I cry.

"Oh hun, we could never do that. This isn't Jay; these are just his belongings. He will forever be in your heart. You're keeping the important things of his. Jay could never be erased; he was far too loud and annoying to let anyone forget him." She smiles.

I wipe my tears and smile, nodding. I know she's right.

We sort through all of Jay's belongings and stack them by the front door ready to take to the charity shop. There's just two black sacks and two boxes. That's it. That's all there is to show for his life.

Sally helps me box up the pictures and things I want to take with me.

After a long day and night going through the whole house, it looks bare.

"You know we could have done this in like a months time. Are you sure you're going to be okay living like this until everything is finalised?" She asks, her voice echoing around the empty room.

"Yeah, I will be just fine." I smile.

Chapter Three

It took nearly three months to get all of the paperwork sorted and finalise the sale. Today is the day I'm flying out. I paid extra so I could take three suitcases. My life is all packed away, ready to take with me.

The butterflies swamp my belly. I feel sick with nerves while I'm waiting for Sally to pick me up to take me to the airport.

"Well this is it Jay, I'm doing it. God I wish you could hold me right now, you'd keep me calm." I say to the empty house.

I check my plane ticket. One way from Heathrow to Halifax Nova Scotia. I check I have my passport. I've done this four times already. The doorbell rings, stopping me from checking a fifth time.

I open the door and Sally barges in.

"Are you ready? Now, have you checked you passport and ticket?" She asks. I give her a look.

"Only about fifty times. I'm crapping my pants Sally. What if no one likes me? What if I put my foot in it somehow and offend the whole town? You know I have a habit of doing that." I whine.

"Yes, I remember that last town you pissed off that chased you down with their pitchforks." Sally says sarcastically.

"You know what I mean. Jay would stop me or at least rescue me somehow. Now I don't have him to do that. This could be a disaster." I sigh, sitting on my case.

Sally perches next to me and wraps her arm around me.

"It'll be fine, I promise. You have every right to be nervous and scared but you've wanted this for so long. Don't write it off before you've even tried."

I sigh and nod, knowing she's right. God damn it! I hate it when she's right.

"Anyway, if all else fails, you just sell up and come back. You won't fail though because you are relentless and never give up." Sally smiles and stands, clapping her hands. "Right, let's go, can't have you missing your plane."

I wheel the suitcases out to Sally.

"Holy fuck Esme, what you got in here, bricks?!" She grunts while lifting them into the boot.

"Yes, I wanted to bring parts of the house with me." I answer sarcastically.

I stand back and look up at the house, our house. I let a few tears fall.

"It's just bricks and mortar. He's still with you, you know." Sally says holding my hand.

I sniff and wipe my tears.

"Yeah, I know. It just holds a lot of special memories." I sigh.

Sally leans her head on my shoulder and sighs with me. I rest my head on hers and we just stand for a few minutes in silence.

"Ready?" Sally asks.

I smile and nod.

"Yeah. Yeah, I think I am."

Sally drives us to the airport and I look out of the window, watching the town I lived and grew up in pass us by. Sally and I point out memories as we go past.

"The skate park where Jay and I had our first kiss." I point out.

"Isn't it also where you first gave him a blowie? Behind the half pipe there." She points out.

"Yes, thank you. Thanks for tarnishing that memory." I laugh.

"OOO look! That craphole B&B where you guys first shagged." She coos.

"Ah yes, what a memorable night that was. There was the guy that had hired a prostitute in the next room, and I believe a crack head drug dealer in the other. It was the most beautiful three minutes of my life." I snort.

We pull up at the traffic lights and Sally smacks my arm.

"Look! There's Jay's mum." She gasps.

I look and see Jay's mum walking along with another man. She's dressed in her finest but I wouldn't expect anything less. I recognise the man she's with.

"Oh that's Jay's father's business partner. It could be harmless, maybe we're reading too much into it." I suggest turning to Sally.

"Something tells me we're not." Sally nods with her head.

I turn and see them share a kiss. I quickly grab my phone and take a picture and then another to clearly show it's them. Cars start beeping at Sally because the lights have turned green.

"Alright, alright! Calm your tits!" She yells, flipping them off.

"Why did you take pictures?" Sally asks.

"Because Jay's father is still legally married to her. She has been fighting his lawyers for more money and they both still live in the marital home. With this he can kick her arse to the curb." I state whilst typing an email to Frank.

He's kept in touch, asking how things were going and making the effort. I just wish Jay were here to see that his father cared and loved him all this time. I attach the photos and click send.

We play the music loud all the way there. Sally had previously stocked up on the must have travel sweets: bonbons, lemon sherbets, and rhubarb and custards.

"Oh yeah this is our jam!" Sally yells, turning up her stereo.

Get Ur Freak On by Missy Elliott fills the car. We jig, bounce, and rap along.

"Holla!" Sally sings.

I laugh. God I'm going to miss her! She's the only one who has been here through everything. She's the only one who has made me laugh since Jay. I'm not sure I would've been able to get this far without her.

After finding a parking spot Sally helps me wheel the cases into the airport to check in.

We go for a bite and a stiff drink. Well, the stiff drink is for me, Sally sticks to coffee.

It's finally time for me to go through to the departure lounge. I grab Sally in my arms and hug her tight. She does the same.

"I'm going to miss you so much." I sob.

"Me too." She sniffles.

"How am I going to cope without you? You've helped me so much, especially since Jay's passing." I sniff.

"You're stronger than you think. Plus I'm only a phone call or a video call away. You better call me a lot. You think you need me, but it's me that needs you, so make sure you don't forget your best friend. Okay?" She wipes her eyes.

"Just try and stop me! I'm going to piss you off so much by calling you day and night." I smile and wipe my tears, taking a deep breath.

"Go on, you got this. I'm so proud of you. Love you." Sally pulls me in for a hug one more time then steps back, smiling with tears in her eyes.

"Love you more!" I yell over my shoulder as I walk into the departure lounge.

I swallow the lump in my throat, push my shoulders back, and take the first steps to the rest of my life.

I'm sitting in my seat on the plane and my leg is jigging nervously. We are taxiing ready for take-off.

"Don't be nervous sweetie. We will soon be up in the air, and then if we crash and burn we won't feel a thing anyway." The old lady next to me smiles and pats my hand.

"Thanks." I murmur, wishing she'd kept that helpful advice to herself.

"Ladies and gentlemen, this is your captain speaking. We'd like to thank you for choosing to fly with us today. Please sit back and relax. Myself and my new co-pilot Ted Striker will ensure you have a safe and pleasant flight." The pilot announces over the speaker.

I snort and laugh, expecting the whole plane to do the same. I look at the old lady next to me and she just looks confused.

"Ted Striker, the character in the movie airplane." I explain.

She just smiles and shakes her head.

"Sorry dear, I haven't seen it. I haven't watched a movie since 1959. The last one I saw was 'Some like it Hot' with Marilyn Monroe, Tony Curtis, and Jack Lemmon. Have you seen it dear?" She asks.

"No, I'm afraid I haven't." I smile.

"Oh you must! It's wonderful, very funny. And of course Marilyn is just stunning! You're like a modern day Marilynn." She states.

The only thing I have in common with Marilyn Monroe is that I'm blonde, but my hair is long. I'm probably around the same size she was. I have a dusting of freckles across my nose and I'm no way near as glamorous and I very rarely wear make up.

"Thank you." I answer kindly.

I try and watch the air steward doing the emergency procedures, or as I like to call it the 'if we crash to our deaths' demonstration, but the elderly lady keeps chatting away.

"So are you visiting family or going on holiday?" She enquires.

"I'm actually moving out there." I say smiling.

"Oh how wonderful! I'm just going to visit my daughter; she married a Canadian man and now lives out there. Not sure how many more trips I will be able to take though. So have you met a hunky man or is your husband working out there?" She asks.

"I'm moving out there on my own. My husband passed away nearly ten months ago." I give her a sad smile.

"Oh my dear girl, so young to be a widow. Can an old lady give you some advice?" She asks, squeezing my hand.

"Sure." I nod.

"From one widow to another, it does get easier. You will never stop missing them and there will always be that hole in your heart for them, but you'll have the chance to find love again and make that hole smaller. I shall always miss my Edward, but one day I will meet him again." She smiles.

"How long were you married for?" I ask.

She pulls out her purse and shows me a photograph of her wedding day.

"This year we would have been married for fifty years. I lost him ten years ago now. I'm just thankful that I got so many years with him; he was the love of my life, oh, and a fantastic lover." She winks.

I choke on my laughter.

"Just because I'm an old lady dear that doesn't mean I don't miss the sex! Let me tell you in our youth we had quite the sessions. I could teach that Mr Grey a thing or too." She states.

"You've read Fifty Shades of Grey?" I ask, stunned.

"Of course, thoroughly enjoyed it too! I've read a lot of romance and erotic novels, keeps me youthful." She smiles.

I smile back. Maybe this long haul flight won't drag so much after all.

"I'm Esme by the way." I say as I hold out my hand.

"Doris." She smiles and shakes my hand.

The plane's engines rev ready for take-off. I grip my seat as my nerves takeover. Doris places her hand on mine reassuringly.

I breathe a sigh of relief once we're in the air. Take-off and landing just scare the crap out of me.

Doris and I continue to talk. She tells me all about her five grandchildren, where her daughter lives in Canada, and that she has a son who lives back in England who is a doctor. I share stories about Jay and I. It's the first time I've been able to speak about him properly with anyone that isn't Sally and not get upset. Maybe it's because I know that Doris has experienced it too, that she understands what it is like to lose that huge part of your life.

Ten and half hours later we land in Halifax Nova scotia.

At the luggage collection I help Doris with her bags and give her a hug goodbye.

"I wish you all the luck in the world, my dear girl. Now be careful of these Canadian men, they have quite the charm." She winks and waves, walking off to her waiting daughter and grandchildren.

I lug my three cases onto a trolly. It just so happens to have a wonky wheel and squeaks the whole time. I struggle to push the bastard trolly to the car hire desk.

"Hi welcome to Maple car hire, how can I help you today?" The nice lady smiles.

I hand over my documents.

"Hi I have a reservation for a car hire. The name is Esme Tucker."

"Okay thank you. Can I see your driving licence please?" She asks whilst typing away on her computer.

I hand her my licence and she types away and then hands me back my documents and keys for the car.

"There you go Mrs Tucker. It's in lot twenty-seven, yellow block. You head straight out of these doors and follow the signs for rental parking." She smiles.

I nod thanks and walk out of the doors. The cold winter air hits me.

"Holy shit it's freezing!" I yell.

I push hard on my wonky wheeled trolly and follow the directions she gave me. I nearly slip on ice patches several times but luckily I'm able to keep myself upright.

I walk up and down looking for the car and

eventually find it.

"You've got to be fucking kidding me." I mutter.

In front of me is a Nissan Micra. A bloody Nissan Micra that I now have to drive in snowy conditions loaded up with three large suitcases! I pull out my phone and take a photo to send to Sally later; she booked the car for me. Clearly she didn't consider that it's winter in Canada!

"I bet you're laughing your arse off right now aren't you Jay." I sigh.

I squeeze my suitcases in, having to put them on the back seat and the passenger side next to me. I set up google maps on my phone and start my journey. It says it should be around a three hour drive.

I drive along looking at the beautiful scenery. I can't stop myself from smiling at how absolutely stunning it is.

I leave the busier city and towns and follow a windy road surrounded by huge trees. The road becomes fairly steep and my little car hates it. I can't go faster than 20mph and that's with my foot flat on the gas pedal!

"Come on you piece of tin!" I yell, hitting the steering wheel.

There is a loud honking sound from behind me a huge truck carrying wood is coming up fast.

He's honking and flashing his lights.

"I'm going as fast as I bloody can!" I yell.

He's not slowing down. He keeps getting closer and closer. I scream and pull over out of the way, skidding into a pile of snow.

I'm shaking, but thankfully I'm okay. The large truck has pulled up ahead. The wanker! Jet lagged and angry I jump out of the car and make my way to the truck to give the guy a peace of my mind. I feel my feet slip out from under me and I go flying, landing on my back and hitting my head with a thump. I groan in pain.

"Son of a bitch." I say, holding my head.

"You got a death wish or something?" A deep voice growls.

I squint my eyes open to see a very angry, yet very good looking, guy staring down. He looks pissed off at me.

"Huh?" I ask in confusion.

He rolls his eyes and reaches forward, pulling me onto my feet. I wobble and grab hold of his jacket.

Gathering my thoughts and ignoring the pounding in my head I step back and cross my arms over my chest.

"Why the fuck would you come up behind me like that?! You ran me off the bloody road! You moron!" I seethe.

"I have a near fifteen ton truck, I cannot ease off the gas when climbing a damn incline! Why in hell would you be driving around in that? You could get yourself killed! Damn tourists." He states pointing to my hire car.

"For your information, I did not order that hire car. It was going as fast as it can up a hill this steep! The only thing that'll kill me on these roads are twat drivers like you. Now if you don't mind, I need to get to my destination before it gets dark." I huff and turn to walk back to my car but my feet slip as I do. I stabilise myself. I hear him mutter something under his breath about tourists so I flip him off over my shoulder.

I slam my door shut.

"Arsehole! Not a great start, hey Jay." I mutter. I wait for the twat with the truck to drive off before I start back on my journey.

It's dark by the time I reach the bakery. It took me nearly four hours to get here. I pull up outside and sigh. I see Cassie the estate agent jump down out of her truck and smile as she walks over to me.

"Hi Esme, glad you made it okay." She states.

"I'm sorry I'm late. There was an incident with a rude truck driver." I state.

"Oh no worries. I guessed you'd take a while, I've only been here for twenty minutes. Come, let me help you carry your cases in." She says helping me to unpack the car.

She hands me the keys and smiles. I unlock the door and step inside. The musty smell hits me from where it's been empty for so long. We walk upstairs to the apartment and I put down my suitcases and switch on the lights. It's a plain and simple apartment. There's a chair in the living area and an old basic kitchen. I smile.

"I hope you don't mind but I grabbed you some coffee and milk. I also left a saucepan on the stove for you." She smiles.

"Oh thank you so much! I really appreciate it."

"No problem, there's a little map I've drawn out for you, and some other paperwork. I shall leave you in peace now. Welcome to Baddeck, Esme." She smiles before leaving.

I smile and a lone tear falls down my cheek.

"I did it Jay, I made it. This is my new life." I whisper to the empty room.

Chapter Four

I passed out on the only piece of furniture that was in the place. I had no blankets so I made use of my entire wardrobe by putting on around five layers of clothing.

I wake up freezing. Shivering I walk to the thermostat and twiddle it to try and turn it up. The knob comes off in my hand.

"Fucking marvellous." I mutter.

Seeing the early sunrise I decide to go out and search for the grocery store and maybe hire a man to fix the heating. I get in the shower to freshen myself up and wash away the jet lag.

Warming up in the hot shower I sigh, relieved to feel the heat from the hot water.

As I step out of the shower I pull back the shower curtain and the entire thing comes away from the wall. I stand soaking wet holding the shower curtain and rail in my hand.

"Seriously!" I say, starting to shiver.

Wrapping myself in the towel I add a shower curtain to the list of things I need to buy. I walk into the living room and rummage through my suitcase, pulling out my thick black leggings and long thick knit jumper. I plug my hair dryer in and switch it on. There is a loud bang and all of the electrics blow.

"What the hell?" I grit.

Giving up on the hair dryer I brush my hair and put it in a side plait. Pulling on my coat I grab my purse and the map Anna gave me and head out. First stop groceries and then the hardware store.

I drive for all of a few minutes when I spot the grocery store. I park up and jump out.

I walk in and the bell above the door chimes.

There are only two people shopping inside and they both turn and stare. I give them a polite smile and grab myself a basket.

I pick up some fruit, a couple of cans of soup, some juice, crisps, chocolate, and a couple of bottles of wine.

I walk up to the counter and I'm greeted by an older lady in her fifties.

"Hi there! I guess you must be our newest resident, you're staying at the old toy shop, right? I'm Nellie." She greets and takes my basket.

I notice the other two shoppers lingering around behind me. They're obviously trying to catch the latest gossip, which I guess is me at this moment in time.

"Yes that's right. Nice to meet you, I'm Esme." I hold out my hand and shake hers in greeting.

"Oh I love your accent! It's like we have Kate Winslet in our store. Eric! Come and meet Esme, she's British! So, how are you finding the town so far?" She asks.

"I only arrived late last night so I haven't had a chance to see much of the town. I'm off to the hardware store after here. Is there anywhere you can recommend for furniture?" I ask.

She rings up my items and a man, who I'm guessing is Eric, comes from out the back.

"Eric, this is Esme. Esme, meet my husband, Eric." She introduces.

"Good to meet you. What are your plans for the shop?" He asks bluntly.

The shoppers behind me lean in and so does Nellie. I bite my lip nervously.

"Well um, I plan on opening a little bakery." I answer.

Nellie smiles and Eric looks relieved that

I'm not opening anything that is direct competition with his store. The shoppers behind me suddenly start chatting too.

"Oh that sounds lovely! Now if it's furniture you need, ask Ted at the hardware store. He has a little there that he buys from a local guy who makes things by hand out of wood. The rest I'm afraid you'll either have to head to the city or order online." Nellie smiles.

"Okay great, thank you. I guess I'll see you around." I say as I leave.

They all smile and wave, even the gossiping shoppers behind me. I guess that's what they were waiting to see: if I was going to come in and ruin their town.

I get in my car and turn up the heat. I know another thing I'm going to need is a clothes store. I definitely need thermal wear. I wonder if I can buy a thermal bra. My poor nipples feel like they're about to snap.

I drive along to the hardware store which is just up the road. I notice all of the beautiful houses; some are painted in bright colours. I smile to myself, this place is so cute.

I park up and jump out. I grab a trolley and slowly walk up and down the aisles, not really sure what I need. I spot the paint and pick out various colours. I grab a drill, saw, and screws. I'm bound to need them at some point. I notice a small homeware section and head straight for it. I grab a shower curtain and pole. I grab a kettle and a couple of pans. I see a blanket I grab two and a pillow.

I walk down and find a camping section with a camp bed. I smile and pile it onto the trolly. Not looking where I'm going I keep looking at the shelves. As I walk around the corner I bump into something, or should I say someone.

"Watch it!" Is yelled in a deep voice. I move around my trolly.

"I'm so sorry, I wasn't looking where I was going. Are you o…it's you." I snap.

"Doesn't surprise me that it's you, I should have guessed when you rammed your trolly into me!" He grumbles.

"I said I was sorry. If you can't tell, I'm trying to push a lot in the trolly right now. So if you could just move out of my way so I could carry on getting the things I need, that would be great." I snap.

I shove my trolly to go around him.

"You going camping in this weather?" He asks, pointing the camp bed.

"No, not that it is any of your business. I have just moved into the flat above the shop, so until I can furnish it I'm buying this to sleep on. You going to give me your opinion on that too?" I ask.

"No opinion whatsoever." He adds.

"Great. Now if you don't mind, I have a lot to get and things that I need to fix." I state as I walk past.

I grab a few other tools and an electrical testing kit, adaptor, and a few other bits I think I might need.

I pay the clerk and ask him about the furniture.

"Mainly benches and a couple of rocking chairs. They're just out back. Give me your keys I will load up your car." He holds out his hand and I dubiously hand over my keys.

"This isn't a city; around here we help each other out. Your stuff is safe, don't worry." He smiles.

"Err, thanks Ted!" I yell.

I walk out back and see the stunning hand carved benches. I take a seat and run my hand along the delicate carved arms. I look up and spot the rocking chair. I immediately fall in love with it. I jump up and sit in it.

It's carved oak, almost gothic in design with its swirls, and almost has a Celtic look about it. I close my eyes and rock back and forth, smiling, I always said to Jay that when we had children I wanted a rocking chair, one that I could rock our baby to sleep in. I twist my wedding band on my finger as I fight back the tears.

I hear a cough. I jump to my feet and sniffle, wiping my eyes. I look up and see it's the tall dark arsehole.

"You're crying." He states.

"Wow, you should become a detective with those kind of skills. You could make it far." I snap sarcastically.

"You want the chair, it's $300." He states.

I frown.

"You work here?" I ask.

"No, I made the chair. Ted lets me sell my work here." He states.

"You made these?" I ask in awe.

"Yes, I just said that. Now do you want the chair or not?" He asks.

"Wow, you clearly have a talent for design, but the same can't be said for your people skills. Yes I want the chair." I hand him the money.

"I will follow you back with it on my truck." He states and walks passed me. He picks up the chair like it weighs nothing.

Before I leave I take down the number on the board for a contractor and an electrician and plumber. By all accounts it was the same number and name for all.

"Ted, are there any other contractors I can

ask for a quote?" I ask.

He bursts out laughing.

"Only one man around here. He's our plumber, electrician, and contractor." He states.

"Ah okay. Thank you." I say. As I head to the car I see tall, dark, and grumpy in his pickup truck waiting, looking as pissed off as ever. I give him my biggest smile and wave just to piss him off. I swear I see him snarl. I laugh, loving that I annoy him that much.

I pull up outside the shop and open up. I start unloading the stuff I had brought and lugging it up the stairs to the apartment.

I hear tall, dark, and grumpy follow behind me. I point to the living room for him to put the chair in.

He looks around the place and blows out his breath, showing the steam from how cold it is in here.

"You got no heating?" He asks.

"Well I don't know. I tried to put the heating on this morning and accidentally pulled the thermostat knob off. That's why I bought the tools and took the number down for the electrician, plumber, and construction worker." I point out.

He spots the knob on the side and picks it up and goes to the thermostat. He pushes it on and fiddles with it a little and turns it.

"There, you should start to feel heat soon. Keep it at that temp, it will keep it nice and warm for you." He states.

"Oh well thank you. I was going to fix it myself, but you've saved me a job. I'm usually pretty handy at fiddling with knobs." I say. Immediately I hear the words back and I blush.

"Oh god, I didn't mean it in that way, as in, a penis knob. I don't go fiddling with them. I meant in terms of the little knobs. Oh for fuck sake Esme, shut up." I ramble.

I look up at tall, dark, and grumpy through my fingers, like when I'm unable to watch a scary part in a movie.

"Good to know. I'm going to go." He states.

"Oh erm, thank you." I mutter as he walks off down the stairs.

I slump in my new rocking chair and pick up my phone and call Sally.

"Well you took your sweet arse time to call! How is it all going?" She asks.

I tell her everything from the truck running me off the road to just now. What does my friend do to support me?! She roars with laughter.

"Sally this isn't funny. I told you I would make a tit out of myself." I whine.

"Okay what does Mr tall, dark, and grumpy look like? Is he all Canadian man, a big lumberjack?!" She asks excitedly.

"Not far off. He's good looking, has dark brown nearly black hair, a nice beard, not too much just the right amount. I'd say he's around 6 foot 4 ish in height. He looks broad, strong, and muscular from what I can tell. Although obviously it's freezing so everyone is wearing layers." I finish.

"Holy hell! My ovaries nearly jumped out of my body and flew to Canada. No wonder you're making a tit out of yourself, he sounds hot." She swoons.

I roll my eyes.

"Yeah, he's good looking but I don't look at him in that way. He would be better looking if he wasn't an arsehole. Plus Sally, I'm not in any way looking for anything like that. I've got my hands full with this place, ideally I'd like it open by spring." I say just as someone knocks on the door.

"I have to go Sally, someone's at the door." I disconnect and walk downstairs to see Nellie from the convenience store waving at me through the glass.

I open the door.

"Hi Nellie, what can I do you for?" I ask.

She hands me a dish.

"This is a proper welcome to the town; it's my famous chicken casserole. It'll keep you warm and I figured you'll be busy unpacking and doing lots of jobs around the place eh? So this is one job you don't have to worry about." She says.

"Thank you, Nellie. That's really kind of you." I state.

"No problem. Now go get back inside in the warm. Bring the dish back when you're done." She says over her shoulder as she jumps in her truck and pulls off.

I take the dish upstairs and start to unpack my things. I unbox Jay's ashes and place them on the mantle.

I finally manage to unfold the camp bed after fighting with the blasted thing for nearly twenty minutes. I use my new blankets and pillows and place some candles I brought around the place. I'm still not sure if I completely fried the electrics earlier.

I sit in my rocking chair looking outside at the people going about their business. I don't miss the people giving sideway glances and having a quick stop outside to gossip about who they think is in here. I smile to myself, wondering what they're saying.

I decide to test a light switch but it's a big mistake: every light bulb decides to blow! I scream and grab my phone and call the number I wrote down earlier.

"Hello, Bob here." A man answers.

"Oh hello, I'm Esme. I moved into the old shop and I wondered if at all possible you could come across? All of the electrics have blown and every light bulb has just exploded." I ask crossing my fingers.

"Sure, no problem. I will be there in ten minutes." He says and disconnects.

I look around for something to use to clean up all the broken glass. I open a big pantry cupboard and a little mouse runs out. I scream at the top of my lungs. It scurries off under the floorboards somewhere. After I've calmed my heart down enough to know that I'm not having a heart attack I spot an old broom and start sweeping. There's a knock and a hello shouted up. I must have forgotten to lock up after Nellie earlier.

"Yes, come on up." I yell.

I carry on sweeping and a guy in his forties walks through the door. His work boots crunch on the broken glass.

"Well my days! You weren't kidding, eh?" He says, looking around.

"I will check your mains and see what I can do." He says and he walks off back downstairs to find the mains box or whatever it is he's looking for. I just carry on sweeping what I can.

I don't have a dustpan and brush so I grab a couple of bits of paper and try and scoop it all up.

I don't do a very good job. I cut my hand quite badly. I hear footsteps come up the stairs and hear Bob talking to someone. I am now standing with my hand cupped with a little pool of blood.

"So Esme, here's the deal…woah there! What did you do?" He asks.

"I tried to clean up the glass and I think a bit got stuck in my hand. It's bleeding a fair amount." I shrug.

It's then I notice tall, dark, and grumpy walk in behind Bob. He sees my hand and walks straight to me. He carefully takes my hand in his and pulls a rag from his back pocket.

"I hope you haven't blown your nose on that." I scrunch my nose up.

He doesn't say anything as he carefully wraps the rag around my hand.

"Ow! Son of a twat waffle that hurts." I wince.

"Well that's a new word for me. Do they use that often in England?" Bob asks.

"Depends what mood we're in Bob." I answer. "So, can you fix it?" I ask him.

"Not right now no, but I can come back tomorrow. I'm told you also want other stuff doing around here?" He states.

Thanks to the towns gossipers he already knew I was going to ask him.

"Yes, I want the whole of downstairs redone. I'm opening a bakery. Of course up here needs a new kitchen too. Ow. Easy!" I state. I look up into tall, dark, and grumpy's eyes as he ties a knot on the rag.

He turns around to Bob.

"I'm gonna take her to the docs; I reckon she'll need a stitch in this. You good staying here to price up?" He asks.

"Yeah, yeah, go." Bob ushers us out.

"Wait what, I'm fine. I have tweezers, I will just pull it out myself. I don't need to see a doctor." I try to argue but I'm already being pushed out of the door and downstairs into his truck.

I notice lots of tools in the back.

"You a carpenter then?" I ask.

"Sort of." He answers vaguely.

"A lumberjack?" I laugh.

"Sort of." He again answers vaguely.

"Okay I give up, what is it you do?" I ask.

"I own a lumber yard and I also do some carpentry on the side." He answers.

"Wow okay. That's like a real alpha manly job. It's like something out of a romance novel. Except the name would be all macho and alpha. That's a point, what is your name?" I ask.

"Gaige Knox." He answers.

I snort with laughter.

"You're kidding me?" I ask.

He shakes his head.

"Well then you have an alpha macho manly name and job. All you need to do now is wear a flannel shirt and walk around with an axe in one hand and throw your woman over your shoulder. You're a bloody walking talking romance novel!" I ramble on.

"You talk a lot." He states.

"I only fill awkward silences. It just so happens there are a lot of those with you." I say crossing my arms.

We drive in silence until he pulls up at the doctor's office. He takes my elbow and escorts me in. As we walk in a young nurse smiles and bats her eyelashes at Gaige. He doesn't seem to pay her much attention though.

"Where's doc, is he busy?" He asks.

"No, he's free right now." She answers.

He doesn't waste any time and drags me

through to the doctor's office, not even knocking.

"Doc, you got a sec to stitch up her hand?" He asks, practically thrusting me forward.

"Hi, I'm Esme." I smile at the doc and turn and give Gaige a pissed off glare.

"Stop shoving me around." I grit my teeth.

The doctor smiles and walks round and gestures for me to sit on the bed.

Gaige goes to pull me by my elbow but I yank it out of his hand.

"I'm quite capable." I snap as I walk to the bed.

"Hello Esme, I'm Dr Alfred Clarke. But you can call me Doc like everyone else seems to. Now, what happened?" He asks as he unwraps the rag.

"I've had a bit of an electrical problem; all of the lights blew and glass bulbs shattered everywhere. I don't have a dustpan and brush, so I used two bits of paper instead, it didn't go too well." I shrug.

"You don't think." Gaige grunts from the other side of the room.

I stare him down. That is until Doc decides to poke around in the cut.

"Woah ow...ow..." I complain.

I notice Gaige crosses his arms over his chest and angrily clenches his jaw. Well excuse me for being in pain! He's such an arsehole.

"Sorry. Gaige, come here and hold Esme's hand while I get this bit of glass out." He orders.

"I'm fine I don't need to hold anyone's haaaa..." I wail and grab hold of Gaige's hand tightly.

I burry my face in Gaige's front and grit my teeth while the Doc rummages around, pulling out little bits of glass.

"There, that should do it. I've put in a couple of stitches. You're all good. The stitches will dissolve." Doc informs me.

I look up. I basically face planted Gaige's stomach.

"Um, sorry about that." I mumble to him and let go of the vice like grip I had on his hand.

I look down at my now bandaged hand.

"Thank you Doc, what's the charge?" I ask.

"No charge. You can bake me something to say thank you when you get your place up and running." He states.

"Oh that's very kind of you. I'm learning that word travels fast around here." I state.

The Doc laughs and Gaige grunts in agreement.

We say goodbye and Gaige takes my elbow again and walks me to his truck.

On the way back I bite my thumbnail nervously.

"Thanks for, um, holding my hand in there. I'm sorry for shoving my face in your stomach." I apologise.

"Think nothing of it." He answers.

We remain in silence the rest of the way until we pull back up the shop.

Bob greets us and give me a run down of what needs doing first and how much it'll cost.

"Great. What sort of time frame do you think we're looking at? I ask.

"Well, with Gaige helping me I'd say anywhere from four to six months." He states.

I smile and shake his hand.

"Great, I will see you tomorrow morning." I say. I'm excited to get started on the renovations.

Gaige leaves without saying a word. He just gives me a nod before getting into his truck. I smile and shut the door. I walk up to the apartment and see that Bob has cleared up all the glass for me.

"Well Jay, I think I definitely made my mark on my first day. It could have been worse I suppose." I shrug, sitting down on my rocking chair. I eat Nellie's casserole.

I just hope everyday isn't this eventful.

Chapter Five

The next few days went by without disaster. I managed to get online and order a sofa and a bed with a mattress that are coming today. To say I was excited to be sleeping in an actual bed was an understatement. I even ordered some soft furnishings too: curtains, bedding, and scatter cushions. Jay always used to moan about my cushions on the bed. He didn't see the point in buying cushions that were never used. I tried to explain that their only purpose was to lay there and look pretty.

I may have got a little bit excited and bought some battery fairy lights to put up around the place. Bob started looking at the electrics further and turns out the whole bloody place needs rewiring! He suggested I stay in a hotel until it's done, but I assured him I wanted to be here and help in any way I can. The fact is there is hardly any furniture to move around so I can stay in one room.

I'm having a nice long hot shower and blaring music from my Bluetooth speaker.

"Whatta man, whatta man, whatta man, what a mighty good man!" I sing at the top of my lungs. I step out of the shower and start to dance. Shaking my arse, still singing at the top of my voice, I wipe the condensation off of the mirror and see a man's reflection staring back at me.

I scream and turn around seeing Gaige standing behind me. I reach for the towel to cover myself.

"What the hell you pervert?!" I yell.

"You left the door unlocked and your bathroom door wide open." He states, standing in the doorway.

"That doesn't mean come on in and join me!" I point out, crossing my arms across my chest while making sure the towel keeps my front covered.

His eyes focus behind me. I look over my shoulder and see the reflection in the mirror: my behind.

"God damn it! Get out!" I yell. I think I catch a twitch of a smile on his lips as he holds up his hands, turns, and leaves.

I march forward and slam the bathroom door. Note to self: never leave the bathroom door open, apparently Canadian men see it as an invite to come in and have a peep show.

I wrap the towel around myself properly and scurry into my bedroom to get dressed. When I walk in Gaige is there.

"Seriously?! Get out!" I yell.

"I was just measuring up the room." He defends, holding up his tape measure.

"Go make us some coffee so I can get some clothes on. Unless you want a second show?!" I ask sarcastically.

He pauses and raises an eyebrow in question.

"I was being sarcastic! Piss off." I point out.

His lips twitch again. He's fighting a smile! He turns and leaves, shutting the door behind him.

What an arsehole!

I quickly get changed, afraid incase anyone else walks in. I walk into the kitchen and towel dry my hair as much as possible. Considering there's no electric I can't dry my hair properly.

Gaige is leaning against the counter drinking his coffee. His eyes come to mine as I walk in. He nods towards the coffee he made for me on the counter. I don't say a word. I just take it and drink it, moaning.

"God that's good coffee." I state.

"I'm sorry for walking in on you like that. If it makes you feel any better, I'd only just walked in when you saw me in the mirror. I only saw your naked dancing for about two seconds, if that." He admits.

"Ah well, that's okay then. No harm done." I roll my eyes.

"I promise I've erased it from my memory. Apart from your singing, I think that has scarred me for life. I don't think I'll ever recover." He says teasing.

"Hang on a minute, are you teasing me? Are you actually fighting a smile, because I didn't know you were capable of it! Anyone would think you're flirting with me." I mock with fake shock.

The twinkle in his eyes immediately disappears and his cold serious face returns.

"I apologise. The last thing I want is for you to think that I was flirting. I'm going to finish taking the measurements and order in the wood." He states. He places his cup down and leaves me standing in the kitchen wondering what the hell just happened.

I shrug and finish drinking my coffee. I hear Gaige leave without a goodbye and watch him jump in his truck.

"There I go again Jay, putting my foot in it

and making a complete tit out of myself. Day six and I've already flashed a local." I smile to myself.

I have to laugh at myself or I'd cry.

A couple of hours later my bed and sofa are delivered. The guys manage to get the sofa up for me and I tell them not to worry about the bed frame and mattress; I can do that myself. They exchange a look of doubt but soon leave.

I practically drag the bed frame box upstairs, huffing and puffing. The thing weighed a ton! I walk back down for the mattress and try to drag it. Well, if I thought the frame was heavy I was in for a treat because this mattress was only moving if I used all my weight! I make it halfway up the stairs, pushing it up with my back to it and squatting up each step. I'm sweating. I remove my jumper and chuck it down the stairs which leaves me in my bra and jeans. I don't care, I just want to get this blasted mattress up the stairs.

I lean against the mattress, out of breath. I move back a strand of hair that's fallen out of my messy bun.

"Well what am I going to do now?" I mutter.

I try pushing back on the mattress but it doesn't shift. Somehow I have managed to wedge it. I snort and think back to that friends episode.

"Pivot!" I snort to myself.

Jesus! I'm going insane. What the hell am I going to do? I decide it's worth seeing if I can climb over the mattress and pull it from the top. The mattress is wedged and not going anywhere and I have nothing to lose.

I start to climb, pulling myself through the tiny gap, the springs of the mattress not giving me much space. Why did I buy a firm mattress?!

"Nearly there Esme, come on!" I pant.

I get a little further up and my top half is near the top of the mattress but my arse is wedged between the mattress and the narrow stairwell. I try wiggling but no luck.

"Oh for mother effing sake!" I yell.

I lay there for I don't know how long.

"This mattress really is incredibly comfortable." I sigh, laying back on it.

I hear someone knock. My head snaps up.

"Hello if you can hear me, HELP!" I yell as loud as I can.

"Esme?!" I hear Gaige shout.

It had to be him didn't it?!

"Yeah help! I'm stuck." I yell.

I hear his large footsteps come closer.

"What the fuck?" I hear mumbled.

"Yes I know. I got wedged trying to get this bastard mattress up the stairs, can you help me please?" I beg.

"Why didn't the delivery company do it for you?" He asks.

"I told them I could do it myself." I mumble.

"Esme, this is a king size mattress; it needs two people to move it." He states.

"Actually it's a super king, and well, I know that now don't I! So can you help me or what?" I ask.

"Yeah hang on." I hear the click sound of the camera on his phone go.

"You better not be taking a bloody picture!" I yell.

"Nope." He answers. I swear he's laughing, the bastard!

"Right, just stay there. I'm going to try something." He states.

"I shall do my best to stay bloody stuck." I snap.

I feel him climb up next to me until he's right alongside me.

"You have no top on." He points out.

"Yes well I got hot and threw my jumper off. You're safe, I have a bra on, the girls are safely tucked away." I say, practically feeling his breath across my stomach. I'm slightly on my side. I look down and watch as he pretty much crawls up over my body. I feel my cheeks blush. Having a guy, a good looking guy, this close to me is something I haven't felt in a long time. There was only ever Jay.

He reaches the same point as me and our bodies are pressed together. We're practically nose to nose.

"So what's you plan?" I ask.

His hand moves down to his pocket, brushing past my breast.

"Sorry." He murmurs.

His hand comes back up and there's a folded knife in his hand.

"Oh no. You are not cutting into my brand new mattress. Do you know how much it cost?!" I argue.

He pauses for a moment.

"Okay. I'm going to try and climb up and push my way through. Can you push against the mattress as hard as you can to create as much room as possible." He states. I nod and try and push all of my body weight back. He manages to climb up and at one point his crotch is in my face.

"Sweet Jesus! We're practically at second base right now." I mumble.

He keeps managing to climb up until he's out.

"I'm through. I'm going to try and reach in and pull you through too." He yells.

I reach my hands up and he grabs hold. He pulls and I move up. He keeps pulling hard, using all his might.

He pulls so hard that I come flying out, knocking him off of his feet and landing right on top of him with a thud.

I burst out laughing.

"Yay I'm free! My hero!"

I look to Gaige and see he's smiling.

"God you have a beautiful smile." I state.

His smile fades and back in its place is his static expression. I cough nervously and get off of him. He stands up, brushing himself off.

"Let's try and get the mattress in the room it's supposed to be in." He states.

I nod and smile.

"Let's do this." I yell, doing a muscle pose.

"Um, you want to put a top on first?" He asks.

I look down and realise I'm still in my bra.

"Oh yeah, right." I giggle.

"Hold that thought." I run off and grab a tank top and put it on.

"Right, let's do this." I clap.

We both heave and pull. Eventually, with Gaige's help, it shifts and we get it up the stairs. I'm pulling so hard I land right on my arse.

I burst out laughing and I hear Gaige laugh too. He helps me to my feet.

"You good?" He asks.

"Yeah." I giggle.

He pulls the mattress into the bedroom and rests it up against the wall.

"Where is your bed? I thought that was delivered as well?" He asks.

I point to the flat pack box and grab the tool belt I bought at the hardware store.

"Yup, and now I build her." I say proudly swishing my hips in my new tool belt.

Gaige shakes his head.

"You want a hand with that?" He asks.

"I'm fine doing it myself but if you have nothing else to do then sure, I guess. I can make you dinner after. I have canned soup." I wink and twiddle my spanner.

It works, Gaige chuckles.

"Ha-ha! I knew I could crack a laugh out of you again. So let's do this, where's the instructions?" I ask.

"We don't need instructions." He states pulling out the parts of the bed.

I spot the bit of paper with the instructions on. If I've learnt anything, it's that you always need the instructions. No man has ever successfully put together any flat pack furniture without needing the instructions. It's usually after hours of getting it wrong and swearing at the thing like a raving loon, but the instructions are always needed. I guess Gaige is the type of man that likes to get frustrated before reaching the final goal. It's a bit like that tantric sex that people do. I giggle to myself at the innuendo. Gaige looks at me and I fake a cough.

"You want a beer or some wine?" I ask.

"Beer if you have it." he answers.

"Sure." I answer, walking out of the room to the kitchen.

"Well Jay, I hope you found today entertaining. I bet you were pissing your pants laughing, huh." I smile as I close the fridge door. Gaige is standing in the doorway looking confused.

"Who were you talking too?" He asks.

"My husband." I answer honestly as I hand him the beer.

"Oh right, when does he get into town?" He asks, walking back to the bedroom.

My steps falter and I go quiet. Gaige turns

around, noticing my unusual silence.

"Esme?" He asks.

I point to the urn on the mantle piece. Gaige turns and looks.

"He died of cancer ten months ago. Sorry, I just still like to talk to him sometimes. I like to think that in some way he's still with me, you know?" I say, blinking back my tears.

"I...I...shit. Sorry Esme, I didn't know. I saw your wedding band and just assumed he was flying in at a later date or something." He places his beer down and surprises me by pulling me into his arms. After a second I relax and hug him back, not realising until that moment how much I needed that hug.

We continue to chat about the town and Gaige tells me which locals to avoid and which ones are okay.

We're soon finished.

"Huh, you didn't need the instructions." I state.

"Never do. I build and make stuff for a living, I know how to put a bed together." He shrugs.

"Alright smart arse." I roll my eyes.

He helps me put the mattress on and make the bed. I can't help but squeal and jump on the bed.

"Oh my god! This is sooo comfy. Gaige, get your arse on here and feel how comfy it is!" I pat the space beside me.

He hesitates for a moment and then lays down next to me. I lean up on my elbow.

"It's comfy, right?!" I asks smiling.

"Yeah it's comfy." He smiles back at me.

I jump up.

"Listen, I don't want to brag but I make a mean can of soup." I smile.

"Wow now that's a promise." He jokes.

I switch on my fairy lights and pull a box over to my new sofa which is still covered in plastic.

"Take a seat on the sofa, I will bring the food in a minute." I yell from the kitchen.

I carry in the two bowls of soup and place them down, going back for some bread rolls and more beer.

I watch Gaige taste the soup.

"Hmmm. That may be the best damn soup I've ever tasted." He says smiling.

I smile back.

"You know, I thought you were a real arsehole at first, but the more I get to know you the more I like you." I say, offering him a bread roll.

"Well, right back at you. I thought you were this posh English girl with no clue. I didn't think you'd last a day." He smiles.

"You were bloody horrible to me." I point out.

"You swore at me so many times even the sailors would've been offended!" He defends.

"Good point. Let's call it quits. Friends from here on out?" I hold my hand up for him to shake. Something flashes briefly across his eyes but he hides it before I can ask what it is. He smiles and shakes my hand.

"So Gaige, have you lived here your whole life?" I ask.

"No, I'm actually American. I moved over here when I was eighteen. Never looked back." He smiles.

"Oh wow…so…" I'm interrupted by my phone ringing.

"Sorry, let me just get that." I apologise.

I see it's Sally on a video call and I quickly answer.

"Hey, I'm kinda busy right now. Can I call you back?" I ask, biting my thumbnail.

"Whoa, why you nervous? You're biting your thumbnail. Is someone there? Ooo is it tall, dark, and grumpy?" She asks.

I look to the sky and sigh. Gaige takes the phone from my hand.

"Hey. Tall, dark, and grumpy here." He smiles.

"Holy mother of fucking Christ! Esme you didn't say he was this hot! How do you do? I'm Esme's better in every way friend Sally." She says excitedly.

"I can see why you're friends." He smiles.

"Alright Sally, we're eating dinner so I will call you later." I say reaching for my phone.

"Okay, but god Esme! He is hot. I swear I nearly had an orga-" I cut her off and smile embarrassingly at Gaige.

"Sorry about that, she can get a little over excited." I state.

"Yeah, I can tell." He smirks.

We finish eating. We talk and laugh a lot. Gaige says he needs to get going so I walk him out.

I stand at my door. Gaige turns with his hands in his pockets and smiles.

"Thanks for the dinner. Maybe I can return the favour sometime." He smiles.

I laugh.

"I look forward to it. Thanks Gaige. I really appreciate your help today."

He learns forward and places a brief kiss on the top of my head and turns and leaves.

I close the door and smile. I'm so happy that I've made a friend.

Chapter Six

Over the next few weeks the shop and apartment are both in utter chaos. There are wires hanging out of the walls and ceiling, holes in the walls where rusted pipes were found, and some of the floorboards are missing. I have a temporary camping stove in the kitchen and my sofa has still got the plastic on. It seems like every time they're fixing something they find a new problem. It's becoming a little draining and taking a toll on the whole living my dream thing.

"You want to come to The Sunken Ship tonight for a bite and a drink?" Gaige asks.

"Is that a pub?" I ask.

"Yeah, it's down by the waterfront. Figured you might want to eat something other than soup." He gestures to my bin of empty cans.

"Oh god yeah, proper food. I was starting to worry that I'd forgotten how to chew." I laugh.

"Great, let me finish up here. I will head home and change and be back to pick you up at seven." He states, going back to cutting up whatever it is he's cutting.

"Bob, you want to finish early? It is two days until Christmas after all." I state looking at the clock. It's 5pm now. Bob, Gaige, and his apprentices have been working till near seven some nights.

"Oh damn right I would. We will be back in the new year. You have a good Christmas now. Where are you going? Are you heading home?" He asks.

"No, I'm just staying here by myself. Oh wait there Bob, I've got something for you." I lift up a dust sheet and open the box where I've hidden the Christmas presents.

"Here you go Bob, that's for you and there's a little something for your wife too. Also boys, here's a little something for you." I hand Bob and the apprentices their gifts.

"Thank you sweet girl, now you take care. Are you sure you don't want to join us for Christmas? I know the wife would be more than happy to have you." Bob kindly offers.

"No, I'm good thanks Bob. I just want to be on my own." I admit with a sad smile.

I haven't told Bob about Jay because he

hasn't asked. I figure they all just think my husband left me. I can't be doing with the town gossiping about Jay. I'm really thankful that Gaige isn't a gossiper.

The guys leave including Gaige. I jump in a quick shower and decide to put something a little smarter on than what I usually wear at the moment. I pull out a jumper dress: it is a cream cable knit form hugging dress. It has a V-neck that shows off a little cleavage. I put on my black thick tights and low heeled brown ankle boots. I put on some mascara and a light pink lip gloss. I spritz on some perfume and grab my handbag.

I walk downstairs to look out for Gaige. I see him pull up so I grab my coat.

I step outside, lock up, and come face to chest with Gaige.

"Opps sorry." I smile, leaning back and looking up at Gaige.

His eyes sweep my body. I hold my hands out to the side and twirl.

"Do I scrub up okay?" I ask.

"Yeah." He answers, his voice gravelly.

I look at Gaige. He's wearing black jeans with a light grey fitted sweatshirt that hugs his broad chest and muscly arms.

"You look very handsome Gaige." I compliment.

He doesn't smile or say anything. He takes my hand and leads me to his truck and opens the door for me.

"Such a gentleman, thank you." I smile.

Gaige jumps in and drives us to the pub. My face is practically pressed up against the window.

"Oh the town is so beautiful." I whisper.

I still haven't had a chance to explore the town properly other than going to the grocery store or hardware store.

All long the bay are fairy lights with red, blue, green and many more buildings. It's so picturesque.

Gaige pulls up outside the pub with fairy lights strung outside. I can't help but smile.

I hadn't even realised Gaige had got out of the truck until he opened my door.

He smiles at me, holds out his hand for me to take, and leads the way into the pub.

We take a seat in a booth and a lady with a kind smile greets us.

"Hi Gaige. I'm guessing this is the famous Esme!"

"Famous?" I ask.

"Yes deary, there are a lot of people talking about you in the town. All good, I promise." She smiles.

"That and you being the only woman to have the balls to stand up to this one." She points her pen at Gaige.

"Thanks for that Eloise. Can you get us two of your famous steak and poutine, a bottle of white wine for Esme, and a light beer for me. I'm driving." Gaige states.

"Sure thing." She says with a wink and walks off.

"Hey macho man, did you think that maybe I wanted to order my own food?" I ask.

"Trust me. Wait until you try poutine. It's the best. If you don't like it, I will order something else. Deal?" He asks.

"Fine. So you never did say why you moved here at such a young age?" I ask.

He pauses for a moment before answering.

"I moved to get away from my family. My father was all to happy to use his fists on my mother or me. I couldn't stay a moment longer so I stuffed a bag full of clothes and moved out here." He answers.

I reach across and place my hand on his.

"I am so sorry, how did you get by? Being so young as well." I ask.

"I asked around for any labouring jobs. The

only one to give me a chance was Tom. He owned the lumber yard. He taught me all that I know. He didn't have a family, no wife or kids. So when he got sick five years ago and passed away I found out he left the lumber yard to me. I've been living here now for fifteen years. Best decision I ever made." He states smiling.

Eloise brings our drinks. I don't miss the look in her eye when she sees my hand on Gaige's.

I ignore it because I couldn't care less about gossip. I'm comforting a friend, that's all.

"Tom sounds like he was a good man; I wish I could've met him." I smile sadly.

Gaige smiles and pours the wine for me.

"He was a grumpy old bastard, but I think you would've broken through that hard exterior of his." He states.

"I do have a way of breaking through barriers." I laugh.

Gaige smiles and I notice he has dimples. He really is a handsome guy. It's a shame Sally didn't move with me, she would be all over him like a rash. I smile to myself.

"So come on then, tell me about your family, your childhood. I bet you were a real hellion." He smiles while taking a drink of his beer.

"Well, I don't have a family. I did, but my mother died when I was seven." I state with a tight smile.

I never really talk about my birth mother to anyone. The only people to know the full truth were Sally and Jay.

"Shit Esme." Gaige says. He looks shocked.

"It's okay. She was a heroin addict, she was dead for three days before anyone came and found us. I never knew who my father was because she, um, put it about a bit. So I grew up in the care system, moved from foster home to foster home. I got put with a decent family when I turned twelve. I stayed with them until I was eighteen and then Jay and I ran away and got married." I smile.

Gaige reaches over and takes my hand in his, stroking his thumb soothingly back and forth.

"I'm sorry you ever had to live through that. No child should have to suffer like that." He says with sadness in his eyes.

"It's okay. I don't remember much of it, I think my mind blocked it out. It happened and if it hadn't I might not have ever met Jay, or Sally, or even be here right now. So I may have lived through some tough times but the happiness and the good I've had definitely make it worth every moment I suffered." I smile.

"You are a truly amazing person Esme." Gaige says sincerely.

I shrug.

"I like to think I'm a normal human being. Until I bake that is, then you'll see I am not a normal human being but a baking goddess." I declare.

"Well I look forward to tasting your baked goods." He says wiggling his eyebrows.

I burst out laughing. Eloise comes to our table with our food, her eyes pinging back and forth between Gaige and I. I roll my eyes and move my hand back from his so she can put our food down.

"Sorry to interrupt. Here's your food." She smiles and places our food down. It smells amazing.

"Thank you Eloise, it smells delicious." I compliment.

"Enjoy you two!" She smiles and walks away.

I look around the bar and notice most of the locals are looking our way and have smiles on their faces.

"Uhh Gaige, I wasn't aware we were a show for the town." I point to the bar.

Gaige looks up and shakes his head.

"Ignore them. It's only because you're still new in town." He states, tucking into his food.

I look down at my dish: sliced steak placed

on top of what looks like chips, cheese, and gravy.

"What's the matter? You a vegetarian?" He asks.

"No, not at all. It just reminds me of chips, cheese, and gravy." I smile.

"Oh I guess it is in a way. So are you a no carb, only salad type of girl? I can order you something else if you'd like?" He asks.

I burst out laughing.

"Do I look like a salad type of girl? Have you seen the size of my arse?! I'm an eat what I want and cry about it later type of girl."

Gaige smiles. "Good. Go on then, try it."

I load my fork up and shovel it into my mouth. Gaige laughs and shakes his head at me.

I roll my eyes and moan.

"Holy flora this is good!" I say while shovelling more into my mouth.

Gaige leans forward and wipes some of the gravy off of my chin. I smile, embarrassed.

"Sorry, I'm a messy eater. I will most likely spill something down my jumper." I say and grab a napkin.

"Don't apologise for enjoying your food." Gaige states, licking my gravy off of his thumb.

We finish the meal and I drink the entire bottle of wine. I feel sleepy and slightly tipsy.

Gaige holds my hand and leads me through the bar and out to his truck. I make him stop at the bar so I can thank the staff for a lovely meal.

I rest my head against the window. My eyes are feeling heavy. Gaige helps me out of the truck and I wobble a little.

"Whoops." I giggle as I fall into Gaige's chest. I bump my head into his chin. I lean up on my tip toes and give him a quick kiss.

"There, all better. Your beard tickles. Did you know that?"

"Come on, let's get you to your bed." Gaige states, walking me into my apartment.

"Ooo steady now, I'm not that type of girl." I giggle.

Gaige helps me to my bed where I flop down and kick off my boots.

"Hhmm, so comfy. Thank you for feeding me." I mumble into my pillow before I fall into a deep sleep.

Chapter Seven

I wake up with the worst headache and groan when I hear my phone going off. I reach for it and answer.

"What?" I groan.

"Jesus you sound like shit. You had wine, didn't you? Why did you drink wine?! You know it gives you a bad hangover." Sally sighs.

"Gaige brought me wine with dinner last night." I mumble.

"Woah hold on, you went on a date and you didn't tell me?!" She screeches.

"Ow! Sally, lower the noise level." I groan.

"Sorry, you went on a date?!" She whispers.

"It wasn't a date! We are just friends. It was only because I haven't been able to eat a proper meal what with all of the work going on. He took me to the local pub and we got some dinner.

That's all there is to it." I state as I slowly sit up.

I notice there's a glass of water on the box beside my bed along with two painkillers and a note.

Esme, you snore. Drink the water and take the painkillers. I will bring you some breakfast to help with your hangover in the morning.

Gaige.

I smile and take the painkillers and drink the water.

"Esme, are you even listening to me?" Sally asks.

"Sorry, Gaige left me a note and a glass of water and some painkillers to take. He said he will be bringing me breakfast to help with my hangover." I state, getting up and getting changed into leggings and a baggy off the shoulder jumper.

"Esme, he's into you! No guy would do that for a woman he barely knows. How can you not see it?! I can and I'm thousands of miles away." Sally fumes.

"Sally, he knows about Jay. He knows I just want friendship. He's just being a good friend. It's no different to what you would do in that situation." I point out.

"Okay but I still think there's more to it. You're a stunner, you have no clue just how many guys want to go out with you. You've always been blind." Sally states.

"Anyway, I'm calling to wish you a merry Christmas and to make sure you're okay?" She says.

"I will be fine, I promise." I reassure her.

"It's just that it's the first Christmas without Jay and I'm going to be at my parents and the phone reception is crap. I will call you as soon as I get back." She states. I can hear the worry in your voice.

"I will be fine. Have you got the presents that I sent over to take with you?" I ask.

"Yes, have you got mine ready to open?" She asks back.

"Yup, I'm looking at it right now." I smile.

"Okay good. Right, I have to go. I'll speak to you in a couple of days. Love ya." Sally says.

"Love ya too." I repeat back and disconnect.

A little while later Gaige turns up with some breakfast and coffee. He's right of course, it definitely helps with my hangover.

I hand him his Christmas present. He takes it and looks surprised.

"Esme, you didn't have to get me anything. I

didn't get you anything." He states and is about to open it.

"No! Save it for tomorrow morning." I smile. "I don't give gifts to receive them. I love giving presents to people; I love seeing the happiness it brings." I state.

"Well thank you. I guess I should be going, have a good Christmas Esme." Gaige states, leaning in and kissing my cheek.

"You too." I smile.

After he's gone I run to the store and treat myself to chocolate, some nibbles, and a few bottles of wine.

Everyone I pass is rushing around getting their last few bits ready for Christmas. The snow is falling heavily too, it's going to be a white Christmas. I suppose that's normal here.

I get back and curl up on my rocking chair just watching everyone walk by in the snow with kids on their sledges being pulled along. I yawn and feel my eyes become heavy and drift off to sleep.

When I awake it's dark and the street is quiet. I look at the time and see it's nearly midnight. I shuffle myself to bed and climb under the covers.

The next morning I make a coffee and pull out the photo album that Sally made for me. It's all of mine and Jay's memories together. Our first Christmas together we had no money and all I could afford was to get him a pair of Santa socks. He got me a big bar of my favourite chocolate. We had nothing but we were so happy. I sniffle and wipe away the tears. In the years after that we always made ourselves a special breakfast in bed, opened our presents in bed, and didn't move for the entire day. We didn't eat a Christmas dinner. Instead we binged on nibbles and chocolate all day while watching back to back Christmas movies.

I sit in bed and do the same but without proper electrics I just keep looking through the photo album and occasionally read some of my book. I cry a lot.

"I miss you so much Jay. God I feel so alone. This isn't the same without you." I sniff.

There's a knock at the door. I frown and walk down to open it, wondering who on earth would be here on Christmas day.

Gaige.

He watches me through the glass with concern on his face. I open the door and force a smile.

"Hey, what are you doing here?" My voice cracks.

He doesn't say anything, he just steps forward and pulls me in for a hug.

I break and start sobbing in his arms. Gaige bends down and picks me up. He carries me upstairs to bed and just sits with me, holding me.

"I'm sorry, it's just it's the first Christmas without him. It doesn't feel right. My heart feels like it has this big open hole that'll never get filled. I'm so alone Gaige. I've never felt so alone." I sob.

Gaige hugs me tighter and kisses the top of my head. We stay like this for a while until I calm down.

"I'm sorry." I apologise.

"You have nothing to apologise for." He states, stroking the hair from my face.

"Why are you here?" I ask.

"I opened my present and I wanted to come and say thank you. I also hated the thought of you on your own on Christmas day." He states.

I look down and realise he's wearing his present. I jump off of his lap and smile, wiping away my tears.

"You're wearing it!" I smile.

"I am but I don't get it." He states.

I got him a Monty Python t-shirt that says 'I'm a lumberjack and I'm okay.' I laugh. I grab my phone and search the clip. When I find it I click play and show him.

I watch his lips twitch while watching it. I giggle.

"See! It's because you're all macho, a butch lumberjack!" I smile.

"I don't wear suspenders and a bra though." He adds.

"Well, in all fairness I didn't know that. This is how I learnt about Canada growing up." I state with a straight face.

"You serious?" He asks, totally falling for it.

"No! That's Monty Python, you've heard of them right?! The comedians? They made the movies Life Of Brian, Holy Grail, and The Meaning Of Life. Have you never seen them?!" I ask.

He shakes his head.

"No, never."

I gasp in shock horror.

"How old are you?" I ask.

"Thirty-three." He answers.

"I'm twenty-three, you have ten years on me. You should know about the Pythons! That being said, you're American/Canadian, it can't be helped that the British awesomeness that is Python didn't reach you. So sit back and get comfy because I'm about to educate you on some proper English humour." I order.

Gaige smiles and kicks off his boots and

shuffles back. I grab the rest of the snacks and my laptop. I sit next to him on the bed.

"Oh, before I start, you're not religious, are you?" I ask.

He smiles.

"What if I was?" He asks.

I nibble my thumb nail nervously.

"Well you would probably end up seriously offended." I state.

"It's a good job I'm not then, isn't it?" He teases.

I smack his chest and click play.

"Wait a minute, how are you able to use your laptop?" He asks.

"Ernie next door tethered me an extension cable so I can charge my phone and laptop." I smile.

Gaige puts his arm around me and I lean against his chest. I keep looking up at him to see if he's enjoying the movie. He smiles down at me.

I laugh at all of my favourite bits and I like hearing Gaige laugh too.

We make it through to the Holy Grail and I feel my eyes become heavy. I cuddle further into Gaige and fall asleep. I feel warm, cosy, and not alone for the first time since Jay passed.

I'm not sure what the time is when I wake up but as I stretch I feel a wall of solid behind me. I turn and see Gaige fast asleep next to me. He looks so peaceful and handsome. I smile, carefully turning back around to get some sleep.

I awake to Gaige stroking back my hair and whispering my name. I stretch and face plant my pillow.

"Go away. I'm sleeping." I mumble into my pillow.

"Esme, I've got to go." He states firmly.

I sit up sleepy and confused and wipe my eyes.

"Huh?" I yawn.

"I have to go. Something has come up." Is all he says. Leaning forward he kisses my head and leaves. I frown in confusion.

I guess he has an invite somewhere. It is boxing day after all.

I lay back down and fall asleep for pretty much most of the day.

I don't hear from Gaige for a while and when Bob returns to work, he returns without Gaige.

"Where is Gaige?" I ask.

Bob looks at me and shrugs.

"No idea. I'm guessing he's at the yard. He rang and said he's too busy to help out and that he has another job." He answers.

"Oh, okay." I shrug. I don't ask any more questions. I guess if he's busy, he's busy.

I go about sorting the kitchen units and ordering in the equipment for the bakery and a new sign for the front of the shop. Finally things are slowly starting to come together. The place still looks like a hell hole at the moment but I figured it wouldn't hurt to order in the stuff now, ready. It's not like I've got much else to do at the moment.

Chapter Eight

It's been three weeks since I saw Gaige. I haven't heard from him, absolutely nothing. I feel hurt and I miss his company like crazy.

I finally have working electrics and fully working heating and plumbing.

Deciding I need a break from it all I go for a walk around the town and down to the shore. It's minus something degrees, blistering cold, and there's snow everywhere, but I just needed the escape. I walk along the docks and see a bench and sit. I have on my new extra thick padded long coat, woolly hat, and gloves. Through all of the layers I can still feel the bite of the ice cold air.

I sit and watch the fishing boats come in and out the dock. I hear giggling and I turn my head in that direction. I see a couple in an embrace, kissing and walking along hand in hand in this direction. I smile, thinking how sweet it is. I remember when Jay and I were like that.

It's not until the couple come closer that I realise it's Gaige. I get up and try to inconspicuously walk away from them as quick as I can. Why wouldn't Gaige tell me he was seeing someone?! That's what friends do, right? I mean he just leaves and I never hear from him. Now he just pops up with some tart!

I am walking too quickly and not paying attention to where I'm walking. I'm angry and lost in my own thoughts. I slip on some ice and fall into the freezing ocean.

I gasp as the freezing cold water hits my body. I desperately try to keep on the surface but the weight of my clothes and jacket are making it hard.

"HELP!" I yell, gasping for breath.

I see Gaige lean over the dock. Reaching in he grabs me by my coat and pulls me up out of the water.

"Thank kkk yyyou." I shiver.

I get to my feet and my whole body is shivering.

"Why weren't you looking where the hell you were going?!" He yells.

I ignore him and start walking back the way I came. I just want to get home, take a hot shower, and forget this moment ever happened.

"Esme!" He yells.

His girlfriend comes running over to me.

"Do you want a ride?" She asks kindly. I shake my head. Even though I would love to be inside a warm car right now, I'm too stubborn to admit it.

"Nnno ttthank yyou." I say waddling my way up the path.

"Esme!" Gaige yells again.

I hold my shaking hand up and flip him off.

I make it back to the shop and thankfully Bob and his men have buggered off. I walk straight to the bathroom and jump in the hot shower. As soon as the hot water hits my skin I moan.

I stay in the shower for as long as I can. Thoughts of Gaige go running through my head. I can't believe he hasn't even bothered to see me for what, nearly a month, and I run into him with his girlfriend. I thought I was wrong about him but I guess I was right from the beginning. Arsehole.

After my shower I put on some extra layers, still feeling the cold. I can't seem to warm up properly. I pour myself a wine and call Sally.

I tell her what happened.

"Oh Esme, thank god he was there to pull you out." She says.

"Is that it? Is that all you're going to say?" I ask.

"Well what else do you want me to say?" She bites back.

"What about Gaige having a girlfriend? Him not contacting me for nearly a month and then me just randomly bumping into him with his new tart?" I fume down the phone.

"Esme, why would you care if he's with someone? Calling her a tart isn't very nice, she offered you a ride home as well remember." Sally points out.

"I don't care that he has a girlfriend, I couldn't care less. I just thought we were friends. Friends don't do that to each other. Friends don't just disappear for a month and then turn up with a new girlfriend." I rant.

"Okay, right. You don't care, just keep telling yourself that." Sally snorts.

"Look, I get that you'd be pissed that he hasn't contacted you but you can't be pissed that he has a girlfriend." Sally states.

God I hate it when she's right. I don't say anything, I just poke my tongue out at her down the phone.

"Listen Esme, it will get better there. Once

the bakery is open and you can settle into more of a life and make friends it will all happen for you okay. Now I hate to leave you, but I have a date in like ten minutes." Sally says.

"Go have a blast on your date and remember to keep your legs crossed until at least date three." I tell her.

"It's Juan from work. I am not making any promises! I've been wanting to ride him since he started back in September. If the opportunity should arise for a thoroughly good ride I shall be jumping on that. It's been too damn long. Got to go, he's here. Love ya, bye." She disconnects.

I sigh and decide to eat junk food in bed and read a book. It's only 8pm but I don't care; I just want to curl up and forget the day.

I try to keep my head down, only waving hello as I pass by people in the town. I'm sure they're all talking about the stupid girl that fell in the ocean. I mean, how can you accidentally fall into the ocean? It's not like you can miss it!

Bob asked me to pick up some bits for him at the hardware store so I jump in his truck. I'm still yet to buy myself one, the rental had to go back. I was going to ask Gaige to help me a few weeks back but because he's been such an arsehole I haven't bothered.

I park up and groan when I spot Gaige's truck. Of course he had to be here.

I jump out and head in with my trolly. I keep my gaze fixated on the task at hand and force myself not to look around for him. I look down at the list and see written is a drill bit with a number next to it. I look up at all of the drill bits. The one Bob wants is about two feet out of my reach. I hold the list in my mouth and step into the trolly to give me the height to reach it. I smile when I grab it. See, I don't need no man to help me.

"What the hell do you think you're doing?" Is yelled at me from down the aisle. I spin around quickly and in doing so rock the trolly.

"Woah!" I yell as I wobble and fall out of the trolly.

"Ow! Son of a bitch, that's going to bruise." I groan, laying back on the hard concrete floor.

Gaige stands over me, looking pissed off. I instantly feel myself getting annoyed. Why the hell is he angry?! He made me lose my balance and fall.

He reaches down and offers his hand but I slap it away and get up by myself, groaning in pain.

"Why the hell do you keep trying to injure yourself?" He asks, crossing his arms over his chest.

"It's your bloody fault! If you hadn't shouted

at me I wouldn't have looked your way and got distracted. Now if you don't mind, you can piss off so I can carry on shopping for Bob." I state going back to my trolly with a slight limp. My arse is killing me.

"Let me see what's on the list. I can help you." He states, holding out his hand.

I laugh.

"No thank you. If I want help I will ask a friend." I see the sting my words have and do my best to walk off without limping and holding my backside.

Gaige storms in front of me and stands at the end of my trolly, forcing me to stop.

"I thought we were friends." He states angrily.

"Friends do not fuck off when their friend needs them. Friends do not avoid their friends for nearly a month and then just bump into them with a new tart on their arm." I spit angrily.

At first he looks apologetic then at my mention of the tart he gets angry.

"Amy is not a tart. Don't go throwing shit at people who are happy together just because you're still in love with your dead husband. You'll forever be widowed and fucking lonely." He yells.

I jolt back, feeling the mental slap of his

words. I feel the other shoppers and the staff member's eyes on me. I swallow back my emotion.

"You're right, I'm sorry. Congratulations on being happy." I mumble. I walk away leaving the trolly and everyone standing around. As soon as I'm outside I practically sprint to the truck. I see Gaige come running out shouting my name. He's too late. I put my foot down and get out of there as quick as I can.

I drive and drive until I see a place to park up. I break and let the tears fall.

He is right, I have no one. I have no friends, no family. What am I even still doing here? This wasn't my dream; this pain wasn't my dream. What the hell have I done to deserve all of this shit being thrown at me?!

"What happened to you being here with me Jay? Huh?! It wasn't supposed to be like this. I could face all of this if you were by my side. I don't know how much more I can take." I sob.

There is a tap at the window and I jump and scream. Gaige is standing there. I immediately go to start the engine to drive off but Gaige is one step ahead of me. He rips open the door and snatches the key.

"Gaige I'm not in the mood, okay? You've made your point now please just leave me alone." I beg.

He reaches forward and cups my face, wiping the tears with his thumb.

"I didn't mean what I said back there. I was angry and I should never have said it." He says.

I refuse to admit how comforting his hand on my face is. I refuse to admit that I want nothing more than to hug him. I won't let myself. I pull my face back and hold out my hands for the keys.

"Esme, I am so sorry, I really am." He apologises.

"Okay, can I have the keys now? I need to get the truck back to Bob." I ask, not looking at him.

He sighs and hands me the keys and steps back. I slam the door shut and drive off, leaving him.

As soon as I get back I tell Bob I'm sorry I couldn't get his stuff and that he can go home early.

"You sure you're okay Esme?" He asks.

"Yeah I'm fine Bob, just feeling a bit under the weather." I give him the best smile I can muster.

He nods but I know he's not buying a word of it. It doesn't matter, the whole town are probably gossiping about it by now anyway. Well I suppose I don't have to worry about telling anyone about Jay now. Gaige saw to that for me.

I climb straight into bed and cry myself to sleep. I call Bob the next morning and tell him to take a break for a while. I just want to be on my own. Sally tries calling me several times but I just ignore her. I sleep, eat, and nothing else. There's been knocks at the door but I've ignored them.

After a few days I answer Sally's call and she gives me an ear bashing for worrying her sick. I break down and tell her what happened.

"That motherfucker! That's it, I'm looking for a Canadian hit man." She fumes down the phone.

"I will be okay. He's just the one person I trusted enough to tell. I thought of him as a friend and he goes and says something like that to me. It hurt a lot but I know he's right. I'm a lonely widow who still loves her dead husband and maybe I'll be that way forever. What if this is it for me Sally? They say you only get one true love, what if I'm alone for the rest of my life?" I sob.

"I swear I'm going to hunt that bastard down myself for setting you back like this. I promise you that one true love bullshit is a lie. We're all destined to fall in love. Sometimes it's more than once, other times it's just one person. Esme you're twenty-three and beautiful inside and out. You will not be lonely forever. Mark my words, Gaige has feelings for you. That's why he distanced himself and that's why he said such spiteful things. He is jealous of Jay." She states.

"How can someone be jealous of a dead man?" I ask.

"Because he's not dead to you. He's still very much a part of your heart. Gaige wants your heart and seeing it belong to someone else is probably torture for him." She sighs.

"I think you're reading far too much into it. He is happy with this Amy. I just think he's a bit of an arsehole." I state.

Sally snorts.

"Okay, have it your way, he's a bit of an arsehole. You going to be okay?" She asks.

"Yeah, I will be in the end." I answer honestly.

"Okay babe. I love ya."

"I love ya too." I say then disconnect.

Chapter Nine

Bob and his apprentices came back to work the next day. I didn't say anything; Bob just walked right up to me and pulled me in for a hug.

"Next time someone speaks to you like that, you tell me and I will give them a piece of my mind. Oh, and the wife baked you a pie." He says reaching over and handing me a pie. I smile and laugh.

"Well thank you. You've definitely made me feel better. Oh and thank you for the pie." I say smiling.

"Now do you need me to run any errands for you today?" I ask.

"No, no, we will manage just fine." He says giving the guys a side glance.

"Bob? What is it that needs doing?" I ask.

"I'm not having you go there, I will go myself." He insists.

"You need something from the lumber yard." I state, guessing exactly why he didn't want me going.

I sigh.

"Bob, it's fine. He can't say anything worse than what he has already said. Give me the keys." I hold out my hand. Bob relents and hands me the keys.

"Fine, he should have the order ready so you won't even need to get out of the truck." He states.

I nod and leave, refusing to acknowledge the butterflies and feeling of dread in my stomach. I follow the directions Bob gave me and spot the sign up ahead. I turn up the dirt track road to the yard. I pull up and park. I notice a house just off to the left, I'm guessing that's where Gaige lives.

I sit for a moment longer. There's no sign of Gaige. I sigh and jump down from the truck. I search for him.

I walk around outside but he's nowhere to be seen. With no other options I walk up the steps up to his house. I knock but there's no answer,

I open the door.

"Hello?" I shout as I stick my head in the door.

I look around. Wow, this place is beautiful.

I hear movement towards the back of the house. I follow the sound. I turn around the corner and see Gaige shirtless. He's kissing Amy who is sitting on the kitchen work top wearing one of his t-shirts. My stomach recoils. I step back and knock into a chair which brings their attention to me.

"I'm sorry, I was out front, Bob sent me. I did knock. I'm just going to go and wait out front." I scramble as fast as I can to get out of there.

"Esme, wait." Gaige calls.

I stop and turn around and hold out my arms.

"Go on then, throw it at me, whatever insult you want. Here's your open target. I'm tired Gaige, I just want to pick up what Bob ordered and go, okay?" I sigh.

He comes to a stop just in front of me. I try to ignore his perfect muscled body. I keep my eyes cast down and refuse to look at him in the eye.

"Esme." He says as he lifts my chin, forcing me to look at him. He sighs.

"I...I just." He tries to say what's on his mind but I just stare blankly back at him.

"Bob's order is over there." He states.

I step back and his hand falls away.

"Great. Thank you." I mutter.

I go over to the order of wood and start lifting it into the truck. Bob failed to mention the amount that he ordered. This is going to take me at least twenty minutes to load.

"Let me help you." He states.

"It's fine, I've got it. Amy is waiting for you. Go back inside or you'll catch pneumonia." I puff, carrying the wood to the truck.

"I said let me help you." He argues back.

"And I said I don't need your help. Go back inside before you lose a nipple to frost bite." I snap.

"God you're a stubborn woman! Fine, do it yourself. I don't give a shit." He walks off.

"Yeah, I'm a stubborn, lonely widow who refuses to stop loving her dead husband. I can live with that." I mumble under my breath.

"I apologised for that."

"Yeah, so it's all okay. Off you pop. Wouldn't want your knob to freeze and drop off." I point.

"God you're infuriating!" He yells.

I smirk and carry on lifting the wood and ignoring him. Eventually he goes back inside. I finish up the load and drive on out of there. Every one of my muscles are aching from lifting all of that wood.

When I return I tell Bob that I'm having a

soak in the bath and ask him to keep the guys downstairs. My achy muscles are screaming for it. Bob doesn't look too impressed. Not by me needing a bath but by Gaige not being there to lift the load onto the truck.

I run myself a nice hot bath with extra bubbles and bath salts. I moan as I sink into the hot soapy water.

"God that feels bloody good." I moan.

I close my eyes and feel my body relax.

I hear arguing and a commotion coming from downstairs. I chose to ignore it. It must be Bob arguing with a delivery driver or something, it wouldn't be the first time.

"Do not go in there Gaige!" I here yelled.

The bathroom door swings open and Gaige barrels in.

"What the hell do you think you're doing?" I squeak, making sure all areas are covered by bubbles.

"I'm sick of the crap I'm getting because of you. People are giving me looks and phoning me up tell me what an ass I'm being."

"You deserved that, boy!" Bob yells from outside.

"My life was simple! It was calm! Ever since you crashed into town it has been nothing but damn chaos!" Gaige yells, running his fingers through his dark hair.

"Well thank you for barging into my bathroom to tell me how I've ruined your life. Would you like me to announce when I next take a shower or go for a pee so you can do the same again? Maybe throw more insults at me while I'm indisposed?" I snap back. My once relaxed muscles start tensing up.

He sighs. He looks tired and stressed.

"I'm sorry, I didn't mean for it to come out like that. This! This is what you're doing to me. You get me so riled up and angry. I can't handle it."

"I'm sorry for making you feel that way but I'm pretty sure we were friends before, even if it was for a short while. You cut that, not me. I haven't done anything to deserve the way you're treating me. Now please piss off. My bath water is getting cold and I want to get out without putting on a show." I state.

"I'm sorry, we can never be friends." He says before walking out and slamming the door behind him.

"Arsehole!" I shout after him.

I rub my chest, feeling hurt.

"Christ, I won't have a heart left at this rate." I murmur.

I get out of the bath and dry off, chucking

on sweats and Jay's favourite hoodie. I crawl into bed.

Bob comes in with a fresh coffee and a slice of pie. I smile.

"Here, don't listen to him. He doesn't mean it, but you know that right?" I shrug and take the pie and coffee.

Bob sits on the edge of the bed.

"Men sometimes can't handle certain feelings. We are simple, stupid creatures and we like to keep it that way. When we meet the right woman that all changes. For example, my wife says men are black, white, and grey. Women are all of the colours of the world. Which is true, us men go about our lives until that one woman comes into it and turns our world completely upside down. Suddenly our dull and boring life becomes this wonderful explosion of colours." Bob smiles and shrugs.

"Bob, I'm not in Gaige's life, Amy is. It makes no sense why he's being such an arsehole to me." I point out.

"Ahh but you are the one that brought the colours into his life, not Amy. That's why he's so bent out of shape about it all. Amy isn't his explosion of colours, you are." Bob pats my leg and leaves.

"But we aren't together! He doesn't want my colours and I'm not giving him my colours. Bob, you're not making sense." I yell at him.

I sigh and take a bite of the pie. I moan.

"Oh my god this pie is amazing!" I yell to Bob.

I need this recipe, it's the best cherry pie I've ever tasted.

I spend the rest of the day sprawled out on my bed searching for wall art for the bakery and other accessories. The work is almost done and I'm one step closer to opening. As soon as my own kitchen is done I will be practicing and perfecting my recipes. I miss baking so much, it has always centred me. I love watching people's reaction and seeing their appreciation of the food I bake for them.

Over the coming days I try to get out more. I head to the Sunken Ship for some lunch on a couple of the days. The people there smile and chat. I'm finally starting to feel more like a resident and less like a visitor.

I walk to the grocery store to pick up some supplies. We are supposed to be getting a snowstorm over the next few days and I don't plan on venturing out when it hits.

I walk into the store and the bell above the door chimes.

"Morning Nellie, morning Eric!" I sing happily as I walk in.

I grab my basket and browse the aisles, grabbing bread, milk, and butter. I turn the corner and walk into a hard chest.

"Sorry." I apologise.

I look up and see it's Gaige. I roll my eyes.

"Damn it, I was in such a good mood." I complain.

Gaige doesn't say anything, he just stands in front of me, looking at me. I wave my hand in front of his face.

"Hello, Gaige, are you in there? Got any insults you want to throw at me while I'm standing directly in front of you?" I ask waving my arms around.

I start to move around him but he reaches out and grabs my arm.

"I am truly sorry for everything." He apologises, his voice quiet.

"Huh?" I ask.

"Gaige, shall I get six eggs or a dozen?" Amy asks as she walks up to us. She stops when she sees Gaige holding my arm. He immediately lets go and turns to Amy.

"Get a dozen, just to be sure." He says.

I shake my head, wondering if I just stepped into the twilight zone.

I grab the rest of my things which of course includes wine and chocolate.

I pay for my things and Nellie reaches for my hand.

"I'm sorry we didn't warn you that he was in here." She apologises.

"Nellie, you don't need to apologise and for future reference, you don't need to warn me either. We are adults and we will learn to live in the same town without tearing each other apart." I states smiling.

"Seems to me what you two need to do is get in the sack, then the town can have some peace." Eric murmurs.

"Eric!" Nellie scorns.

"Err, bye. I will be in next week." I wave as I leave.

I asked Bob earlier to come with me to get a new truck so after dropping my shopping back Bob pulls up and takes me to a local dealership.

"Now let me do the talking. They catch on that you've got money and have no clue about trucks and they will sell you the biggest load of crap going."

"Gotcha! My lips are sealed. Not a peep. Just one thing though Bob, heated seats and bluetooth are a must." I state.

We pull up and jump out and look around the lot at the trucks.

"Welcome to Donald's Real Deals. What can I help you with today?" A guy greets us with a bright smile.

"Hello Donald." I greet.

The guy laughs.

"I'm not Donald, I'm Wyatt."

"Okay. I'm Esme, it's nice to meet you." I hold out my hand and shake his.

"I want to buy a truck, what you got?" I ask.

He walks us through a few but I can't take my eyes off of the bright red one.

"I like the red." I whisper to Bob. He nods.

"Lets talk shop Wyatt. What can you do the red truck for?" Bob asks.

He crosses his arms over his chest. Meanwhile I'm like a kid in a candy shop, climbing in the truck. I turn on the sound system and music blares out really loud.

"ITS GOT A GREAT STEREO BOB!" I yell.

"Well, it has got all of the latest extras." Wyatt says to Bob.

"Those things don't interest us." Bob states.

"Oo Bob! There are cup holders! And a built in sat nav!" I yell excitedly from the truck.

"Jesus Christ! Give me strength." Bob sighs and pinches the bridge of his nose.

"Oooo shiny!" I sing from the truck.

"Just give us a damn price so I can get the hell out of here." Bob moans.

"It's $20,000. It has ten thousand miles on the clock and it's only a year old. I think you'll agree that it's a very good deal." Wyatt states.

I start honking the horn.

"Out the way bitches, I've got me a new truck." I laugh.

"She'll take the damn truck." Bob sighs.

I sign the paperwork and pay for the car in the office with Wyatt while Bob walks around looking at the trucks.

"There's the keys and the paperwork. Enjoy your new truck." He smiles.

"Thank you." I beam excitedly. I stand up to leave but Wyatt stops me.

"Esme, I wondered if maybe you'd like to go out for a drink with me sometime?" He ask.

"Oh, um. As in, a date?" I ask.

"Yeah, a date." He states.

I bite my thumbnail nervously. "I...well the thing is I'm not ready to be dating right now. Sorry." I apologise.

"Don't be. When you are ready, call me." He says and hands me his card.

"I will." I smile.

I follow Bob home and park up my new truck outside. Overall, today has been a good day. I just have to take each day as it comes.

Chapter Ten

Today is the anniversary of Jay's death. I've given Bob the day off and I've switched my phone off. I don't want to speak to Sally or anyone else. I just want it to be me and him.

I walk along the docks. The ground is covered in thick snow left over from the storm. It's quiet out. With it being so cold people are only going out when they really need to. It's peaceful.

I sit on a bench and look down at my wedding ring. I feel my bottom lip begin to tremble as the tears fall. I'm not sure how long I sit for in the freezing cold. I get up and wipe my eyes. Deciding I need a drink I walk to The Sunken Ship.

"Hey Esme, what can I get you?" Jack asks.

"How many shots are left in that bottle of vodka?" I ask.

Jack looks at the bottle.

"Maybe twenty?" He shrugs.

"Great. I'll take the bottle." I state handing him my card.

He hands me the bottle and I walk over to a booth. I'm tucked away in the corner alone with the bottle of vodka.

"To you Jay." I state. I raise the bottle and down some vodka. I squeeze my eyes shut as it burns my throat.

"To leaving me on my own." I raise the bottle again and drink some more.

"To making me live my dream without you." I do the same again.

I drink and toast Jay each time. When half of the bottle is gone I stand and yell.

"Happy first anniversary to my dead husband! May he be having fun in heaven while I'm suffering all alone here! Cheers!" I yell and down some more before flopping back into the booth.

"Esme honey, I think you've had enough. Do you want me to take you home?" Eloise asks.

"El-ou-is. I'm fine. I can get myself home absolutely fine. Do you know why? Because I'm a widow! Being a widow means you're allll alone, it means you have to do it alllll by yourself." I slur.

"I think we all need a hand sometimes. Maybe I could call someone for you?" Eloise offers.

I shake my head and laugh.

"I don't have anyone. No family, no friends, just little old me! You know my husband lied to me? He said he would love me forever and always. Where is he now? Dead! He's dead. A year ago today I watched him die. I held him so he wouldn't be scared, so he wouldn't be alone. Now who's holding me?! Who's comforting me so I'm not scared and alone? No one!" I yell sobbing.

I sit back down. Wiping my tears away I drink more vodka. I ignore the sympathetic gazes I'm getting. Eloise leaves me to it and I curl myself into a ball, hugging the vodka bottle. I close my eyes.

"Forever and always Jay." I mumble.

I feel myself being moved and I jolt awake.

"It's okay sweetie, Gaige is taking you home." Eloise soothes.

"Put me down." I demand.

"What and watch you fall on your ass and hurt yourself? Not a chance." Gaige answers as he carries me.

I huff.

"Why did you call him? You're a traitor Eloise. He will probably dump me in a ditch and leave me for dead. He hates me." I yell back.

"Shut up." He snaps.

He dumps me in the passenger seat and puts my seatbelt on for me. Walking around he jumps in and starts up his truck to drive me back to the shop.

I feel my stomach roll.

"Gaige pull over, I'm going to be sick." I gag. He slams the truck to the side of the road and I practically fall out onto the floor and start throwing up. Gaige rubs my back soothingly and makes sure my hair is out of my face.

"Oh god. I think I threw up a lung." I groan.

"Here, sip some water. Rinse your mouth out." Gaige hands me a bottle of water and I rinse my mouth out. He helps me back into the truck. I rest my head against the window, feeling my eyes start to close.

I wake up and it's the middle of the night. When I open my eyes I don't recognise where I am. I start to panic. I turn and see Gaige asleep next to me, topless. Did we sleep together?! I lift the cover slowly and peek under the covers: he has bottoms on. I'm desperate for the toilet but I'm only in my underwear and I have no idea where the bathroom is. I slowly creep out of bed and tip toe out of the room in search of the bathroom.

After opening a few doors I eventually find it. I do my business then decide to search for my clothes and get the hell out of here. I creep back into the room and try to hunt for my clothes in complete darkness. As I creep forward my foot catches on something and I go flying and land on the floor with a thud. The light comes on and a sleepy looking Gaige stands over me.

"Hi." I smile. I'm almost curled into a foetal position to try and cover my modesty.

"What are you doing?" He asks.

"Trying to find my clothes so I can go home." I state.

"You're not going home. Come back to bed." He states.

"Err, Gaige, I am going home. I want to go home to my bed and take some painkillers and sleep." I argue back.

"I put pain killers and water next to you. I'm not driving you home at 3am. It's snowing heavily and I'm tired so just get your ass back to bed so I can sleep." He sighs.

I look out of the window and see the snow falling rapidly. I sigh and get up.

"Fine." I grumble.

"But keep your hands to yourself." I warn.

"I will try." He answers sarcastically.

I take the painkillers and drink some water. Feeling dehydrated I drink the lot.

I curl up and tuck the cover around me so I'm not touching him in anyway. I lay in bed listening to Gaige's breathing and waiting for him to fall asleep.

"Go to sleep Esme." He murmurs.

"Don't tell me what to do." I snap.

He sighs and ignores me. As much as I fight it, sleep wins.

I stretch out and groan as the daylight beams through the windows.

I blink a few times and then I remember where I am. I sit up a little too quickly and the room starts spinning. Why the hell did I drink so much vodka?

I spot a dressing gown hanging up so I grab it and try and find Gaige so I can get my arse back to the shop.

I find him in the kitchen dressed only in a pair of low hung sweatpants, leaning against the counter drinking coffee. I go to speak but then I realise he's on the phone.

"Yeah Bob, she's here. No it's all good, she's

safe. Will keep her here for a few days until it's sorted. Catch you later. Bye." Gaige disconnects.

"I am not staying here for a few days." I state, crossing my arms.

Gaige spins around.

"Ah you're awake. Do you always eavesdrop on conversations or just as and when you feel like it?" He asks.

"I don't know. Do you always walk in on women when they're naked or is that just me?" I snap back.

"Just you." He answers quickly.

His answer has me stuttering.

"Eh, what?"

"Ah I've finally found a way to shut you up." He smiles.

"I'm not staying here Gaige, I have to get back. I have deliveries coming and work being done. I need to get back." I state.

Gaige walks towards me and grabs my hand, pulling me to the patio doors. He slides them open and points.

"There's already ten foot of snow out there and there's more coming in today and tomorrow. No one is going anywhere." He states.

I stare out at the view of the white blanket covering the entire town.

"The view is amazing from up here." I whisper.

You can just about make out people's roofs and the smoke coming from their chimneys. Even the boats in the distance are covered in snow. The town is silent; everyone is staying indoors and keeping safe and warm.

I go to step out onto his decking but Gaige grabs my arm and stops me.

"You take one step you'll fall ten feet into the snow." He states.

"Huh, I thought this was decking." I answer.

He smiles and shakes his head.

"No, there are steps down to the decking just there." He points.

I can't see a thing, there's snow everywhere.

I feel Gaige's thumb gently stroking my arm. I shiver, must be the cold air.

"Come in, you're getting cold." He slides the door shut.

Gaige makes me a coffee and some toast.

I perch at his breakfast bar, unable to stop looking at his well defined muscly body. Every time I make myself look away to focus on something else my eyes trail back to his glorious body.

"What am I supposed to do without

clothes?" I ask.

"I have jumpers and t-shirts you can borrow. I just can't help you out in the underwear department." He states.

"Does Amy keep any clothes here that I could borrow?" I ask.

"She doesn't stay here." He answers back.

"Oh." I answer because I'm not sure what else to say.

"I'm sorry Eloise called you last night to pick me up. I...I wasn't in the best place and I should have just gone back to the shop. If I had I wouldn't be here now and you wouldn't be stuck with me." I apologise.

"Eloise didn't call me. I was on a date with Amy in the bar the entire time." He states.

I slam my head down on the counter and head butt myself over and over.

"Oh god. I'm so so sorry. How busy was it in the bar?" I ask, my face pressed against the counter.

He moves around and lifts my face, cupping it in his hands.

"Don't apologise, ever. It doesn't matter who was there. I'm the one who is sorry. I left you alone for my own selfish reasons when you were still in so much pain. You're not alone Esme."

He wipes away my tears, tears that I hadn't realised were falling. He pulls me to him, holding me tight. I wrap my arms around him and let the tears fall.

I need this: to be held, to be comforted, to feel safe.

I lift my face up to look at him. His eyes are searching mine.

"Thank you." I whisper.

He wipes my tears away with his thumb. The air shifts around us.

My eyes drop to his mouth and he moves slowly closer. His lips are just millimetres from mine. I close the distance and kiss him. He kisses me back. I moan as his tongue strokes mine. He trails kisses along my neck, nipping at my skin.

I freeze. What am I doing? I'm such a slut. Gaige notices and stops.

"Esme." He rasps.

"What am I doing? I can't do this. The day after the anniversary of Jay's death! And Amy! Oh god, I'm a horrible person." I push at Gaige's chest. He steps back and I run past him to the bathroom.

I slam the door shut and lean against the sink. Shit, shit, shit! My heart is beating wildly in my chest. I enjoyed the kiss, too much, and I wanted more. Oh god! He's with someone else and I'm not ready for a relationship. Am I?

"Esme." Gaige knocks on the door.

I open the door and see a deflated Gaige standing in front of me.

"Gaige...I..." I sigh.

"I'm sorry. It shouldn't have happened. It won't happen again. Please don't repeat this to Amy." Gaige says before walking away.

I feel like I've just been slapped. He's right, of course, it shouldn't have happened. He's with Amy. Why am I so disappointed by that? Maybe it's because he's a solid figure. He held me and comforted me. Maybe it's that. Yes, it has to be that. I'm just missing that part of life.

After my mental pep talk I go around the house in search of Gaige. I find him sprawled out watching ice hockey in the lounge.

I sit next to him.

"So which team do you want to win?" I ask.

"The Maple Leafs." He answers, his gaze never leaving the screen.

"Cool. The red team?" I ask.

"The blue team." He corrects.

"I went ice skating once. I wasn't very good, couldn't even skate holding on the side. I slipped over and split my jeans." I say, nibbling my thumb nail.

"Doesn't surprise me." He answers,

We sit in awkward silence for a while longer. I tap my foot anxiously.

"Esme?" He asks.

I spin round to face him, curling my legs under me.

"Okay. Just let me get this off my chest. Please don't interrupt me because I'm trying to get my words out without messing it up or making you mad." I rush out and pause, waiting for him to answer.

"Well?" I ask.

"You said not to interrupt." He states.

"Right. Anyway what I'm saying is, I liked us kissing. I did. It was nice. You're a good kisser." I say. His lips twitch, fighting a smile.

"You're right though, it shouldn't have happened. You are with Amy and she's a nice girl. I mean, it wouldn't make it okay if she were a bitch but we probably wouldn't feel so bad about doing it." I say not looking at him. I focus on the top of his t-shirt instead.

"The final thing is, I'm not ready for any of that yet. Well, I don't think I am."

"You don't think?" He interrupts.

"Shh, don't interrupt me. I just don't know. I mean it was the anniversary yesterday. That makes me an awful person, like a total slut bag. Shouldn't there be this massive sign that says 'you're ready to move on'. I know I'm crazy but I still love Jay. I don't know when I will stop loving him, and that's not fair on you or anyone, right?" I ask.

"Esme, look at me." He demands.

I look at him.

"I enjoyed the kiss too, a lot actually. I think when the time comes and you're ready, you will know. You shouldn't feel guilty for moving on. Now as much as I liked our kiss, I'm with Amy and I'm not the cheating kind. You will find the right guy one day. You'll be happy again Esme." He states.

I give him a small smile and hold out my hand.

"Friends?"

"Friends." He smiles and shakes my hand.

We sit there a moment longer until I get an idea.

"Do you have any baking stuff? Flour, eggs, etc?" I ask excitedly.

He smiles.

"I have some, yeah. I'm not sure what's in date."

"Yes!" I jump from the sofa and run into the

kitchen.

I run back into the lounge.

"Do you mind if I do some baking?" I ask.

Gaige laughs and shakes his head.

"Knock yourself out."

"Awesome!" I yell over my shoulder and start pulling out lots of ingredients.

Chapter Eleven

"Dinner!" I yell. It turned out Gaige's kitchen was loaded with baking ingredients. When I was digging through the back of the cupboard I found an old mixer and I may have screamed with excitement and made Gaige crap his pants thinking I had cut a finger off.

Gaige walks in smiling.

"Do take a seat sir. Tonight, your taste buds will be alive with pleasure." I twirl with the towel.

"Smells good, what is it?" He asks.

"I have made you a traditional English roast dinner. You have slow cooked minted lamb, seasoned roast potatoes, sausage meat stuffing, and pigs in blankets, which are usually for Christmas but I got excited. Oh, and not forgetting Yorkshire puddings! Accompanied by a selection of seasonal veg." I state as I point to each dish.

I sit next to him.

"Come on then, eat up." I elbow him, grinning.

"Oh shit, I forgot." I jump up and grab a dish and place it down.

"What's that?" He asks.

"Mint sauce." I state as I pour a load onto my lamb.

"But we've already got gravy." He states.

"Yes but it's delicious. Trust me. Hhmm." I moan.

He shrugs and pours a small amount onto his lamb. I watch him try it and smile when he nods.

"See! Anyway, cheers to new beginnings." I smile.

Gaige grabs his beer bottle and clinks it with my water.

"No wine tonight?" He asks.

"Um no, funnily enough my stomach isn't really feeling alcohol right now." I state, shovelling food into my mouth.

"But it's ready for that." He smiles pointing to my plate.

"Oh yeah, stodgy food is the best cure for hangover. Normally it would be a takeout but a roast will do. If I were really hungover and dying

I wouldn't have been able to do this." I state.

"Stodgy food?" He asks.

"Yeah, like high fat, sugar, and carbs to soak up the alcohol."

"Ah okay." Gaige smiles and continues eating.

When we finish I go to clear up the plates.

"Sit down. You made the dinner, I will clear up." Gaige orders and takes the plates to the sink.

"Holy hell I think I just had an orgasm." I blurt out.

Gaige bursts out laughing and shakes his head.

"Is there any thought process before you speak?" He asks.

I laugh.

"Not usually, what's the point of holding back? People can't accuse me of being two faced then, can they? If I air all of my thoughts I'm not hiding anything." I smile.

"Very true." Gaige smiles and finishes loading the dishwasher.

We move into the lounge.

"Wait! Are you ready for pudding?" I ask.

"Yes I think I can squeeze it in." He says patting his belly.

I smile and skip back to the kitchen. I come back in with a Victoria sponge cake.

I place it down on the coffee table.

"Viola! It's a classic Victoria sponge cake. Made with fresh cream and strawberries with homemade strawberry jam. We wouldn't normally have this for pudding but I thought why not show you a bit of England." I shrug as I cut him a piece.

I stand and just watch him take that first bite. He moans.

"Good?" I ask.

"So good." He answers. I clap and cut myself a piece.

"I don't think I've seen you this happy about something before." He states.

I smile.

"I love baking, it's like my therapy. Truthfully I haven't baked since before Jay got ill."

"It has been that long?" He asks.

"Yep, it has been eighteen months and seven days since I've baked." I state.

"We're still talking about actual baking right? You're not using it as a euphemism?" He smirks.

"Ha-ha, actually it's the same for both. Last time I baked chocolate orange muffins, Jay's favourite, it got a little messy." I smile at the memory.

Gaige reaches over and wipes some cream off of my face with his thumb. Then he places it in his mouth and sucks it clean off.

I feel my breath hitch and I lick my bottom lip, watching him. His eyes become heated. I look away and cough.

"Oh it's a little hot in here isn't it? I'm just going to grab a cold drink." I say jumping up from the sofa and walking into the kitchen.

"God Esme! Get a grip. You're stuck here for I don't know how long. Keep your damn libido in check." I say to myself.

"Err, thanks for the cake Esme." Gaige says, making me jump.

"Shit." I gasp and spin around.

Gaige smiles.

"Not funny! I could have had a heart attack or worse, pissed myself!" I state, my hand over my erratic heart.

"Pissing yourself is worse than a heart attack?" He asks.

"Yes, there is nothing to be ashamed of if you have a heart attack but if you piss yourself that's pure embarrassment. Don't even get me started on if you were to shit your pants." I state seriously.

Gaige bursts out laughing and shakes his head.

"I love how your mind works Esme." He says walking off.

I smile.

I decide to go to bed. Gaige offered to sleep on the sofa but I refused and said it would be fine. This time instead of just being in my underwear I'm wearing Gaige's t-shirt. I climb into bed. I feel my eyes get heavy and soon fall asleep.

Sometime later I feel the bed dip and Gaige leans over and kisses my head.

"Night Esme." He whispers and lies down.

I smile and drift back off to sleep. The next day I bake some cupcakes, cookies, and brownies just to pass the time.

I make us fajitas for dinner and Gaige makes us a batch of margaritas.

"I feel like we should have a sombrero or at the very least some Mexican music playing in the background." I point out.

"That can be arranged." He gets up from his chair. He walks over to a little speaker in his kitchen and Mexican music fills the room.

"Amazing." I smile.

We finished our dinner and are just talking. I start to feel a happy buzz from the margaritas.

"How about a game of never have I ever?" I ask.

"Okay. Want to make it interesting with tequila shots?" He asks.

"Hell yes, bring on the shots!" I yell.

Gaige smiles and comes back with some limes, salt, tequila, and shot glasses.

"Okay, ladies first." He says pouring the drink.

"Okay. Never have I ever eaten liver." I state smiling.

Gaige rolls his eyes, picks up his shot, and downs it.

"Playing it like that are we? Okay then. Never have I ever been married." He states smiling.

"Bastard." I smile. I pick up my shot and down it and cough.

"Christ that's strong." I murmur.

Gaige refills our shots.

"Okay, my turn. Never have I ever had a threesome." I wink and laugh.

Gaige downs his drink.

"OH my god! You've had a three way?!" I screech.

He shrugs.

"Yeah, many years ago when I was traveling here." He states.

"And?" I ask.

"A gentlemen never kisses and tells." He states.

"I think you lost the title of gentlemen when you had that threesome." I state.

"I'm still not telling you. My turn, never have I ever been to England." He says smiling.

"Oh that's a low blow." I state, downing the shot.

"God damn!" I rasp, shaking my head.

"Right! Never have I ever peed standing up." I smirk.

Gaige shakes his head and downs his shot.

"Never have I ever got it on in an elevator." He smirks.

"Ha! Neither have I! You drink!" I laugh and point.

"Shit." He says before downing his shot.

"My turn. Never have I ever masturbated in the shower." I blush a little at my own words.

"Woah! You're taking it real personal and dirty aren't you?! Sorry, nope. I haven't." He smiles smugly.

"What? Come on!" I complain.

"Drink it." He smirks.

I sigh and down the shot.

Gaige refills the shot and sits back, watching me.

"Never have I ever had no strings attached sex. Sex without a commitment. Just two people in the moment sex." He says. His eyes are heated.

I clear my throat and feel my cheeks heat. I look down at my hands.

"Esme." Gaige rasps.

I grab my shot and down it. Then I stand and take off Gaige's t-shirt and remove my jeans. I stand in front of him in just my underwear. Gaige clenches his hands into tight fists.

"I haven't Gaige, but maybe, just maybe, we could tonight. We could be each other's no strings attached. Make me feel again. I trust you Gaige." I state.

"You've been drinking, a lot. You don't know what you want." He grits.

"I'm not drunk, I'm just buzzed. I am well aware of what I'm doing and I know I want this." I state.

Gaige stands and walks towards me slowly.

"You sure about this?" He asks, tucking a strand of hair behind my ear.

"I'm sure. What happens while we're snowed in, stays snowed in." I smile.

Gaige leans in and brushes his lips slowly across mine. I grip his t-shirt in my hands.

"Say you want it Esme. Tell me you want tonight." He whispers across my lips.

I lick my lower lip. My heart feels like it's about to beat out of my chest.

"I want this Gaige, I want tonight." I whisper.

That is all Gaige needs. He takes my mouth, kissing me passionately. His tongue caresses mine. I moan into his mouth. His hands stroke down my back and he cups my behind. He kisses along my neck and shoulder, pulling my bra straps down my arms. His hand reaches around and unclasps my bra, letting it fall to the floor.

"Fuck." Gaige groans.

He kisses along my collar bone and down to my breast, taking my nipple into his mouth. Moaning I reach for his button and undo his jeans. Gaige stands in front of me and removes his t-shirt. I bite my thumb nail nervously as he removes his jeans and boxers, freeing his hard, long length. He strokes himself.

"You just gonna stand there and watch all night?" He asks.

"I – I um…I've only ever been with one person." I state nervously.

Gaige's eyes alight. He takes my hand and wraps it around his cock and kisses me. I start stroking him up and down, gently squeezing. He moans into my mouth. I kiss along his chest and down his stomach, dropping to my knees in front of him. Before he can say anything I take him in my mouth, swirling my tongue around his hard length. I take him deep. Hitting the back of my throat, he moans.

"Fuck Esme."

I moan and keep sucking him, taking him deeper each time, over and over. I feel him tense.

"Esme I'm gonna come." He grits out. I just moan and don't stop. I feel him pulse. He groans, coming. I lick and take every last drop of him.

I stand and remove my lace knickers, smiling at Gaige. I swear I hear him growl at me. He moves me back to the couch, I wobble and fall onto it. I giggle, but my laughter soon dies as his mouth is on me, his tongue on my clit.

"Oh God." I moan.

He continues to lick and tease me with his tongue. I can feel my orgasm building.

"Gaige, I'm going to come." I moan.

He continues with his mouth while he places his finger inside me, rubbing the perfect spot and sending me over the edge.

"Oh god Gaige!" I cry as I climax.

I'm panting, my orgasm completely taking hold. I'm not even aware that Gaige has moved until he's on top of me, the tip of him at my entrance. He strokes the hair from my face and kisses me as he slowly fills me. We both moan.

"Fuck you're tight." Gaige groans.

"Sorry." I pant, trying to adjust to his size.

"Shut up Esme, you feel incredible." He states, slowly moving his hips.

Gaige kisses me as he moves in and out. I can already feel my orgasm building. Gaige groans, feeling my walls begin to tighten.

"Christ you're killing me." He moans. "Fuck Esme."

He starts moving faster and faster, thrusting in me harder and harder. I can't take anymore, I feel my walls clamp tight around him as my orgasm hits me hard.

"Gaige! Fuck!" I cry out.

"Shit, fuck!" Gaige groans as he finds his release.

We're both panting. I don't think I can move. Not having an orgasm for over a year and having two in an hour has killed me.

Gaige kisses along my neck and up along my jaw to my lips. He kisses me softly.

"You okay?" He asks.

I smile.

"Hell yeah, I'm pretty sure I can't walk but yeah, I'm good." I giggle.

He smiles.

"Well the night is still young. We only have tonight after all, we'd better make the most of it." He states, kissing my neck.

Gaige carried me up to his bed and we made love well into the early hours of the morning.

I'm laid on his chest and his hand is stroking up and down my back in a soothing motion.

"Night Gaige. You've given me the most amazing night in so long. Thank you." I murmur sleepily.

Gaige doesn't say anything back. He continues to stroke my back. I fall fast asleep after that.

∞∞∞

I awake to bright sunshine pouring in through the window. I groan and face plant my pillow. I reach my hand out to cuddle into Gaige but he's not there. I frown and wonder if he's in the shower or making breakfast.

I think back to the night before and smile. It was the most amazing night I've ever had. I know I said one night but I'm not sure that my heart only wants one night. I need to think this through and talk to Sally. I thought I would wake up feeling guilty like I'd cheated on Jay or something, but I don't. I just want more.

I jump out of bed smiling. I can't remember the last time I woke up smiling. I chuck on Gaige's t-shirt and go downstairs in search of him. I find him with his back to me. He's on the phone. I tip toe behind him so he can't hear me.

"Yeah, I missed you too." He says into the phone. I freeze.

"Yeah, I will see you tonight. No I will come and stay at yours. Yeah, I can't wait." He smiles into the phone.

I feel like I've been punched in the gut. I quietly step backwards, walking straight into the shelves and knocking a plant all over myself. I'm covered in dirt. Gaige spins round, his smile fading.

"Yeah I've got to go. See you later Amy. Bye." He says with his eyes on me.

God, it was Amy. Sucker punch number two.

"You okay?" He asks, brushing some of the dirt off of my hair.

"Yep, yep, yep. Totally fine. Was, err, just

going to ask if you mind if I jump in the shower first?" I ask.

His lips twitch.

"Well, seeing as you are covered in dirt, I think you call dibs." He smiles.

"Good, good. So roads are open again?" I ask.

"Yeah." He answers. For a moment I think he looks sad, but then he smiles.

"Great! Can't wait to get back home." I state.

"That's the first time you've called it home." He notices.

I start walking backwards to get the hell out of there.

"Ah-ha so it is! Well, off in the shower now, then I can be out of your hair." I laugh nervously. I walk as quickly as I can, tripping up the stair as I go.

I stand under the water and chastise myself.

"Stupid Esme! You knew he was with Amy. One night, that's what was agreed. You have no right to feel hurt, upset, or angry. Nope. Get a grip girl." I talk to myself.

Once out of the shower I borrow one of Gaige's big hoodies. It drowns me but it's warm and comfy.

I walk downstairs and wait for Gaige to be ready.

I sit biting my thumb nail anxiously. I just want to get back home and hide away for a while. I need to hide my embarrassment, gather my thoughts, and regroup.

Gaige comes downstairs and smiles. I grab my coat and purse.

"Want to go so soon?" He asks.

"Yeah, best get back. There's lots to be getting on with." I smile.

"Okay, let me just get the key for the truck and we will get going." He states.

On the ride home there's an awkward tension in the truck.

"Listen Esme, about last night. I…" I interrupt him.

"It's fine, honestly. I promise I won't say a word to anyone. I promise you that. Amy seems like a nice woman. I won't ruin that for you. As Eric said, maybe we just needed to get it out of our system to clear the air." I smile.

He pauses for a moment.

"Yeah, thanks. I appreciate that." He says firmly.

We pull up outside the shop and I sigh.

"Thanks Gaige, for the baking and, well, you know." I blush.

I lean forward to kiss him on the cheek. He

moves so our lips connect. We kiss each other softly.

"Bye Esme." He says softly.

I frown, confused at the way he said bye.

"Bye Gaige." I whisper as I climb down out of the truck.

I don't look back, I get inside and lock the door behind me. I rub my chest, feeling my heart hurt.

"I need Sally." I mumble to myself.

Chapter Twelve

"So that's it. What do I do?" I ask.

I rang Sally as soon as I got in and woke her up in the middle of the night. She was pissed at first but then when I mentioned that I slept with Gaige, she was all ears.

"Well first off, next time you want a few days of no contact, let me know in advance. I was worried sick on Jay's anniversary. You do that to me again and I will jump on a plane just to punch you in the tit." She threatens.

I roll my eyes.

"Don't you roll your eyes at me, my tit punches are deadly. Now back to the matter in hand: you finally having your way with the delicious lumberjack, who, by the sound of it, has a very impressive bit of wood." She snorts at her own joke. She knows me too well. She doesn't have to see me to know how I react to what she says.

"Sally." I beg.

"Right, sorry, anyway. Number one: shame on you two for bumping uglies when he's clearly dating this Amy girl. Whether they're exclusive or not, it's still not cool." She chastises.

"I know, I know. You know I've never done anything like this. I don't know what came over me." I sigh.

"The dick. The dick is what came over you." She states.

"His dick did not come over me!" I point out.

"Fine, the dick came in you then. Potato/Patato." She sighs, clearly irritated.

"Jesus Christ Sally! Can you stop focusing on his dick and where he came and focus on the matter at hand." I sigh, pinching the bridge of my nose.

"Okay, but you saying dick and matter in hand all in the same sentence doesn't exactly help take my mind off it." She mumbles.

"God damn it Sally! Focus!" I yell.

"Alright, alright. Bloody hell! You know, for someone who just had an amazing night of multiple orgasms you're surprisingly snappy." She points out.

I don't respond. She will make anything I say about Gaige's dick.

"Okay. Firstly, did you use protection? Because otherwise you're likely to have little baby lumberjacks running around the place." She asks.

"Yeah I still have the implant, never got it taken out. I have another year in it I think. We used condom at the start but then I told him I was clean and covered." I answer.

"Okay good. So now for the emotionally traumatised side of it. Here's what I think: I think he has feelings for you but you made it clear that it was just for one night. You've said you're not ready for a relationship and he's seen that first hand. Men are very literal beings Esme. You both had one amazing night together and he's taken that. I'm guessing he's wanted it for a while so he would've taken whatever you offered him. You didn't realise your feelings were growing for lumberjack and now after last night they've blossomed. Now he's gone back to his woman to make a go of it with her because he doesn't think you want him, or any relationship for that matter. He can't wait around forever, especially when he has feelings for you. It's got to hurt." She states.

I sigh and face plant my pillow.

"Esme, answer me this, when was the last time you spoke to Jay?" She asks.

I pause and think.

"His anniversary." I answer.

"So the entire time you were with Gaige you didn't speak to him? Doesn't that tell you something?! You're ready to start dating! Of course you love Jay but there is room for you to start over. My advice is run like a crazy bitch chasing down Christian Grey and tell him before it's too late." She states.

"My god, you're right." I whisper.

"I have to go!" I disconnect and grab the keys. I run out in search of Gaige. I ask Nellie if she's seen Gaige and she says she saw him about twenty minutes ago and he was heading to the Sunken Ship. I run as fast as I can and slip over a lot.

I see the pub lights up ahead and I spot his truck. I smile. I reach for the door and swing it open. I'm panting.

I walk in and search for Gaige. I spot him and walk to him.

I watch as he laughs and then leans down and kisses Amy. I freeze. Can I tell him how I feel? Can I tell him that I'm sort of ready to see how things go? Even though I can't guarantee it will work out because I'm a mess of a human? He has a chance of happiness with Amy; she can give him everything without holding back anything.

I turn quickly so he doesn't see me and walk

straight into Eloise carrying a tray of food. I end up absolutely covered in food and then slip over on some soup.

"Fuck!" I yell.

Gaige stands over me.

"You okay Esme?" He asks, his lips twitching.

"Perfect." I mutter as he helps me up.

"Oh Gosh Esme, I'm so sorry. You're not hurt are you?" Eloise asks.

"Not physically." I mumble.

"What?" She asks.

"What?" I ask back.

"My mistake, no problem at all. I shall just be going." I step back and slip a little. Gaige's hand shoots out to try and steady me.

"I'm fine thank you." I reassure.

"Why did you run in here like that?" Eloise asks.

Thanks for bringing that to everyone's attention Eloise.

"I, err, um, wanted to ask Gaige if I'd left my keys at his. But look ha-ha silly me, here they are. Okay then. Bye bye now." I say while jingling the keys in my hand.

God I wish the ground would swallow me

up. I walk out as quick as I can and head back home. I feel so deflated.

I stop by the grocery store and buy the biggest tub of ice cream I can find and a bottle of wine.

"Oh! It looks like you've had a fight with a buffet table." Eric so kindly points out.

"Yeah well, I kinda did." I mumble.

"A litre of ice cream and a bottle of wine can only mean one thing: man troubles, or as the wife says, blow job season." He smiles.

I stare back at him, clueless.

"Sorry Eric, I don't understand. What do you mean?" I ask. I'm confused and ever so slightly scared.

"You know, when women are jamming? Carrie at prom, massacre at the Y, decorators are in." I hold my hand up to pause him.

"Do you mean when a woman is on her period Eric?" I ask.

"Yes. The wife and I call it different names. Helps to spice things up a little." He smiles.

God, if you can hear me, I know I'm not religious but if you could just strike me down right now that would be just peachy.

"Great talking to you Eric, bye!" I yell over my shoulder and leave quickly.

I make it back home and open the wine and the ice cream. I pick up the phone and call Sally.

"So was it all romantic? Did he swoop you up in his arms and tell you he's loved you since you first met?" Sally coos down the phone.

"I didn't tell him." I mumble with a mouthful of ice cream.

"What do you mean you didn't tell him?!" She screeches.

"I got there and he was with Amy. He was laughing. He was happy. I wasn't about to ruin that. I'm still a slight mess. What if it got to it and I just couldn't commit? Or Gaige felt inferior to Jay? He deserves stability and happiness. I, my dear, don't come with that guarantee." I say and shovel more ice cream into my mouth.

"You absolute twat Esme! That is not your decision to make, it's his. You just shot yourself in the foot." She sighs.

"Well maybe it's for the best. I mean, I have the bakery opening soon and if it was meant to be it would happen, right?" I ask.

"Yes fate blah, blah, blah. What ice cream are you eating?" She asks.

"Christ Sally. It's kind of spooky how well you know me. I'm eating cookie dough and I have a bottle of rosé to wash it down with." I state.

"Ha-ha good girl! You can't get anything past me, I know you better than you know yourself."

We say our goodbyes and I continue to sit and wallow in my self-pity.

The next day Bob is back with more men to get the work done. He is ahead of schedule. He thinks the bakery and apartment will be done in four weeks, which is amazing! He says the kitchen should be done first so I can start cooking as soon as it's done. It's exactly what I wanted to hear.

The next couple of days all of my deliveries arrive. I have all of my baking equipment, accessories, and the rest of the furniture for my apartment.

I practice baking and give some to Bob and the guys to try. They all say they're delicious. I take samples round to the grocery store and The Sunken Ship.

"Oh my days sweetie, these taste delicious! You know who you need to take these to?" Eloise says.

"Who?" I ask.

"Ted! Oh he loves eclairs. He's working now and I'm sure he would appreciate it." She smiles.

"Okay, sure. I will go there now." I state.

I hop in the car with butterflies in my stomach. Every time I've been to Ted's hardware store I've bumped into Gaige. It has been two weeks now and I'd rather not bump into him.

I park up and don't notice his truck, thank you god. I jump out and head inside. I spot Ted over the far side.

"Ted, I made these. I was told they're your favourite." I hand him the box.

He opens the box and smiles. Taking one out he takes a bite and moans.

"Good?" I ask.

"Darling, if I wasn't already a married man I'd be asking you to marry me." He smiles.

"Well if they are that good I want to try them." A voice behind me says.

I turn around and spot the guy I bought the truck from.

"Oh hi, um, Wyatt?" I ask.

"She remembers my name!" He mocks shock, holding his hand on his heart.

"Boy I'm telling you now, you are not getting your hands on these. They are mine and mine alone." Ted grumbles as he walks away with the box.

"He really likes eclairs." I smile.

"So, you're looking good Esme. I hear your bakery will be opening soon?" He asks.

"Yeah, not long now. All depending on the final checks. Should be good to go in three weeks time." I say excitedly.

"Wow that's great. Let me take you out for a bite to eat and drink to celebrate?" He asks.

I think about it for a minute. Wyatt is a nice guy, he's good looking, and I've got nothing to lose.

"Sure, okay, great." I smile.

"Okay. I will pick you up at seven tonight." He says, taking my hand and kissing it.

I smile.

"See you at seven."

I turn around to head back to the truck and see Gaige. My steps falter and I quickly paste on a smile.

"Hey." I greet awkwardly.

His eyes are following Wyatt.

"Gaige?" I call, waving my hand in front of his face.

His eyes come to mine.

"You're going out with him tonight?" He asks.

I frown.

"Yeah I am, why? Is he not a nice guy?" I ask.

"No, he's a nice guy. Just didn't think you

were ready to be dating yet." He states.

I look down at the ground.

"Well I've got to start sometime right?" I shrug.

I look up at him and see that he looks pissed off.

"I will see you around." He states and walks off.

Huh, I wonder what's crawled up his arse. I shrug and head home to get ready for my date.

Chapter Thirteen

I video call Sally to ask her which outfit I should wear.

"The deep emerald green long sleeved wrap dress with your cute heeled brown ankle boots." Sally orders.

"Okay but my legs are going to freeze! It's still -5 out here and that's fairly mild."

"No pain no sex. Have you shaved?" She asks.

"Yes I've bloody shaved! Cheeky cow! I'm not going to sleep with him. It's just a date." I point out.

"You never know. Now just go and have fun and don't forget to call me tomorrow to tell me all about it." Sally demands.

"I will. Bye." I hang up and get changed.

I put on the green dress and a pair of black tights. Sod what Sally says, she's not the one that'll freeze her hoo-ha off in this weather! I style my hair and keep my make up simple.

There's a knock at the door and I quickly grab my bag and coat and head downstairs.

I open the door to a smiling Wyatt. His eyes do a sweep of my body.

"Esme, you look stunning." He compliments.

"Thank you." I say as I lock up. Wyatt takes my hand and leads me to his car.

He drives us to The Sunken Ship which I've learnt is the only place to go locally.

We walk inside and the place is packed out.

"Wow, I don't think I've ever seen it this busy." I say as Wyatt takes my coat and hangs it up for me.

"Yeah, there's live music tonight so everyone in town has come out." He states. We move through the packed out pub and find a free table.

Eloise comes over and drops off two menus.

"What do you guys want to drink?" She asks, clearly flustered.

"Just a wine for me, please." I answer.

"Beer please." Wyatt answers.

"You're swamped tonight Eloise." I state.

"You ain't kidding. With the bad snowstorm

the other week folks are desperate to get out and have some fun." She smiles and leaves.

"So Wyatt, have you lived here your whole life?" I ask.

"Pretty much, I moved here with my family as a child." He answers.

Eloise comes back with our drinks. She smiles and waves someone over. I turn around and see Gaige with Amy.

"You guys don't mind sharing a table do you? We're all out of space." Eloise asks.

"Sure thing. It'll be like a double date." Wyatt smiles.

The worst date ever is about to commence in 3, 2, 1.

"Hi!" I beam enthusiastically.

Amy smiles.

"Thank you for letting us join you guys. It's so busy tonight! Oh gosh, are you guys on a date?" She asks.

"We are! You?" Wyatt asks.

"Yes. Oh this is cute! It's like a double date." She claps.

I down my wine.

"Eloise, I'll have the bottle." I yell with my hand in the air. I point to my glass.

"So I hear you're opening a bakery in town Esme?" Amy asks.

"Yep, that's right." I smile.

"We will have to come by when it's open. I've heard wonderful things about your baking; Gaige says you have a very moist sponge." She compliments.

Gaige's eyes are on me the entire time.

"Eloise! Wine!" I yell.

"God damn it, go and get it yourself if you're that thirsty." Eloise shouts back.

"Excuse me, I shall get our drinks. It'll save Eloise the hassle." I stand.

"I will give you a hand." Gaige says following me.

I walk to the bar and Gaige comes up and stands right beside me. He's so close I can smell his cologne and his natural scent of the outdoors and pine.

"You look beautiful tonight." Gaige whispers in my ear.

"Thanks." I mutter.

"Jack, when you have a minute!" I yell, tapping my hand on the bar.

"Sorry about that. What can I get you?" Jack asks.

"Can I have a bottle of rosé? Actually, make that two. Oh and a beer for Wyatt." I ask.

"I will take a beer and a bottle of rosé too." Gaige asks.

Jack nods and gathers our drinks.

"He's not right for you." Gaige states.

"Sorry?" I ask.

"He won't be able to keep up with you; he's too boring. He won't get you." Gaige informs me.

"Thanks for the heads up but I think I can work things out for myself. I'm a big girl." I snap.

"Only trying to be a good friend." He retorts.

The way in which he says friend pisses me off. Jack comes back with our drinks. I hand over my card and tell him to keep a tab open. I pick up my wines and Wyatt's beer and turn to head back to our table.

"You're even buying his drink!" Gaige says as he walks past carrying his and Amy's drinks.

God this night needs to hurry up and be over.

Eloise comes back to take our orders. Amy orders a salad and I order a steak and fries.

"You sure you don't want the salad?" Wyatt asks.

I turn to him, shocked that he would say such a thing.

"I'm happy with my steak and fries thank you." I smile sweetly.

Gaige snorts into his beer. My gaze shoots to him.

"What?" I snap,

"Just that if I'd asked you that you would've told me to piss off." He states.

"That's because Wyatt is nice and kind to me and you can be a twat sometimes." I bite back.

"Okay. I'm changing the subject, have any of you watched that new reality show 'It's me or the Car'?" Amy asks.

"No Amy, I haven't. Is it any good? I ask.

"Oh it is! The guys have to choose either the car of their dreams or their wife." She giggles.

"It's funny, I've seen it." Wyatt smiles fondly at Amy.

I roll my eyes and catch Gaige staring at me. I poke my tongue out like a pissed off toddler. His lips twitch, clearly fighting a smile.

"So tell me, how do you make your cake so moist? Gaige couldn't stop talking about it." Amy says, cutting me from my thoughts.

"Sorry what?" I ask.

"Your sponge; Gaige said it was very moist." She states.

"The best I've ever tasted, I could eat it all day and night." Gaige states, his eyes searing through me. I choke on my wine.

Wyatt pats my back.

"You alright?" He asks. "You've gone a bit flustered."

"I'm fine thank you. It just went down the wrong way." I rasp.

"Umm, well Amy, it's just about getting the ingredients just right and not over baking. Over baking can dry a cake right out." I say.

"Maybe you should give baking classes when you open. I know I'd sign up for that!" She says smiling.

"It's certainly something to think about." I smile.

Eloise brings our food and we tuck in.

"Wow, this steak is delicious." I mumble with a mouthful of food.

"Slow down Esme or you'll choke on your meat." Wyatt states.

"Don't worry Wyatt, I've seen her with more meat in her mouth than that before." Gaige points out.

I immediately start choking on my steak.

Wyatt pats my back again. He probably thinks I'm some kind of toddler that doesn't know how to eat and drink properly.

"Excuse me, I'm just going to the bathroom." I state.

I just need to get away for a moment. I have no idea what's gotten into Gaige but if he's not careful Amy will catch on and that'll be the end of them.

I wash my hands and place my cold hands on the back of my neck. This has to be the worst date in the history of dates.

I walk out of the bathroom and come face to chest.

"Sorry." I mumble as I try to move around them.

"Esme."

I look up and see that it's Gaige. He takes my hand and pulls me around the corner, out of sight.

"Gaige what are you…" I don't get to finish my sentence because Gaige's crashes his mouth on mine, kissing me hungrily. It's like he needs me as much as he needs his next breath.

My brain finally decides to kick in and I shove at his chest, pushing him away.

"Gaige what the hell?!" I pant. "I'm on a date with Wyatt and your girlfriend is out there right now!"

"I'm...shit. I'm sorry. I can't think clearly when I'm around you! Especially with you looking as beautiful as you do in that dress." He states while running his hands through his hair.

"Gaige, you're with Amy. This can't happen." I state as I walk past him and back to the table.

I notice Wyatt and Amy are huddled close laughing and smiling together when I return.

We finish our meal. I avoid looking in Gaige's direction and continue to chat about random shows and crap I have no idea about. By this point I'm on bottle number two and the live band have started playing. They start playing Mr Brightside from The Killers. I'm British, I'm drunk, there's only one thing for it: I have to dance. I find myself jumping up and down.

"Cause I'm Mr Brightside!" I yell.

I try to drag Wyatt up with me but he shakes his head in mortification. I shrug and leave him and dance on the small part of the dance floor. There are a few others dancing, just not quite as enthusiastically as me. The band finish and I cheer and whoop.

"Thank you, especially to the pretty lady in green." The lead singer says over the mic.

"Whoop!" I scream with my hand in the air.

They go straight into their next song: Spin Doctors. God I wish Sally were here, she would be up dancing with me right now.

I swing my hips with my hands in the air and dance. I'm loving the live music. Sally and I used to go and see bands all the time. I miss it.

I dance the night away. Eventually I stop and go back to the table for a drink. I'm feeling thirsty.

I walk over and drink my wine. I notice Wyatt and Amy have disappeared.

"Where've they gone?" I ask.

"Amy wanted to go home because she felt tired and Wyatt offered to take her." Gaige states.

"Oh, that's odd. Why didn't you?" I ask.

"Wyatt offered and she accepted." Gaige shrugs, not caring that another guy took his girlfriend home.

Gaige looks like he's about to say something but the band start playing Kings of Leon's Sex On Fire.

"Yes!" I yell and start dancing. I don't even bother to return to the front this time, I just dance where I am.

"Sex is on fire." I sing and point to Gaige smiling.

I move my body seductively. Sally would say I was shaking what spin class had given me.

Not what my mother gave me, of course, because she gave me jack shit.

I feel a hand come around my waist and smile, still dancing.

"Come on, let's get home." Gaige whispers in my ear.

"Bye Eloise!" I yell over my shoulder.

Gaige grabs my coat and bag and leads me to his truck. The whole way I'm singing sex is on fire.

Once in the truck I lean my head on the window and yawn.

"God I'm an awful date." I mumble.

"Best date I've ever been on." Gaige smiles.

"It's your fault. You and your moist sponge made me nervous, so I drank." I whine.

"Noted. I won't talk about your moist sponge again." He laughs.

We pull up outside the shop. Gaige opens my door for me and I practically fall into his arms.

He guides me to my door and unlocks it for me and takes me upstairs to my bedroom. I start stripping off.

"Esme." Gaige warns.

"What? I'm going to bed. I'm not nakey!" I giggle.

"Christ." Gaige helps me into bed and tucks me in with the cover right up to my chin. He leans over me, his eyes searching.

"Night Esme."

I lift my head and kiss him, slowly.

"Night Gaige." I mumble before falling to sleep.

Chapter Fourteen

I awake the next morning and groan. My head feels like it's been steam rolled. I squint my eyes open and see water, pain killers, and a note. I grab the water. My mouth feels like the Sahara desert. I swallow the pain killers then slowly sit up to read the note.

Esme,

I'm not sorry I ruined your date.
Gaige.

"What?" I say. I turn the note over to see if there's anything on the back: nothing.

I groan and lay back down. My phone rings and I answer it.

"What's up slapper?! You have a good date?" Sally shouts.

"Shhhh Sally. Esme dying." I groan.

"Oh Jesus, how much wine did you drink?" She asks.

"Two bottles." I state.

"Christ, please tell me you didn't shag him that drunk." She pleads.

"No, no. The date was a disaster. Gaige and Amy were there and the pub was that busy we had to share a table." I tell her.

"No way?!" She gasps

I tell her about the rest of the night and about the note I woke up to.

"Well any ideas Sherlock?" I ask.

"None. I mean if he wanted to confess his undying love for you he had perfect opportunity by the toilets with that hot kiss and then again either last night or this morning. He could have stayed and woken you up with a romantic breakfast in bed. I'm sorry Watson, I just don't get it." She sighs.

"Arggh! I thought it was us women who were supposed to head fuck the guys, not the other way around." I state, frustrated.

"Maybe he's just one of those guys that doesn't want you but doesn't want anyone else to have you either? Or maybe he's planning something romantic and will come back today or tomorrow and surprise you?!" She swoons down the phone.

"I doubt it. Look, I'm going to go. You should know, I'm going to scatter Jay's ashes tomorrow." I inform her.

"Wow, are you sure you're going to be okay?" She asks.

I sigh.

"Yeah, it's time. There's this spot down on the front where the boats dock. It's stunning. We are where we wanted to be and I think he would be happy with that. I'm going to go at sunrise tomorrow." I tell her.

"I think he would like it too." She says sadly. "Call me if you need me, okay?" She adds.

"I will, love ya." I say before disconnecting.

I decide to go and have a long shower and wash away the hangover. I don't plan on going anywhere or seeing anyone over these next couple of days. My focus is on finally saying goodbye to Jay and moving forward.

I thought I would struggle to fall asleep tonight but I didn't. I smile to myself.

"It's the right time."

My alarm wakes me and it's still dark out. I get changed and grab my truck keys and pick up Jay's urn. I head out to the truck and drive down to the docks.

I get out and shiver at the freezing cold

morning air. I walk down to the bench where I've sat a few times.

I take a seat with the urn in my hands.

"Well, this is our final goodbye. I know people thought your death or your funeral was the final goodbye but I still had you with me after that. I am finally moving forward. I'm learning to live my life without you. I'm finally used to not talking to you like you're still there with me. I know I'm doing it now, but this is different, this is goodbye forever. I will still think about you, I will still love you and hold you in my heart, but it's time for me to let you go. I should have done it a while ago, but I just wasn't ready." I sniff and wipe away my tears.

"Be free Jay, wherever you are. Be happy. I will love you forever and always." I say sobbing.

I open the urn and tip it, shaking his ashes into the sea. A gust of wind catches and blows his ashes back into my face.

"Fuck!" I screech and splutter, wiping my face. "Son of a bitch."

I spit and hold out my tongue, desperately wiping it with my hand.

"Esme?" I hear a deep voice call. Of course I would bump into him now.

I turn with my tongue still hanging out.

"Uh, you okay?" He asks.

I quickly put my tongue back in my mouth.

"Yes. Fine thank you." I smile.

He looks me up and down and smirks.

"Erm, you have, um, I'm guessing it's Jay, all in your hair." He points.

"Yes well thank you for that. I was trying to give him a nice send off and then there was a gust of wind which blew him back into my face." I say annoyed.

Gaige bursts out laughing.

"This isn't funny!" I yell.

"Oh Esme, I think it is. It could only happen to you." He laughs.

I smirk and fight my own smile. Jay would be absolutely pissing his pants laughing at me right now. Bastard! I burst out laughing.

"Damn it, I was trying to give him a nice send off and it backfired. Literally." I laugh.

Both of our laughters die down. The air becomes thick with tension and awkwardness.

"Well I have to go. I shall leave you to it." He says while jogging off.

I slump back onto the bench and sigh.

I sit with my own thoughts and watch the sun rise. I look at the time and figure I best get back to let Bob in. I ring Sally on my way.

"It go okay?" She asks.

"You'll never guess what happened." I say to her.

I update Sally on what happened and she cries with laughter and fully expects Jay was behind the whole thing.

I don't see Gaige again. I ask Ted at the hardware store where all of Gaige's furniture has gone. Apparently he has gone out of town for a while, no one seems to know where he's gone or if he's coming back.

I'm gutted as it's coming up to the opening of the bakery and he's the one person I want there.

"Little to the left. No that's too much, down a bit. Yeah, yep! Stop! Perfect!" I clap. I'm watching the guys put up the sign for my bakery. Bob climbs back down the ladder.

"Tiers Of Joy eh?" He says smiling. "Where did you come up with that name?" he asks.

"My late husband wrote it to me in a letter." I say smiling. I wipe away a stray tear.

Bob puts his arm around me and gives me a squeeze.

"You did good darling." He says smiling.

I rest my head on him and sigh.

"I'm opening in three days Bob. I'm crapping

myself." I say honestly.

"Well that's good, it shows that you care enough not to mess it up." He laughs.

"Well I'm not counting my chickens yet. This is me we're talking about. I have this amazing ability to fuck things up." I laugh. "Pardon the language."

"That's true." Bob agrees.

∞∞∞

It's finally here: opening day! I handed out flyers with a ten percent off coupon attached, I have balloons for the kids, and I put up a poster for a part time salesperson.

I put on my brand new apron with Tiers of Joy stitched across it. I look in the mirror and smile. I have my hair up in a messy styled bun.

"You've got this Esme." I reassure myself.

I take a deep breath and walk downstairs. I check that everything is in it's place, all of the price tags are correct, and the till is working correctly. I look at the clock, five minutes to go.

I tap my feet, anxiously watching the clock

tick down.

It hits 9am. I smile and walk to the door, open it up, and turn the sign. I step out and see nearly the whole town has turned up for the opening.

"Oh my god!" I sob.

Nellie and Jack walk over with a giant yellow bow and ribbon.

They stand either side of the door and hand me some scissors.

"Now it's a proper opening." Nellie whispers.

"Thank you." I whisper.

"Speech!" Bob yells.

"Oh crap, really?! Okay, well, I would like to say thank you to all of you for making me feel so welcome in your town. I know I haven't been the best I can be. I came here alone and scared." I pause to wipe a tear that has fallen. "For those who don't know, it was mine and my husband's dream to move over here. He was going to do what he loved, restoring boats, and I was going to do what I loved and own my own bakery. Sadly, our dream changed when he died of cancer. In a letter he left to me he told me to go and live our dreams, to go and make a life without him. Instead of crying tears of sadness I was to cry tiers of joy." I sob. I wipe away my tears and smile.

"So with the help of Bob and his guys I've done just that. Everyone, I would like to officially open the Tiers of Joy bakery!" I yell.

I cut the ribbon and everyone cheers. I sob and wipe my eyes, welcoming everyone in.

The day was a huge success; I pretty much sold out of everything. People loved the cakes and bread. People constantly hugged and congratulated me and I couldn't wipe the smile from my face.

After I've cleaned down I go and slump in my chair with a glass of wine and call Sally.

"How did it go?" She asks excitedly.

"Amazing! I pretty much sold out and I had a few people pick up an application for the part time job too. I'm having a break with a glass of wine now and then I'm getting to bed ready to get up at 3am and bake for tomorrow." I sigh, rubbing my foot.

"Did he show?" She asks.

"No." I answer.

"A card, letter, anything?" She asks hopeful.

"Nope." I sigh.

"Oh hun, I'm sorry." Sally says.

"It's okay. It's not like we were madly in love or anything. I mean, we had one great night and argued a lot. I don't know, I just thought he would be here."

"Well regardless, you did it. I am so proud of you. Don't let that dick weed bring you down. You're amazing and I love you." Sally sings happily down the phone.

"Thanks babe, love you." I say before disconnecting.

I lay in bed and hope that wherever Gaige is, he's okay. It has been three weeks and no one has heard a word from him. I'm so worried that something bad has happened to him. I worry that he went off hiking somewhere. What if he's been eaten by a bear? I just don't understand why he would up and leave like that without a word?

Chapter Fifteen

It has been two weeks since Tiers of Joy opened and I've been rammed. Ive been selling out nearly every day and people are starting to ask if I do birthday cakes as well. I've been saying that until I hire more staff then it will have to wait.

I'm sitting with the two applicants I've narrowed it down to. There's Josie, a sixteen year old high school girl who I just adore. She is cute and nerdy. Unfortunately, she can't work the mornings in the week because she's at school. The other candidate I have for those mornings is Amy. I thought it was going to be awkward but it's not. Her and Wyatt actually hooked up and are now an item. They work really well together.

"Okay so I have you both here because there has been a slight change of hours. Because the demand is so high I'm going to need someone here in the mornings from eight until two Monday to

Friday and then I will need someone to help me at closing down and clear up from three thirty util six each night. Then because Saturday is our busiest day I will need you both in all day Saturday. However, we shut earlier on Saturdays: four. So you can go then and not worry about cleaning down. How does that work for you both?" I ask.

They both smile wide and nod their heads.

"Great! Here are your aprons, please wear smart but comfy clothes. I know it's Sunday tomorrow but if you could come in at eleven I will go over till training and show you where everything is." I smile.

"Thank you Esme! I won't let you down." Josie promises excitedly before running out of the door to her mum who is waiting in their truck.

"Thank you Esme! I look forward to working here. Gaige was right, your sponges really are moist." She smiles.

I feel terrible for lying to her all of this time. I can't keep it in any longer.

"Amy, come and sit down with me for a second." I gesture to the chair.

"Okay, did I do something wrong?" She asks.

"Oh god no, not at all. I owe you a massive apology and I hope it doesn't effect you working here because I really think you'll be great." I smile.

"Okay." She says cautiously.

"I slept with Gaige." I blurt and wince, waiting for her reaction.

"Okay." She shrugs.

"No honey. I slept with Gaige when you were dating him." I clarify.

"Oh well I know that." She states, surprising the ever loving crap out of me.

"What?!" I ask confused.

"Gaige told me straight away. I wasn't bothered as we were only dating. We never even slept together. He was nice and all but a bit quiet and grumpy. I saw how he was with you though. He was different with you." She states.

I sit back in my chair. I'm stunned. The whole time I felt guilty, why didn't he tell me?!

"I thought you knew that he told me. Oh gosh, you've been carrying that guilt on your shoulders the entire time?" She says sympathetically.

"The bastard. Why would he not just tell me that?" I ask.

"I don't know, maybe because he wanted you to think that him and I were more." She states.

"I was going to try with him. I ran to tell

him. Then I saw you two together and thought he was happily involved with you." I say, feeling gutted.

"That time you came into the bar?" She asks.

I nod.

"Oh Esme." She hugs me.

"Well who knows if we will see him now? Considering that he's gone back to Chicago." She says.

"What?!" I yell.

"Oh hell, you didn't know that either, did you?" She sighs.

"No I fucking did not! Where did you hear that?" I ask. I stand up and open a bottle of wine.

"You keep wine in the bakery kitchen?" She asks in disbelief.

"Yes, for moments just like this one." I open the wine and drink a large amount. "Who told you he was in Chicago?" I ask.

"Bob. He called Bob a week after he'd gone. His mother had been in contact. Well, apparently she'd been tracking him down for years. Anyway, she sorted herself out and become a high profile councillor. She has a book and everything, even does those radio call in shows." She says.

"Who's his mum, Dr Phil?!" I ask.

Amy laughs.

"You're funny Esme. I don't get it, but you're funny." I roll my eyes.

"So, what now?" I ask.

"I'm not sure, Bob is the only one who has spoken to him." She states.

I slam the bottle down on the side and grab my keys. "Come on Amy, I'm locking up." I say ushering her out of the bakery and locking up.

"Oh god. You're mad. Are you going to fire me before I've even started?" She asks.

"God no! See you tomorrow." I yell over my shoulder, running to my truck.

I jump in and speed to Bob's. When I arrive I pound on the door. Bob swings the door open and sighs when he sees my face.

"Who told you?" He asks.

"Amy." I answer.

He walks out, shutting the door behind him.

"Look, I didn't want to hurt you anymore than you were already hurting. I know you had feelings for him. You weren't handling it well and what with the bakery and everything, I didn't want to ruin your big opening." He apologises.

"Okay I get that, but maybe you could have said he was visiting family or something so I didn't worry myself at night thinking he'd been eaten by bloody bears?!" I point out.

"Fair enough. I should have said something, but I don't think he's coming back Esme. He's making a life out there for himself. He's building a relationship with his mom. I don't want you waiting around for him. You're doing great with your life. Please Esme." Bob begs.

"How did you know I had feelings for him?" I ask.

"I have eyes. I saw the way you looked at him and he you. If things were different then you guys would have been great. But they're not. You can't wait around for a guy who may or may not come home." He points out.

I nod and nibble my thumb nail.

"He's okay though, happy?" I ask.

"Yeah, he sounds it." Bob asks.

I nod and start walking back to my truck.

The whole way back I can't help but be angry that he didn't even have the decency to drop me a letter, a text, a bloody email?! I woke up to a note saying I'm glad your date was ruined and then saw him jogging. He didn't say anything then, not even a clue.

I pull up at the bakery and grab the wine and head up to bed, I'm exhausted from the day. Hearing that has just topped my day off superbly.

Over the next coming weeks me and the girls get on great. We work really well together and I love going to work everyday .

I have to pop to Ted's hardware store to grab some more baking trays. He started getting more homeware stuff in when the town started demanding it rather than waiting weeks for something they had to order online.

I walk to the section I need, saying hi to people as I pass. I pull my list out of my bag and read it to make sure I get the right things. Not looking where I'm going I walk straight into a hard wall of man. I fall backwards and land on my behind with a thud.

"I'm sorry. Here, let me help you up." In front of me is a guy wearing faded ripped jeans and a t-shirt that stretches across his broad chest. My eyes travel up to see a handsome guy with warm brown hair, stubble, and blue eyes.

"Um thanks." I blush. I stand up and brush myself off. "Sorry, I'm a bit accident prone." I smile.

"No, I should have looked where I was going. I'm Tanner by the way." He holds his hand out and I shake his hand.

"Hi Tanner, I'm Esme." I smile.

"I know who you are; people in this town talk. You're the pretty English girl who owns the bakery. Am I right?" He asks smiling.

"Well aren't you a smooth talker? Yes, that's me." I laugh.

"Do you live in town?" I ask.

"No, I live just outside. Sort of in between the two towns. I just started working for Bob." He says.

"You picking up a new hammer?" I ask.

Oh my god, did I really just ask that question?

He laughs.

"No, Bob is picking up some bits. Why are you here? Picking up some baking trays?" He asks smiling.

"Actually I am. Who knew you were psychic?" I laugh.

"I have to come clean, I saw your list." He winks.

I giggle and nibble my thumb nail nervously.

"Well come by the bakery sometime and I may just offer you a free cupcake." I smile. Good god, am I flirting? I am! I'm flirting.

He smiles brightly. God he's cute!

"Sure, I would never miss an opportunity

for a free cupcake." He says winking. "See you around Esme."

I wave like a giddy schoolgirl and practically skip to the trays.

When I get back to the bakery I tell Amy.

"Oh I've seen him, he is really cute. Do you think he will come in?" She asks.

"I don't know but I'm kinda excited to see if he does." I state.

I'm going to have to make sure I'm not a total mess now just in case he walks in.

Chapter Sixteen

It's a busy Saturday and the customers have been coming in thick and fast. Easter is approaching and the customers can't get enough of the bunny cookies and chocolate egg basket cakes I've made.

"Oh and I will have two of those and three of them and two rolls please dear." Nellie asks.

I bag up her goods and smile.

"Thanks Nellie. Next!" I yell.

"Do you have any vegan, gluten free, sugar free cupcakes?" I swear everyone gasps.

My head whips round. This isn't the first time someone has asked for some think like this.

"Do you have allergies?" I ask.

"No." He smiles.

"Then why the hell are you asking for that crap?!" I snap.

"Well I am a vegan." He states.

"Very good. Now I can make Vegan cupcakes if ordered in advance. I can even do sugar free and gluten free if ordered in advance. But what you are asking sir is something impossible. Especially from a bloody bakery! This is a place of goodness, it's a place people come to buy treats for themselves. What you are asking for sir is a bloody stick of celery! Now I shall ask you one more time, what can I get you?" I smile sweetly but with a definite undertone of threat. Everyone in the bakery can see it.

"I don't think you understand miss, I want something vegan, sugar free, and gluten free." He says, irritated. He pushes his glasses up his nose.

"Right that's it, you've been warned. Get out!" I yell.

"What?" He asks in disbelief.

"I said GET OUT!" I repeat.

"Right, that's it. I want your full name. I will be ringing the papers and telling them about how you treated me." He continues to rabbit on.

"Nellie, door please." I ask her kindly.

"Josie, piping bag." Josie hands me a piping bag full of chocolate frosting.

"Amy, be ready with the flour." I order. She grabs the bag.

I walk towards him and hold my piping bag up like a gun.

"What do you think you are doing with that?" He asks.

I continue to walk towards him. I twist the end of the bag tighter, so a tiny bit of frosting comes out.

"Get out or you'll get frosted." I threaten.

"Right, that's it, I'm call the cops! How dare you treat me in such a way?! Never…"

"Three." I count

"You cannot be serious." He says while walking backwards towards the door.

"Two." I continue.

"Well, you shall be hearing about this from my lawyer!" He screeches, tripping back out of the doorway and landing on his backside on the curb.

"One." I smile.

"You wouldn't…"

He doesn't finish. I squeeze the piping bag full of chocolate frosting and cover the guy. It goes all over his clothes and face.

I drop the bag and the guy jumps up and

starts running.

"You crazy bitch!" He yells.

"Amy, flour." I hold out my hand and throw it, hitting him right on the head and covering him in flour.

"Now, you can bugger off and never dare to step foot in my bakery again or next it will be custard tarts!" I yell.

The girls in shop all cheer and laugh.

"Esme?"

I turn round and see Tanner.

"Well shit." I mutter.

"I didn't catch you at a good time?" He smiles.

"Uh no, it's a great time, just throwing out a hooligan." I state.

"A hooligan huh? He didn't seem like the type to cause trouble." He says smiling.

"Oh believe me, he did. I mean, what kind of sicko walks into a bakery and asks for a vegan, gluten free, and sugar free cake?!" I ask.

"You're right, my mistake. He seems like a complete dick." He smiles.

"You want to come in for a cake and coffee? I'm due a break anyway." I offer.

"I thought you'd never ask." He smiles.

We turn to go in and Amy, Josie, and the customers are all in the doorway watching us.

"Umm folks, the show is over." I state. They all quickly scurry back to acting like they weren't being nosey arseholes.

"What cake do you fancy?" I ask, sliding around the counter.

"Surprise me." He says.

I bite my lower lip and grab two chocolate and salted caramel muffins.

"I'm taking a break." I inform the girls as I walk out the back with Tanner.

I make us a coffee and hand him his muffin. I watch as he takes a bite and moans.

"Good?" I ask.

"So good! I can see that dating you is going to be dangerous." He states.

"Oh, how so?" I ask.

"I'm either going to gain fifty pounds or become a diabetic." He laughs.

"Well live a little! Life is too boring." I smile, licking the caramel off of my finger.

If I could see myself now I would wonder who the hell this was; I don't flirt like this. It's something about Tanner, it's like he has this sexual magnetism.

"Well I guess you're right there." He says as he walks towards me. I hold my breath as he cups my face and kisses me tenderly.

He pulls away slightly.

"I will pick you up at seven tonight. Wear comfortable shoes." He licks his lips. "Best muffin I've ever tasted." He smiles and leaves.

"Huh?!" I stand still. I'm stunned like a deer caught in headlights.

Amy comes rushing in.

"So?" She asks excitedly.

"He kissed me and told me to be ready at seven tonight and wear comfy shoes." I whisper.

"Holy hell that's hot!" Amy says, fanning her face. I nod in agreement.

"Let's serve these customers so I can lock up and get ready." I smile.

I'm excited and nervous. Tanner is cocky, smooth, and a little arrogant but he carries it off well. I just want to throw my panties at him and tell him to take me. It's like he's my celebrity crush. I need to calm myself down.

It's just a date Esme.

I rush around trying to find the right outfit to wear. I'm guessing we're walking somewhere since he told me to wear comfy shoes. I grab my nice skinny jeans and pair them with a blood red long sleeved body wrap. I chuck on my converse and spritz my hair, leaving it in natural waves. I decide to wear my bright red lipstick to jazz up my outfit a little. It is a date after all. A quick spritz of perfume and I'm done.

There's a knock at the door. I grab my cute cropped leather biker jacket and a scarf. Even though we're in April, it's still cold out.

I open the door and smile.

"Hey." I breathe.

"Wow Esme, you've managed to make casual hot." He states.

His eyes sweep my body.

"So come on then, tell me, where are you taking me?" I ask.

"That's a surprise. Come on." He says and takes my hand.

"Oh shoot, hang on. My shoelace is undone." I reach down and tie it.

"She's going to kill me." He groans.

"Huh?" I ask as I stand.

"Esme, your ass in them jeans. Seriously fucking stunning." He states, biting his bottom lip.

"Thanks I guess." I blush.

He takes me to his truck and drives out of

town and up the hillside to a forest.

He pulls up and I'm not going to lie, I'm crapping myself a little.

"Come on." He holds the door open for me.

"What about bears?" I ask.

"Don't worry. You're safe with me, I promise." He winks and holds my hand.

He leads us through the trees and down a bit to a clearing. I lose count of the amount of times I nearly fall on my arse.

The view from the clearing is unbelievable.

"Wow." I breathe.

"Come on, I made us dinner." He says pulling me towards a tent.

When he gets there he unzips it and just inside is a small picnic table with a food cooler.

"Wow, this is some date." I smile.

He points for me to sit as he opens the cooler and places down a bottle of wine and foil wrapped sandwiches.

He sits and points outside.

"Watch the sun go down, it's amazing. The stars you'll see will blow your mind." He smiles as he bites into his sandwich. I watch the sun set slowly. It is so beautiful up here.

We chat and laugh. Tanner flirts a lot and it's

nice. Being paid compliments all the time is refreshing and I would be lying if I said it wasn't working.

He pulls out a blanket, lays it on the floor, and lights some candles around us. He grabs a thicker blanket and wraps us up in it, with me in between his legs, my back to his chest. He wraps his arms around me. He slowly circles his thumb against my stomach. I take in a shuddery breath.

He starts placing soft gentle kisses along my neck. Without thinking I tilt my neck back. His hands move up and cup my breasts. I moan.

"Esme, I want you. Right here under the stars." He whispers in my ear.

I refuse to let myself think or worry. I just want to feel. I'm fed up of everything. Right now I'm letting myself be in the moment.

I spin around and straddle his lap. His eyes alight.

"Let's do this right now." I state as I roll my hips, rubbing against his erection.

"Fuck me! English girls are wild." He groans as I stand and undo my jeans. I step out of them and shiver from the cold.

Tanner quickly unzips his jeans and pulls out a condom. He frees his length. It's impressive. Not quite as impressive as Gaige's, but still. I freeze. How could I even think that?! I shake my head and straddle Tanner's lap.

I slowly slide down on him and start rocking my hips. He moans and grips my behind.

"Oh God yes." I moan, taking complete control.

"Yes, take it you filthy whore." He groans.

I open my eyes and stop.

"What?" I ask.

"Don't stop Esme." He groans.

I shake my head, thinking maybe I misheard him.

I continue to ride him, harder and harder, feeling myself build more and more.

"Fuck yes, ride my cock mommy!" He shouts.

I stop. What the fuck?

Tanner rolls me onto my back, kissing and nipping my neck, rolling his hips. Okay shake it off Esme, it's just dirty talk. There's nothing unusual about that. Just concentrate on enjoying the moment.

Tanner starts pounding into me.

"Yes!" I moan.

"That's it you filthy fucking whore, take daddy's cock." He groans.

And there goes my orgasm.

Tanner stills as he reaches climax.

"Yes mommy, take my come." He yells.

Holy fuck, wait until I tell Sally.

"That was unbelievable." He states, kissing my neck.

"I'll say." I mumble.

He pulls out and I quickly pull on my jeans and do a fake watch check.

"Wow, would you look at the time. I really should be getting back." I fake sigh.

He gets up and kisses me. I try not to cringe. I've heard what comes out of that mouth buddy, I certainly don't want to be kissing it.

He leads the way back to the truck with a flashlight.

Eventually we pull up outside of the bakery. Thank Christ.

"Thanks for a lovely evening and a great date." I say, ready to jump out. He grabs my hand to stop me.

"Can I have your number? I'd really like to see you again." He smiles.

I gag slightly.

"Sorry, um, I'm just not in that place right now. I'm still not over my dead husband. Sorry, I hope you find the woman for you." I smile and jump out of the truck and practically sprint to my door.

I'm definitely going to hell for using the dead husband excuse but surely in that situation it is acceptable.

"Oh my god. I'm dying." Sally roars with laughter down the phone.

"Right? I mean, the boy has issues. Oh god Sally, what the hell was I thinking just sleeping with him like that?!" I groan.

"You were being a healthy, sexually active woman who saw a hot bit of man meat and took it. Sure, the guy clearly has mummy issues beyond repair, but he was pretty." I hear her giggle.

"Well I didn't even get an orgasm out of it. What a waste!" I complain.

"Yup, it's a waste of a hot looking guy alright. They are always either gay or have issues that run deeper than the grand canyon." She sighs.

"That's true." I yawn. "I'm getting to bed, I'm exhausted." I say as I climb into bed.

"Night mummy!" Sally giggles and disconnects.

I smile and shake my head and lay down. It could only happen to me.

Chapter Seventeen

A month! It took me a month to shake off Tanner. He kept trying and trying to ask me out again. I was being nice but then I got pissed off and was horrible. Sally said I must have some kind of voodoo pussy. In the end Bob had a word with him and said I would forever be on my own as a lonely old spinster and that I was going to join the nunnery. I did tell Bob that I'm sure he will notice when I'm not actually gone, or a nun for that matter, but Bob said he couldn't give less of a shit. We left it at that.

I had a new sticker put on the side of my truck to advertise the bakery and I've started doing delivery for larger orders. I got an order last night for Bob. I pull up outside and carrying the large box of cupcakes I knock on the door.

Bob's wife Ruth opens the door.

"Hi Ruth, delivery." I smile.

Her smile slips briefly.

"Come through." She opens the door wider for me.

Odd. I walk through, hearing voice chatting and laughing.

"If you could pop them in the kitchen that would be great. Thanks Esme." She smiles.

"Sure, no problem. So are you guys having a little celebration?" I ask.

"Err sort of. More of a reunion." She smiles.

"Ahh that's lovely, well there's twenty cupcakes there. I'm sure that'll keep you going." I state, finishing off unloading them onto the cake stand.

"Thank you Esme. You want to say hello to Bob?" She asks.

"Sure." I shrug.

I follow Ruth into the living area, looking at the family photos on the wall as I pass them.

"Bob look who came to see you!" She says excitedly.

"Hey Bob, I just dropped you some cup..." I pause.

Standing next to Bob is Gaige. I feel the colour drain from my face.

"Jesus Ruth, you ordered the cupcakes on purpose didn't you?" Bob chastises.

"I don't know what you're talking about. I just thought it would be nice to have some special cakes. That's all."

I haven't moved or said anything. My eyes are still firmly fixated on Gaige. He is wearing smart jeans boots and a fitted jumper that clings to his delicious body.

"Esme." He says, his voice gravelly.

"I have to go." I rush out.

I walk to my truck but before I make it Gaige grabs my hand. I snatch my hand back.

"Don't touch me." I fume.

"Esme, I'm sorry I left without saying goodbye and telling you what was happening. I didn't think I would be gone this long." He apologises.

"I trusted you! I let you worm your way in. I had feelings for you. After our night together I came to tell you but you were with Amy. I saw how happy you were and I thought I couldn't ruin that for you or her so I never said a word. That was a lie though, wasn't it? You and Amy! I carried on feeling guilty about it, thought I had done the right thing. It was all a bloody lie!" I seethe.

I jump into my truck.

"I'm glad you sorted crap out with your mum. Just do me a favour, do not come near me. Stay away from me and the bakery. You're not welcome there." I state before slamming the door shut.

I speed off, gripping the steering wheel tight.

"Hey Esme, I'm back. Sorry I just fucked off and left you hanging. Sorry I gave you the best sex of your life then made you feel like a home-wrecking whore afterwards for no fucking reason at all." I yell angrily in the car to myself.

"I'm sorry I ever let myself fall for you Gaige fucking Knox!" I yell and sob.

I pull up at the bakery and storm through the door. All eyes come to me and all conversations stop.

"Amy, I don't feel too good, I'm going upstairs. Can you close up for me." I say, not giving her time to answer.

I shut myself upstairs and sit in the rocking chair; his fucking beautiful rocking chair.

"Cock sucker!" I yell randomly.

There's a knock on my apartment door. I get up and open it to see Amy with a box and the keys to the shop.

"Here, there were a couple of cakes left. I figured you might want them. Might make you feel better. I have cleaned up as well, so you don't have to worry about that later." She smiles kindly and give me the box.

"Thank you Amy. I will pay you for your overtime." I state.

"Don't worry about it, just see it as one friend helping out another. Plus I've got your back. We won't let him in the bakery, I promise." She smiles.

"How did you know he was back?" I ask.

"Ruth came to see if you were okay and to apologise." She shrugs.

"Ah okay." I nod.

"See you tomorrow." Amy says, walking down the steps.

I shut the front door and go to the kitchen and pour myself a large wine. I open the box and there is a mini Victoria sponge cake inside.

"Son of a bitch."

I pick it up and open the window and throw it onto the street, narrowly missing a person walking past.

"What the?!" The guy yells, looking around.

"Sorry! My bad!" I yell and hide.

I slump down in the rocking chair and stare out of the window, drinking my wine. My phone pings with a text. I frown. I don't really get text messages as the only people local to me who have my number are Bob, Amy, and Josie.

I unlock my phone and see it's a message

from an unknown number.

It's good to see you still like the rocking chair. G x

I look out of the window and see him standing next to his truck. He's looking up at me. I pick up my phone to reply.

How did you get my number?

I drink my wine and watch him type and then look back up at me. I flip him the bird and he just laughs. My phone pings again, alerting me.

Bob gave it to me. He begged me to tell you not to kill him or worse, cut him off from your cakes. Can I come in and talk to you?

I roll my eyes and reply.

I will deal with Bob. No you can't, you can piss off.

I keep glancing outside to see him writing a text. What is he writing? An essay? Eventually my phone pings with a text.

Fair enough. You can't blame me for trying. There is what looks like a smashed up cake on the ground. You get an angry customer in or did you throw one at me and miss?

I snort and quickly type my reply.

It was a Victoria sponge. I didn't throw it at you. It was a symbolic protest against you. A warning if you like. Now please leave me alone. I have to get up early in the morning for work.

I hit send and wait.
My phone pings.

What if I were to camp out in my truck all night to show you how serious I am about you? To show you how sorry I am? I could bring you breakfast in the morning? I could make you lunch, dinner, supper. Anything. Just hear me out. x

I read his message and my heart lurches just a little. I have to protect what little bit of my heart I have left.
I reply.

Go home Gaige. Goodnight.

I get up and switch the light off so he can't see in. I watch him sigh and look up.

"I'm not giving up Esme!" He yells before getting into his truck and driving off.

I climb into bed that night and curl up into a ball. It's almost as if I'm protecting my heart. I was broken and fragile after Jay and Gaige helped to fix that broken part of me. But when he up and left, he undid the part of me he had fixed. He killed any hope I had. After the date with Tanner I resigned myself to just being alone. I need to look out for me and focus on my business, at least I can enjoy that.

Chapter Eighteen

I open up the bakery and see a parcel on the step in front of the door. I look around for who might have delivered it. I pick it up and bring it inside. I place it down and open it. There's a card that reads.

Esme,

> *I'm sorry. Do you forgive me?*
> *Gaige.*
> *X*

Inside the box under some tissue paper is a lumberjack gnome holding a flower.

Josie walks in and looks over my shoulder.

"Aww cute!" Amy comes over next.

"Oh you got a present." She states. "Aww, that's cute." She smiles.

I take the gnome and grab my sharpie. I write on his hat and put it back outside the shop.

"What did you write on it?" Amy asks.

"Go and have a look for yourself." I suggest.

She picks it up and reads it out.

"Gnome trespassers." She laughs.

"Right girls, it's Saturday and it's Easter tomorrow so action stations. Prepare for a crazy day." I clap.

I wasn't wrong. The morning was unusually busy; we had a queue outside the door. I had to get Josie to give people number tickets because it was getting too much.

"Number twenty-three?" I yell.

"Oo that's me! Out of the way Margery." A little old lady elbows her way to the front.

"What can I get you?" I asks smiling.

"Do you make chocolate penis cakes or cookies?" She asks.

"Umm not on Easter. Try valentine's day." I laugh.

"Excuse me cutting through, thank you, sorry." I hear. I look up and see Gaige working his way through to the front of the queue.

"Okay dear. Could I have three of the bunny cookies and three of the chocolate nests please."

She asks sweetly.

"Sure thing." I get the ladies order and ring it up at the till.

"That will be $12." I state as I hand her the box.

"Here, allow me." Gaige says handing me the money. "Keep the change."

"We don't accept tips here." I hand him back his change.

"Thank you for your custom. Please come again." I smile to the elderly lady.

"Twenty-four!" I yell.

"That's me." Gaige smiles and holds up the ticket.

"How in the he…" I start to ask.

"Paid a customer $100 for it." He smiles.

"You paid a customer $100, just so you could come in here?" I ask.

"Yes." He smiles.

"Phillis will you move out of the way? You have your order." An elderly woman moans.

"Back off Margery, I want to see how this works out." Phillis points to Gaige and I.

I pinch the bridge of my nose.

"Christ."

"It's the only way I could get you to hear me

out." He begs.

"If you're not buying anything then you can leave." I state.

"Fine, I have $20. I will have three of the mini Victoria sponge cakes." He smiles.

I growl, which just makes him smile more.

"$15 please." I hold out my hand.

He places the $20 in my hand I go to take it but he keeps hold of it, forcing me to face him.

"Esme, I am sorry. You have no idea how much. I didn't know you liked me too. I would never have treated you that way otherwise. I'm begging you, let me take you out tonight for a drink. I just want to talk, I promise." He begs.

"Do it stupid girl! He's a hunk!"

"Yes do it!"

"If she doesn't go I will!"

Is all yelled from various customers. I try and fight a smile but can't. Gaige smiles.

"Is that a yes?" He asks.

"Fine. You have one hour, come back at closing." I relent.

"Well done girl. You'll only need five minutes with this one, I can tell." Phillis says.

"I will see you later." Gaige smiles and leaves.

"Okay the show is over. Number 25?" Amy shouts, giving me a minute to collect myself.

Shaking myself off I continue to serve the customers. We were actually all sold out by four, an hour before closing. I had to turn people away.

The girls help me clear up and I hand them both an Easter basket I made and kept aside for them as a thank you gift.

"Here. It's just a little thank you for all of your hard work and a happy Easter too."

"Oh wow, thanks Esme." Josie says, looking in the hamper.

"You're too kind." Amy smiles.

I hug them both.

"Go. Have a couple of days off. I'm keeping the bakery closed Sunday and Monday for Easter. I'm not sure what you guys here do but it's the norm in England. Plus I think we've earnt an extra day off." I smile.

"See you Tuesday." They both say as they leave.

I continue to clean and wipe down all the surfaces. I notice a large bag of flour has been left out. I grab it and try to put it on the shelf but I can't reach and I don't know where Amy put the bloody steps. I grab a chair and stand on that. I manage to put the flour on the shelf.

"Christ, what are you doing?" Gaige says.

I spin around too quickly and wobble and fall. Gaige moves fast and catches me.

"Thanks." I mutter.

He helps me stand and I brush my hair out of my face.

"The shop was still open so I came through. Sorry, didn't mean to frighten you." He says apologetically.

"It's fine." I smile tightly. "Just give me a second to get my apron off and I will grab my coat and purse." I say, undoing my apron and hanging it up.

I lock up and start to walk to Gaige's truck.

"I thought we could go somewhere a little quieter without the town listening to us." Gaige suggests.

"Sure." I smile.

Walking with him is hard. He smells amazing and he looks good too in his worn jeans and thick black jumper.

We walk for a while down to the docks. We sit on the bench. The same bench where I scattered Jay's ashes.

"Esme, I've made a mess of things. You came into town like this ball of fireworks. You captured my attention and no matter what I just couldn't look away. I was in awe of you, of your strength. I know this is going to sound completely insane but when you broke down and I held you, I wanted to strangle your husband for making you feel pain like that. It freaked me out feeling that way. I knew you weren't ready for a relationship, so I tried doing the friend thing. If I couldn't have you as mine I would take what I could get." Gaige sighs, rubbing his jaw.

"Then that night Esme, fuck. It killed me. I knew you wanted just a one time thing, so I shut it down. I wanted nothing more than to wake you up that morning and make love to you. But I didn't. For you, I didn't." Gaige tucks a piece of my hair behind my ear.

"Seeing you on a date with Wyatt, that was a massive kick in the crotch. I'm glad it was a disaster. I was planning on staking my claim but then I got the call from my mom and I had to go. I just hoped you would still be here when I got back." He smiles.

"Why didn't you text me? Or tell Bob to tell me that?" I ask.

"I wanted to do it myself like this. Just you and me."

I nod and take a deep breath.

"Then I think you should know I went on a date and slept with someone." I state honestly.

His jaw clenches and he closes his eyes.

"Who?" He asks.

"Tanner. He works for Bob." I answer, nibbling my thumb nail.

"Is it serious? Do you like him?" He asks.

I burst out laughing and shake my head.

"Well, let's just say I've given him a wide birth since. That guy has serious mummy issues." I snort.

Gaige sighs in relief.

"Thank fuck. I thought I was too late and you were with someone else. I have no right to complain about you being with someone else. We weren't together. Do I like it? No, but you're free now and I have my chance." He takes my hand and kisses it gently.

"You have your chance huh?" I ask smiling.

"It means I will stop at nothing to prove to you that your heart is safe with me. I will do anything to make you happy. I will kick anyone's ass who upsets you even a little bit." He promises.

He cups my face in his hands, his thumbs softly stroking my cheeks.

"You, Esme, are the best thing that ever came screaming and swearing into my life. I'm not about to give you up." Gaige says sincerely.

I lick my lower lip and his eyes drop to my mouth.

"I'm not going to kiss you Esme. Not until you say that you trust me with your heart." He states.

"I'm sorry, what?" I ask in disbelief.

He smiles.

"I'm not kissing you. I'm going to prove to you that you can trust me, that I will never break your already fragile heart."

"You're serious, aren't you?" I ask.

He nods.

"Wow, I'm kinda happy but also annoyed because I want to kiss you right now." I sulk.

He laughs.

"Do you trust me not to break your heart?" He pleads.

I pause because the truth is, I don't. Damn it!

"Well it looks like it's a case of blue balls for you and blue clit for me. Happy days." I state.

Gaige roars with laughter.

"Come on, let's get you back to the bakery before it gets too cold." He takes my hand in his.

We walk back up to the bakery. A few people walk past and they all take note of us holding hands.

"We are the town's gossip." I point out.

"Yep. Let them have their fill."

We reach the bakery and I fiddle with my key.

"Um, do you want to come in for some dinner?" I ask.

He smiles and shakes his head.

"No. I don't trust myself around you in private. I'd like to take you out tomorrow though?" He asks.

I bite my bottom lip and nod.

"Bye Esme." He says kissing my hand and walking back to his truck.

I quickly unlock the door and run straight upstairs to ring Sally.

"So let me get this straight, he isn't going to even give you a little tickle, a fondle, a squeeze, a nibble?! Not even a kiss?!" She asks, sounding perplexed.

"That's right, no touchy." I affirm.

"Well I mean I agree with him in the sense that you are messed up and he needs to tread carefully with your heart. But isn't falling head over heels for a guy helped along by them giving us a few of the big O's?"

"Well I know he's good in that department. I've already fallen for him. Do I think he will let me down and hurt me again? Most definitely but god damn I just want to kiss him so bad." I whine.

"I want to kiss him and I've never even met him. The guy is a walking wet dream. You need to send me a picture of him." She sighs.

"Eww no, you'll use him as wank bank material." I say, disgusted.

"Hey now, you know I don't call them that. That sounds disgusting."

"Sorry, my apologies. Your gallery of happy endings." I say rolling my eyes.

"Yeah, it's an impressive gallery. Right my blue clitted friend, I have to go to work. Don't forget to send me a picture! Speak soon."

"Bye cow bag." I say and disconnect.

I make myself some dinner and sit and watch a movie. I'm not really paying much attention to the film. The main thing running through my mind is what will tomorrow's date bring? He didn't say what sort of thing to wear. I decide to text him.

You didn't say what to wear tomorrow? Esme x

I don't have to wait long for him to reply.

Wear whatever you want, there's no dress

code. G x

I roll my eyes. Bloody men don't get it because they don't have a lot of options, especially when it comes to shoes.

Okay, but what shall I wear shoe wise? Are we doing a lot of walking or can I wear heels?

He replies straight away.

We aren't walking that far so it's up to you. I won't be wearing my heels, just so you know. ��

I snort and roll my eyes.

Good to know. I will see you tomorrow. Night xoxo

I get up to go to bed when my phone pings again.

Hey, I said no kissing until you trust me! Night beautiful x

I smile and shake my head. He's such a dork.

I go to bed feeling nervous and excited for our date tomorrow.

Chapter Nineteen

Fed up with trying to decide what to wear I finally decide on my grey off the shoulder jumper dress with tights and dark brown boots. It is sexy with how it clings to my body yet stretchy and comfy. It'll also keep me warm in the crisp spring air.

I leave my hair down and grab my jacket and head downstairs for when he knocks. I check my bag and as I do he knocks on the door. I smile as I open it.

"Come in a second, I'm just seeing if my gloves are in my bag. Will I need gloves?" I ask.

He doesn't answer. I turn around and see his eyes fixed on me. I smile and walk towards him, putting an extra sway in my hips. When I reach him I place my hands on his chest.

"Gaige, are you okay?" I whisper.

His eyes come to mine.

"You look fucking stunning. You don't play fair." He says, his voice gravelly.

"Thank you, although I have no idea what you're talking about. I'm British, we are all about good manners and playing by the rules." I laugh.

He takes my hand and pulls me outside to his truck. Taking my keys from me he locks up.

"Slow down! You didn't answer my question about my gloves." I rush out, practically having to run to keep up with him.

"Fuck your gloves, I will buy you some." He states, opening the door for me.

I climb in and he shuts the door and walks around to his side. Jumping in he starts up the truck and quickly pulls off.

"Why the rush?" I ask.

"Because I need to get us in a public place so I'm not tempted to kiss you or anything else." He grits.

I laugh.

"Hey, don't go complaining. It's your rule."

That earns me a glare which just makes me laugh more.

He parks up and I look at the sign.

"You have to be kidding me." I mutter.

Gaige comes round and opens my door.

"Ice skating?" I ask.

He just smiles and holds out his hand.

"You know I hate ice skating and that I can't skate for shit, I told you that. So far mister, you are getting nul point!" I say, ending in a French accent.

Gaige looks at me like I'm insane.

"Eurovision song contest. When a country doesn't get any points. Do you know what, never mind, it doesn't have the same effect if I have to explain it to you." I wave my hand, disregarding my statement.

We walk in and Gaige pays for us. We get our skates and I can already feel the pain coming my way. It's been a little while since I caused myself an injury so I know it's coming.

Once we have our skates on Gaige takes my hand. He walks with ease and I wobble like Bambie after too many shots of tequila. I grip hold of his arm like a vice.

"Ease up there. I need blood flow to my arm." He teases.

I roll my eyes and flip him off which only makes me wobble.

Gaige steps onto the ice and helps me. As soon as my skate touches the ice it slides. I grab hold of Gaige to stop myself from landing on my arse.

"I'm seriously not liking you right now." I mutter.

"Okay, you need to trust me. You need to relax your body." He states laughing.

"Um here's the thing Christopher Dean, my body isn't relaxing because it knows when there is pain coming my way. The pain will be coming as soon as I try to move. I will be flying arse over tit. It's inevitable." I sigh.

"Christopher Dean?" He asks.

"Really? Out of what I said that's what you ask me about? He was an olympic gold medallist ice skater with Jane Torville. It was an iconic moment for us Brits! We still relish it thirty plus years later." I smile.

"Right, now bring your other foot onto the ice and hold on to me." Gaige directs me.

I wobble and hold onto him so tight that I don't think I can unclench my hands.

"See! You're still upright. Now I'm going to skate backwards. Just relax and glide across the ice. Oh and keep your eyes on me." He instructs.

I nod and tense as soon as he starts skating backwards. My eyes go wide in fear. Gaige laughs.

"I've got you, relax." He reassures.

"See! You're skating." He states.

"I'm gliding. You are my skating tow truck." I

laugh.

He stops.

"Right. Now you're going to move your feet. I will say left, right, and so on. Just follow that. Keep your eyes on me, not your feet. Okay. Are you ready?" He asks.

I shake my head. He smiles.

"Left, right, left right." He continues and I follow his instructions.

I resist the urge to look at my feet.

"You're doing it!" He smiles.

I smile.

"Holy shit, I'm doing it." I breathe.

We continue like that for a while.

"Right, now I'm going to let go of one hand and stand to the side of you." He says as he lets go.

"What? What are you doing you psychopath?" I screech.

Gaige laughs.

"Right ready? Left, right, left, right." He repeats as I move slowly and wobbly around the ice rink. I can't believe I'm skating.

Some young teens whizz past us, making me wobble.

"Hey! Watch it!" I yell.

They spin around to face us.

"Oh look boys, it's true. You can teach an old dog new tricks." He mocks.

My head snaps up.

"Oh piss off pimple dick. I could eat a bowl of alphabet soup and shit out a smarter statement than that!" I snap.

Gaige bursts out laughing. The teen looks like I slapped him as his mates laugh at my comeback.

"Fuck off." He strops off, his mates following him.

"Esme?" Gaige calls.

"Yeah." I turn my head in his direction.

"You're skating." He smiles.

I look down at my feet and realise I'd been so distracted by teen twat I hadn't realised I'd been skating.

"Oh fuck!" I smile excitedly.

As I say that my foot slips and my feet come out from under me. Gaige moves fast and grabs me. He takes the brunt of the fall with me landing on top of him.

"You stopped me from hurting myself." I smile, laying on top of him.

He tucks my hair behind my ear.

"I promised you I would never let you get hurt, even if that means protecting you from yourself." He winks.

I move quickly so he doesn't have time to stop me. I crash my mouth on his. He moans and kisses me back.

"Oi! None of that on the ice rink!" Is yelled over the speaker.

We break the kiss.

"You caught me off guard there." He states.

"Maybe, or maybe I just trust you." I say honestly.

His eyes darken.

"Are you serious or are you just trying to get me into bed?" He smiles.

"Both." I answer.

Gaige rolls me onto my back and takes my mouth.

"Right, that's it, you've been warned. Security!" Is yelled over the speaker.

We ignore it and carry on kissing. We don't move until we are escorted off of the rink. The entire time we are laughing.

He drives us to his place and parks up.

"I will make us some dinner since we didn't get to have any after skating." He states.

I lick my bottom lip.

"I'm not hungry for dinner."

The muscle in Gaige's jaw ticks. He jumps from the truck and opens my door. He grabs me and drags me up to his front door.

Once it's unlocked he pins me to the wall. His eyes search mine.

"Do you trust me Esme?" He asks.

"I trust you with all of my heart Gaige." I whisper.

He picks me up and I wrap my legs around his waist. He takes my mouth, kissing me, owning me.

He carries me upstairs and lays me down on the bed. He removes my boots, tights, and panties. I sit up and remove my dress while Gaige takes off his clothes.

He crawls on top of me and kisses up my body. I moan.

"I need to feel you." He says before sliding into me.

I gasp, feeling him stretch me.

He kisses me slowly, nipping my bottom lip. He doesn't move.

"Gaige. Please." I beg.

He moves his hips slowly as he kisses and

bites my neck. I scratch my nails down his back. The feeling is almost too much to bare.

"Gaige, more please." I moan.

"You want this?" He groans, thrusting hard.

"Oh god yes!" I cry.

"More?" He asks, swivelling his hips.

"More." I moan.

He thrusts harder, his relentless power hitting my g spot over and over. I can't take it anymore; my orgasm crashes over me, hitting me hard.

"Gaige! Fuck!" I scream.

"Fuck." He groans deep in his throat as he climaxes.

We both are panting. There's a sheen of sweat covering our bodies. Gaige lifts his head and kisses me softly.

"It didn't take much for you to trust me." Gaige smiles.

"Are you saying I'm easy?" I feign offence.

"Beautiful, you are anything but easy." He laughs.

"Are you saying I'm hard work?" I tease again.

"Jesus Christ." He sighs.

"Honestly, I was already pretty close to trusting you enough not to break my heart. I know that what happened before was unintentional but I was still pissed off and hurt. I'm not stupid enough to think you intentionally did it to hurt me. You made me take a risk today, a risk that would have normally seen me in the emergency room. But you were there. You stopped me from hurting myself and I trusted you enough to lead me onto the damn ice. You should have known from that point that I trusted you." I admit.

"You mean to tell me I didn't even have to actually make you ice skate, just getting you on to the ice rink was enough?! I've wasted so much time! We could have been here fucking all along. Well beautiful, we are going to make up for that now." Gaige says, wiggling his eyebrows before kissing me. I burst out laughing.

After we made up for lost time, we curled up on his sofa to watch Sherlock. It was the only series we could agree on.

"He's pretty hot." I state, eating popcorn.

Gaige twists his body round to me.

"I'm sorry, I thought I heard you say another guy was hot?" He says dramatically.

"He is. I never saw what the fuss was about Cumberbatch before, I like my men a little beefier." I say whilst winking. I squeeze his bicep. "But there's something about him as Sherlock. His quirky behaviour, his intelligence, his perfect bow shaped mouth." Pausing, I sigh.

"No, don't stop on my account. Please, tell me more about this guy that makes you swoon." Gaige huffs.

I burst out laughing.

"Swoon?! What, are we in the 1950s?"

Gaige laughs.

"I do apologise me-lady. Maybe you would prefer the word smitten instead." Gaige says trying his best English accent.

"Oh sir! I do believe it is you I am smitten with." I say in a posh accent while fanning my face.

"Is that so? Well me-lady, I do believe I am very fond of you too." Gaige says in his English accent while placing the popcorn on the floor and crawling on top over me.

"Oh sir, I am feeling all of a quiver." I mock laughing.

"Shut up me-lady and fuck me." Gaige says bluntly and kisses me.

I giggle but that soon dies while sir gives me a right good fucking.

Chapter Twenty

I spent the next night with Gaige too. I swear I've never shagged so much in all my life. Then I had to come back to the bakery to start prepping for opening the next day. Gaige said he would be back a little later. He had some wood to deliver first.

I have my music on full blast while I'm kneading dough, listening to Cypress Hill's Insane in the Brain. I'm dancing around doing my best hip hop moves. The music stops suddenly and I jump. I turn around to see Gaige standing there leaning against the doorway with the biggest smile on his face. God, he's so bloody handsome.

"Hey." I smile.

He pulls me to him and kisses me. His thumb wipes flour from my cheek.

"Let me take you upstairs." He kisses my neck.

"Hmmm. Sorry, I can't." I breathe. "I have to finish preparing for tomorrow."

"After then! Let me help so I can get you upstairs."

I place my hands on his chest and push slightly to stop him from kissing me.

"You want to help?" I ask.

He smiles and nods. "Yeah, especially if it means I can get you naked quicker."

"Okay, have you ever baked before?" I ask.

He shakes his head.

I bite my bottom lip and smile.

"Okay. Here, you're strong, you can do the kneading. Wash your hands and I will show you what to do." I instruct.

I click my music back on, turning it down slightly. War's Low Rider comes on and Gaige looks at me with his eyebrows raised.

"What? I have a vast taste in music. Don't diss War." I start dancing my way back to the counter.

Gaige laughs. "Do you always dance?" He asks.

"I do if I hear music. Any music. I can't stop my toe from tapping or my hips from wiggling." I shrug.

Gaige comes up behind me. He wraps his arms around me and rests his chin on my shoulder.

"So chef, show me what I need to do."

"Okay. Make sure your surface is floured and sprinkle a little on top of the dough. Then you knead it like this for around ten minutes." I say showing him.

"Okay, let me try." He says stay where he is and kneads the dough.

"How's this?" He asks, placing kisses along my neck.

"Hhmm. Perfect." I breathe.

He smiles against my neck and nips me before moving and slapping my behind.

I give him an evil glare.

"Not cool man, not cool." I say handing him some dough.

Gaige laughs and kneads the dough.

"I'm going to have to change now. I have a giant handprint on my arse cheek!" I state.

"Beautiful, after this you're not going to be wearing or needing any clothes." Gaige states.

I bite my lip and smile. Bob Marley and the Wailers come on and I can't stop myself from dancing.

I move and sway my hips, kneading the dough. I look to Gaige who is smiling and shaking his head at me.

With all twenty loafs of dough proofing I clean up and wipe the side down.

Gaige comes up behind me and spins me around and lifts me onto the counter.

"I don't think this conforms to health regulations." I smile.

Gaige takes the cloth from my hand and throws it across the room. He grabs my ponytail and pulls, tilting my head back. Then he crashes his mouth on mine. I moan into his mouth.

My hands move quickly. I undo his jeans while he removes mine. We are both frenzied, the sexual tension has been building since he arrived. He pulls me forward. Tilting my hips he drives into me.

"Fuck!" We both moan.

"This isn't going to be slow and sweet beautiful. It's going to be hard, intense, and fucking phenomenal." Gaige grits.

"Promises, promi…" The word die in my throat when Gaige surges forward.

He grips tightly on my hips and he relentlessly pounds into me. Each time filling me to the hilt. He releases my hip and circles his thumb over my clit.

"Gaige!" I cry.

His hand slides up my body, pushing me to lie down. He pinches my nipple and wraps his hand around my throat, gently squeezing as he continues to slam into me. I don't feel it coming. My orgasm hits me like a freight train. I buck and my whole body tenses.

"Fuck! Gaige!" I scream.

"Fuck!" Gaige groans.

We are both panting. I'm coming down from the most incredible orgasm I think I've ever had. Gaige is leaning over me with his head on my chest. I stroke my fingers through his hair.

"Gaige." I whisper.

"Yeah beautiful." He says between trailing kisses across my chest.

"I think I'm falling in love with you." I say honestly,

Gaige's body freezes and his head snaps up.

"What?" He asks.

Feeling my cheeks heat and my heart rate pick up.

"No sorry, I don't mean that. What I meant to say is that I've fallen in love with you Gaige Knox. I'm head over heels in love with you." I say softly. I'm anxious; he hasn't said a single word. He just stares ahead, not saying anything or moving.

"Gaige, say something." I beg.

His eyes come to mine.

"You love me?" He asks.

I nod. I'm scared he's going to bolt or say he doesn't feel the same.

"Thank fuck for that." He sighs.

"What?" I ask, my voice wavering.

He strokes my face.

"Esme, I've loved you for what feels like forever. From the moment I met you I haven't been able to get you out of my god damn head. You came into my predictable boring life with your fire, your kind heart, and your fucking hot body. I couldn't handle it. I couldn't stop myself from loving you even if I tried." He admits.

My tears fall.

"Well fuck me." I sob.

Gaige laughs.

"I was your explosion of colour." I state.

"What?" Gaige asks confused.

"It's something Bob mentioned a while back." I shrug.

Gaige smiles and takes my mouth, kissing me softly.

"Suppose we better finish cleaning up this

flour, then we better clean ourselves." I state smiling.

"I vote we go straight to the shower now." Gaige whispers across my lips.

"Lead the way." I giggle.

After our very long, very hot, incredible shower Gaige helps me finish cleaning the kitchen.

He stands and talks to me while I decorate some cupcakes and biscuits.

"You're incredible." He says watching me pipe.

I smile and bite my lip.

"There are far more talented people out there than me." I state.

"I disagree." He comments.

My phone starts ringing with a video call.

"Brace yourself." I warn. I put down the piping bag and answer it.

"Hiya Sally." I smile.

"Well what the hell happened? You went on the date with the hot lumber jack and I haven't heard from you since. I nearly called the Mountie's to start a search party! I mean, what is he, bloody Christian Grey? He didn't make you sign anything did he?!" She questions.

I laugh and shake my head. Gaige laughs and

takes the phone from me.

"Hi Sally, I'm Gaige. It's good to see you again, well, sort of." He smiles.

"Holy shit! Don't move, let me just screenshot you a sec." She states.

"No you bloody don't!" I yell.

"Oh alright, selfish cow now sharing. Sorry Gaige, where are my manners? It's a pleasure to speak to you again, the guy that's had my friend tied up in knots. Honestly, she has not shut up about you." Sally sighs.

"Okay that's enough. Calm your hormones." I state, taking the phone from Gaige.

"Okay you can see I'm alive and not kidnapped. I'm totally fine. Now you can go and I will call you later." I say gritting my teeth while smiling at her.

"Oh I can see that you're more than okay. The fact you're freshly showered shows me you're one happy and thoroughly fucked friend." She laughs as I cut the call.

Gaige laughs.

"She really does seem nice."

"She's the best. She just has less of a filter than I do." I point out.

Once I finish all of the prep Gaige suggests going for a bite and a drink at The Sunken Ship.

Before we walk in we pause.

"Ready for this?" He asks.

I laugh and nod.

We walk in and I swear every person in there swings their gaze to us. I curl and hide my face in Gaige's chest. He laughs and kisses the top of my head.

We reach the bar and Eloise has a massive grin on her face.

"Well, well, well. Look at you two! Finally pulling your heads out your asses and getting it together. Damn good to see you both happy." She states as she gets our drinks.

She places them down.

"I'm guessing it's the usual. Unless you're wanting something fancier like champagne?" She asks.

We both laugh.

"No, we are good with our usual." Gaige states.

We find a table, sit down, and look over the menu. I'm not sure why, I'm already planning on having poutine. I want nothing more than carbs covered in delicious gravy and cheese. My stomach rumbles. Gaige raises an eyebrow at me.

"Well we have worked up quiet an appetite. I'm starving." I smile and pat my belly.

We place our order and while we are waiting Tanner walks in.

"Oh you have to be fucking kidding me." I groan.

"What?" Gaige asks looking in the same direction.

"Tanner. The guy I, um, you know." I mumble.

"Ohhhh, the momma's boy." Gaige laughs.

I slap his arm.

"Don't be horrible please."

Tanner spots me and smiles.

"Hey Esme."

"Hi Tanner, how are you?" I ask.

"I'm good. I was wondering if you wanted to come for a drink with me another time?" He asks.

Gaige stands up in front of Tanner. He has at least four inches in height on Tanner and his build is much bigger.

"Hey there Tanner. I'm Gaige, Esme's boyfriend, lover, sexual partner, date, old man, whatever you want to call me." Gaige holds his hand out in greeting.

Tanner is taken aback for a moment. Then he smiles and shakes Gaige's hand.

"No harm man, I didn't think it would take long for her to settle down, she's something special. Best damn sex I've ever had." Tanner states smiling.

I grab Gaige's hand to stop him from landing one on Tanner, who is too thick to realise he's pissed Gaige off.

"Bye Tanner." I smile.

Tanner leaves and I tug Gaige's hand to get him to sit back down.

"He's a little umm, dumb. He didn't mean anything by it." I state.

I grab Gaige's chin and force him to focus on me.

"Don't get into a fight over nothing. He means nothing to me. What do I have to do to change your angry face into a happy one?" I ask smiling.

Gaige grunts.

I lean in and kiss him softly and whisper 'I love you' across his lips.

He grabs the back of my head and deepens the kiss and groans.

"Well I was going to warn you that the food is hot but I can see you guys don't mind it being a little hot." Eloise says giggling.

She places down our food and leaves.

We stop kissing and I smile up at Gaige.

"You still angry?" I ask.

"If I say no does that me you'll stop kissing me like that?" He asks.

"No, but I'm going to stop kissing you now because your woman is hungry." I smile and peck him on his lips.

"Can't have my woman being hungry." He smirks.

We eat our food and decide to share a pie and ice cream after.

"Here, try this pie. It's delicious." I say, holding out my spoon with pie and ice cream on it.

He opens his mouth and I feed him. He hums in approval.

"That is good, but I happen to know of something that tastes much better." He says low.

I lean in and kiss him.

"Want to go home? You can eat as much as you like." I tease.

"Move your ass now, your man is hungry." He orders.

I jump up giggling as he chases me out the bar.

Chapter Twenty-one

Gaige has promised to help Bob out with a couple of contracts and he has deliveries to catch up on. We only manage passing visits through the day and by the time Gaige comes back to mine at night I'm out cold, too tired to stay awake.

The next day the shop is just as busy. What doesn't help is I'm not feeling great either. I'd rather be in bed sleeping but Amy has called in sick so I'm on my own until Josie can get here after she finishes school. Thankfully everyone is being patient and understanding.

"Next please?"

"Hello Esme, could I have a fresh loaf and two of your red velvet cupcakes please?" Nellie asks.

"Sure thing." I answer.

I reach for the loaf of bread and wobble slightly.

"You okay Esme?" She asks.

I stand still for a minute to stop myself from feeling dizzy.

"Yeah, I think it's just low sugar levels. Being on my own I haven't had chance for a break yet." I say as I bag her bread.

I grab her cupcakes and that's when the room spins and turns to darkness.

I wake up laid on my bed in my apartment with the doc sat next to me.

"The bakery." I say sitting up too quickly. The room spins again.

"Calm down, it's taken care of. Here, drink some water. When was the last time you ate?" He asks.

"Um I grabbed a cookie for breakfast." I answer.

"It's now 2pm. You need to eat. Also I need to ask you, is there any chance you could be pregnant?" He asks.

I shake my head vigorously.

"No doc, I have the implant in." I say pointing to it in my arm.

"Right, and when did you have it fitted? Can

you remember?" He asks.

I set it on my laptop calendar. I pull out my laptop and look.

"I've had it in for four years and eight months." I state smiling.

"Esme, that implant is over a year out of date." He informs me.

"No doc, I was told five years."

"I'm sorry. The coil is five years but the implant is only three." He affirms.

My hands start to shake and I feel like I can't breathe.

"It's okay Esme, deep breaths. Let's do a test first. Here, can you go to the bathroom and wee in this pot for me." He hands me a little pot and I go to the bathroom.

I can't be pregnant, I just can't be. I go to the bathroom and come out with the pot and hand it to doc.

He dips a little strip in it and then turns to me.

"This can take a minute or so to show...oh never mind. Congratulations Esme, you're pregnant!"

"WHAT?" I screech.

"Esme sit down." Doc orders.

I take a seat and he sits next to me and holds

my hand.

"I take it the father is Gaige?" He asks.

"Yeah, I mean I slept with Tanner a while back but he used a condom. I told Gaige I was covered with the implant. Oh shit, he's going to think I've trapped him isn't he?" I sob.

"Calm down. I'm sure he will be over the moon. Now, if you like I can book you in for a scan at the county hospital to determine how far along you are. Shall I ring through now and see when we can get you in?" He asks.

I nod. He makes the call and has managed to get me in for tomorrow.

I'm pregnant, fucking pregnant. God, this is a nightmare!

Doc packs up his bag and goes to leave.

"Doc!" I call after him.

"Yes Esme?"

"Please don't mention this to Gaige, the pregnancy, I mean." I ask.

"I wouldn't have divulged anything to anyone unless you specifically told me too." He affirms.

"Thank you." I say, staring out of the window.

About an hour later Gaige comes barrelling up the stairs looking all panicked.

"Esme?" He calls.

"Yeah." I answer back.

He comes straight to me on my bed and cups my face.

"Are you okay? I heard you blacked out while working." He asks concerned.

I smile.

"I'm fine, just low blood sugar is all. I hadn't eaten much and Amy was off sick. Doc checked me over and I'm good." I lie.

"Thank god. Why didn't you call me?" He asks.

"I knew you were busy with work and knew it would take a while for you to get here. Plus who needs to phone anyone? This town's gossip spreads quicker than the speed of light." I laugh.

Gaige smiles and kisses me softly.

"Let me order in. I will go pick it up for us." He says kissing my head.

He rings Eloise and I feel awful lying to him but I can't tell him yet. I don't know how far along I am or anything. We've technically only been seeing each other properly for what, a week? It's insane! That one fantastic night has to be the cause of this. So that would mean I'm around ten weeks! Holy shit. I need to keep it together tonight and I will tell him after the scan tomorrow.

"Just tonight." I mutter to myself.

We eat our dinner and Gaige can tell something isn't right with me. I tell him I'm just not feeling right.

He's sweet and attentive. He writes a sign and puts it on the bakery door. He also texts Josie and Amy telling them bakery is shut tomorrow.

"Come on beautiful, let's get you to bed." He holds his hand out for me and leads me to bed.

He pulls me into his arms and holds me until I fall asleep.

The next morning Gaige makes me some toast and orders me to eat it.

"I will call Bob and tell him I won't be in. You're more important than work." He states.

"I will be fine, go. I'm just going to laze about and rest. I have a new book I want to read anyway so you being here will just get in the way of that." I smile.

"Fine. I will call you when I'm on my break." He kisses me goodbye and leaves.

I creep to the window and watch him drive off. I look at the time and quickly get dressed and grab my bag and keys. I jump in my truck, hoping none of the town have seen me and are gossiping about where I'm going.

I park up at the hospital and follow the signs to the prenatal unit. As I walk in there are pregnant women everywhere. Some look huge and so uncomfortable. There's one woman who is heavily pregnant and has a toddler with her who is running around like he's just injected sugar into his veins.

She sits next to me and groans. She's rubbing her stomach.

"How far along?" She asks.

"Oh um, not sure. Waiting for the scan to tell me. You?" I ask.

"Thirty-five weeks today, four more weeks to go and that's if I don't go overdue." She says smiling. Smiling?! What has this woman got to smile about? She is the size of a buffalo and she still has four weeks to go! I mean how much bigger can she get?!

"You still have 4 weeks to go?" I asks stunned.

She smiles.

"Your first pregnancy, right?"

I nod.

"Well, I hate to tell you this but the last weeks are when the baby gains weight. I was twice this size with junior over there."

"You are shitting me?" I ask, my jaw hitting the floor.

She laughs.

"No, I was huge. Let me tell you one piece of advice, it's the best and the worst time of your life all rolled into nine months. It's the most amazing feeling in the world having a life grow inside you, but it's the most exhausting and uncomfortable time too. It's worth it though when you hold that tiny baby in your arms. There is a bond and a love so strong, so powerful, you will never feel that way about anyone else. Believe me."

"Ms Tucker." A nurse calls.

I stand and turn to the woman.

"Good luck and thank you." I smile.

"You too honey."

I walk in the room and the doctor greets me.

"Hi there, I'm doctor Rosie Fealan. Please lay down on the couch and lift your top and lower your waistband." She asks.

I do as she said and she squeezes some cold gel liquid onto my stomach. I suck in a breath at the coldness.

"Sorry. It always catches people off guard. Okay, let's have a look shall we." She says, moving the wand like thing around my lower stomach.

"Ah there we go! One healthy looking baby." She says and she turns the screen for me to see.

There on a screen in black and grey is a tiny baby. A baby bean. I can see its little nose and its little arms and legs moving about. I can't keep back the tears from falling.

"Wow, that's really my baby." I whisper.

She nods and smiles.

"Let's just take some measurements and see how far along you are." She says moving the wand in certain angles.

"Okay I would say you are around eleven weeks pregnant today. Baby is lovely and healthy. If I turn this up you'll be able to hear the baby's heartbeat." She smiles and suddenly the room is filled with the sounds of my baby's heartbeat.

"That's the baby?" I ask.

"Sure is." She smiles.

"Would you like some photos to take home?" She asks.

"Yes please." I say, wiping my tears, unable to take my eyes off the screen.

She prints them off and hands them to me while the nurse wipes the remaining gel off my stomach.

"Right, I would like to see you back here in a weeks time for blood tests. Then there will be another scan at twenty weeks. And you will be able to find out the sex of the baby if you choose." She smiles.

"Thank you." I say staring at my photos as I leave the hospital.

I get in my truck and I cry. I place my hand over my stomach.

"I'm going to love you so much." I whisper.

I wipe my tears and start up the truck.

"There's just one slight glitch. We have to tell your daddy about you and I'm not sure how that will go because we've never spoken about children before. But don't worry bean, whatever happens you will have me, I promise."

Chapter Twenty-Two

I decide to cook Gaige and I a nice meal. I bake a Victoria sponge for dessert just like that night.

I'm so nervous I think I'm going to throw up, or is that part of the pregnancy? On my way home I swung by the pharmacist to pick up some pre-natal vitamins. There was a tiny little bib that had the Canadian flag on it and said 'Canadian eh'. I had to buy it.

I look out of the window. I'm waiting for his truck to pull up. When I see it I squeal.

"Calm down Esme. Jesus, it's not good for the bean. Is it?" I ask an empty room.

I hear him come up the stairs and I nibble on my thumb nail nervously. If I don't tell him soon I won't have a nail left.

He walks in and sniffs.

"Something smells good." He states.

"I cooked us dinner and made us a dessert." I say smiling.

He pulls me to him and kisses me.

"You should have been resting, but you actually look better." He says opening the fridge and getting a beer. He hands me one.

"No thanks." I state.

"You still not feeling right?" He asks.

"No I feel fine. I just don't feel like a beer. Gives me gas." I blurt.

Gaige's lips twitch.

"I have some news to tell you later. Exciting news actually." I ramble.

"Yeah? What is it?" He asks.

"Let's wait until after dinner, save the best till last as they say."

"Christ Esme. Whatever it is you're wired like a coil." He states smiling.

He kisses me softly.

"I could get used to coming home to you every day." He says between kisses.

The timer beeps on the oven and I jump.

"Dinner is ready." I sing.

I bring our food and place it on the table.

"Lasagne and homemade garlic bread."

I sit down and we eat. We chat about his day. Then he asks about mine and I nearly choke on my food. After we've finished I bring out the Victoria sponge. Gaige smiles and winks.

"Ahh! My new favourite cake." He winks.

I cut us each a slice and I can't keep it in any longer. I need to tell him before I give myself a stomach ulcer from the stress.

"Gaige, that thing I need to tell you, are you ready for it?" I ask.

"Sure beautiful." He smiles.

I jump up and grab the little box I put the bib and the scan pictures in. My hands are shaking as I place the box down.

Gaige takes my hand and kisses it.

"Whatever it is, don't be nervous. I love you and that's all there is to it." He states. I smile.

I feel my nose begin to sting as tears fill my eyes. I watch him open the box. He frowns in confusion at first looking at the bib. Then he sees the photos. He freezes completely and just stares at them.

"I'm pregnant. That's why I fainted. I had the scan today, the baby is healthy and -"

"I thought you said you had the implant." He interrupts.

"I do but I was misinformed; I thought it was

five years of protection when in fact it was only three. I feel like a total idiot." I admit.

"And it's mine?" He asks.

I feel like I've been kicked in the gut with that question.

"Yes of course." I answer.

He sits in silence, gripping the picture in his hand.

"Gaige, say something." I whisper, tears running down my face.

"I've got to get out of here."

He storms out, dropping the scan picture on the floor. I hear the door slam and his truck screech off.

I sob and pick up the scan picture. I go to bed and lay down. I thought he would be shocked but happy. I didn't expect that. He promised me he would never hurt me, he lied.

I lay there for I don't know how long, crying until there's nothing left in me. Exhausted, I fall asleep.

I feel the bed shift next to me and it makes me jump.

"Shhhh, it's just me." Gaige whispers.

I wipe my puffy eyes and get up out of bed.

"Esme, I'm sorry." He apologises.

"Sorry? Sorry for what? Accusing me of being pregnant with someone else's child and palming it off as yours? Or sorry because instead of talking to your pregnant girlfriend you decide to piss off, leaving her wondering if you would even come back?" I yell.

Gaige grips his hair.

"I'm sorry for all of that. I was shocked! I wasn't even thinking about kids anytime soon. We haven't even had any time for just us. I'm scared! I mean, what kind of parents are we going to be? We didn't exactly have the best role models growing up. We know nothing about parenting. I don't know how to change a nappy or feed it! What if I mess it up and it ends being a drug dealer? Or worse, a politician!" Gaige smiles.

I laugh whilst wiping my tears. He walks towards me and pulls me to him.

"We learn, Gaige. Don't worry, you won't mess up its life, I won't let you."

"There is one upside to this. Apart from the baby of course." He states.

"Oh yeah, and what's that?" I ask.

"Your tits are going to get even bigger." He laughs as I hit him.

He kisses me.

"I mean it, I'm sorry. I just…I don't know…

I couldn't think straight. I needed time to breathe, to think." He whispers.

"I get it, but in future don't just leave me like that. It hurt a lot. I didn't know if you were coming back. You're not the only one who's scared you know." I point out.

"I know and I'm sorry." He kisses me softly.

Gaige held me all night with his hand placed protectively on my stomach.

****

"I think you should move in with me." Gaige says drinking his coffee.

It's the next morning and I've decided to keep the bakery closed for another day so I have time to cook and prep for the next day.

"What?" I ask.

"I think you should move in with me." He says seriously.

"But we barely know each other." I point out,

"Esme, we've known each other a few months now. We slept every night together there last, what, ten days. Oh and we're having a baby." He states in matter of fact voice.

"Wow, you're such a romantic." I mock.

"Look, I love you. For me this was going to happen at some point anyway. You must have thought about it? I want you in my bed every night, I want to make love to you whenever we get the chance, I want to wake up to you every morning." He says cupping my face.

"That romantic enough for you?" He smirks.

I hit his chest.

"Jerk."

"I will think about it, okay. I've only just got this place sorted." I point out.

"You can rent it or keep it. It's up to you." He states.

I nod.

"Um, when are we telling people? I was thinking of telling the girls today because of work. I'm going to need them to help out further down the line and of course with things now like lifting the ten kilo flour bags and things like that." I ask.

"Tell them. The good thing about this town is that if you tell one person the rest of the town will know by lunch time. You better call your friend too; I'm sure she will want to know."

"Oh shit, I forgot about Sally. I better call her now." I state, picking up my phone.

"Isn't it the middle of the night there now?"

Gaige asks.

"Yes but you don't get it. If she found out that others knew before her there would be hell to pay. Like Carrie but without the blood." I state.

"Hello, you better be dying right now." She grumbles.

Gaige laughs.

"You're on speaker Sally. Gaige is here." I inform her.

"Hey Gaige." She yawns.

"Listen I will let you get back to sleep. There is just something I want to tell you first." I pause.

"I'm pregnant." I say smiling.

"Well done, bye." Then she disconnects.

"Wasn't expecting that kind of reaction." Gaige says.

I hold up my hand and count down from five. By the time I get to three my phone is ringing again.

"What the ever loving fuck?! You're knocked up?!" She screams.

I laugh.

"Yes!"

"Oh my god! This is incredible. How far gone are you?" She asks.

"Eleven weeks." I answer.

"Oh the hot fucking night! He knocked your arse up! High five on the spectacular sperm Gaige." She compliments.

"Err thanks." He mutters.

"Look I have to go but I wanted to tell you before people in the town found out." I state.

"Glad you bloody did too, no one wants to see me go all Carrie." She laughs.

I mouth the words 'see, I told you' to Gaige.

"Bye Sally!" I yell.

"Bye my beautiful pregnant friend!" She yells back.

Gaige puts his arm around me and kisses my head.

"You two are batshit crazy." He states.

"Yes, yes we are." I laugh.

Chapter Twenty-Three

I close the door to the kitchen and hand Amy and Josie a coffee and a cupcake each.

"What's going on Esme? Are you closing?" Amy asks, clearly panicked.

"No, no, not at all. I'm definitely not closing." I reassure them.

"Okay. So obviously you both heard about me collapsing the other day?" I ask.

They both nod.

"Well, Doc found out why." I pause smiling.

"Oh my god, you're dying?!" Amy cries.

"Amy...I'm - " I try to tell her.

"Don't you worry about a thing. We will take care of the shop for you. We could do a fundraiser and get the local network here too? They could do a whole piece..."

"Amy." I try again.

"And don't worry if you lose your hair, I

know a great wig maker! He makes them out of dog hair. I know that sounds mad but have you seen a retriever's coat?! Practically the same as your hair now, very glossy."

I pinch the bridge of my nose.

"Jesus Christ." I mutter.

"Ooo! I also know a great shop that sell the most amazing scarfs if you'd prefer? We will make you look amazing." She beams and leans over, squeezing my hand.

"You done?" I ask.

Amy smiles and nods.

"I'm not dying. But if I were, then I'd be glad I had you to make me at least look good while I shrivelled up and died." I give her a tight smile.

"What I am trying to tell you is that I'm pregnant!" I announce.

Both Amy and Josie's mouths hang open. They look like goldfish.

"Say something." I say.

"Wow! I mean: congratulations." Amy says, giving Josie a side glance.

"What?" I ask.

Josie shakes her head.

"No, come on, what is it? Spit it out." I ask.

"It's just, well, is Gaige the father?" Amy asks.

"Yes of course he is! Christ! What does this town think I am? Some kind of massive slag?!" I screech.

"I told you not to say anything." Josie mutters.

"No one thinks that Esme. It's just that we all know about Tanner and, well, you know." Amy shrugs.

"How do you know about Tanner?!" I ask.

"I never told you we slept together! Also, not that it's any of your business, but we used protection! I am eleven weeks pregnant now. Not only did we use protection, but we also hadn't sleep together then, so it's fucking scientifically impossible." I rant.

"Sorry Esme, we shouldn't have assumed." Amy apologises.

"Who told you?" I ask again.

"Tanner told anyone that would listen one night down at the Sunken Ship." Amy says, biting her lip.

"He did what?!" I whisper.

"Oh that's not good; she's whispering. My mom does that when she's really pissed." Josie points out.

"Is there a live band this week at the pub?" I ask.

"Um, yes, this Friday. Why?" Amy asks.

"I just want to go is all. I need you two to promise me that you will keep my pregnancy quiet until then. Can you do that?" I ask.

"Sure." They both answer.

"I mean it, no one is to know. Gaige and I would like to announce it to everyone then." I smile sweetly.

"I think she's planning something." Josie mutters.

"Most definitely." Amy agrees.

I smile to myself as I walk out of the kitchen. Picking up my phone I ring Gaige.

"Hey beautiful." He answers.

"Hey. We are going to the pub on Friday. There's a live band and I think we should tell everyone there that I'm pregnant. The whole town will be there so it'll be easier that way." I state.

"Why do I get the feeling that there is more to it than what you're saying?" He asks sceptically.

"Oh there is. I just think it's best you wait until then. Trust me on this." I say.

"Okay, I trust you." He replies.

"You do? You don't think it'll be something that will cause a scene or be a disaster?" I ask.

"Oh I know that what you have planned will definitely cause a scene! It may even be a disaster, that's a very high probability. But if it is, I will be there to clean it up." He assures.

"Gaige Knox, I bloody love you." I smile into the phone.

"Love you too beautiful." He replies.

We disconnect and I get the girls to help with the preparations ready for tomorrow.

"While I have you both here, when it gets too much for me further down the line I'm going to have to employ a baker. I might also increase your hours if you want the extra." I query.

"Um Esme, I've been going to evening baking classes. If you wanted to, you could teach me your recipes and I could bake for you while you're on maternity?" Amy asks.

I stop piping and look up.

"Why didn't you say anything?! I would have helped you, I could have shown you different techniques!" I grin.

"I didn't like to bother you. You've had a lot going on." Amy points out.

"Yeah but I would always offer to help! I would love to train you up to cover me! I would much rather have someone I know I can trust than hire someone from outside." I say while pulling her into a hug.

When we open the next day there is actually a queue waiting before we even open. I'm guessing they've all really missed the bakery these past couple of days.

Everyone was asking how I was, if I was feeling better, and telling me about their aunt's cousin twice removed who had fainted and it turned out to be malaria. I did point out that I haven't visited Africa at all, as in not once in my life, but they all came back with the same.

"Well you can't be too careful these days! You can hop on a plane anywhere."

By the end of the day I'm exhausted. If the days don't start calming down I will have to hire someone in to help me so that I have time to train Amy up. I flop down on the bed and yawn.

"Beautiful, wake up." I hear whispered.

"Hmm." I moan.

Gaige kisses along my neck.

"Hhmm. What time is it?" I ask.

"Seven." He answers.

"I finished work and laid down; I must have passed out." I yawn and roll over, cuddling into Gaige.

"Are you hungry?" He asks.

"Yeah, I will cook us something." I say.

"No, I will cook. You rest." He states.

"But you can't cook." I point out.

"Leave it to me." He says kissing my head before climbing off of the bed and going into the kitchen.

I lay back and switch on the TV. I can hear a lot of banging and crashing around.

"Are you okay in there?" I ask.

"Absolutely fine, just rest." He yells back.

I bite my lip to stop myself from laughing.

"Ow! Son of a bitch!" He yells.

I giggle as more banging and crashing comes from the kitchen, followed shortly by the smoke alarm.

I burst out laughing, covering my face with the pillow so that he can't hear me.

"Shut up you mother fucking shit!" He yells.

Eventually it stops. I wipe my tears.

He walks in a moment later with some kind of sauce spilt down his top and a burnt towel thrown over his shoulder. He looks like he's just come out of a war zone.

He smiles, proudly placing down the tray.

"Ta-da! A toasted cheese sandwich." He smiles.

I burst out laughing.

"All that banging, crashing, and the smoke

alarm was for a cheese toastie?" I laugh, wiping my tears.

He smiles and shrugs.

"So what's the sauce down your shirt?" I point.

He looks down at his shirt.

"Oh, a jar of sauce fell out of the cupboard and it smashed. It must have splattered on my shirt." He shrugs.

"Thank you for cooking for me." I lean over and kiss him.

I take a bite of the toasted cheese sandwich and moan.

"Gaige, this is delicious! What did you put in it?" I ask.

"Ahh, now that would be telling. It's a secret recipe." He wiggles his eyebrows.

I giggle and lean in and kiss him.

We eat some of the leftover cakes from the bakery and in less than two hours I'm asleep again. I feel Gaige pull me into his arms and place his hand over my stomach again.

Chapter Twenty-Four

I'm getting ready for the night at the Sunken Ship. Gaige keeps giving me side glances, especially when I sing Pink's So What.

"You're scaring me, do you know that?" Gaige says. Coming up behind me he sweeps my hair to the side and kisses my neck.

"Hhmm. Nothing to be scared of. Just sit back and watch the show." I smile and wink.

"Jesus Christ. I'm going to call my lawyer just in case." He smirks.

"I'm not the one who will need the lawyer." I state.

I grab my bag and coat.

"Let's go." I smile.

We walk into the Sunken Ship and as expected, it's packed out. Gaige automatically becomes protective of people coming too close and bumping into us. He guides us to a table.

"I'm just going to talk to the lead singer for

a moment. He's just there." I point and Gaige frowns curiously.

I walk over and tap the singer on his shoulder. He spins to face me and smiles.

"Well if it isn't our number one fan." He jokes.

I laugh.

"Crap, you remember me then?!" I ask.

"Oh yeah, I'm not going to forget such a pretty face any time soon." He winks.

"Thanks." I brush off.

"Listen, I have a big announcement to make tonight. Is there any chance you would let me up on stage to make it, say, when you take a break or something?" I plead."

"Sure, I will call you up when it's time." He smiles.

"Ah brilliant, thank you." I say and go back to Gaige.

"I don't like that asshole." He grumbles.

"He is nice enough." I state.

"Nope. He was eye fucking you, still is." Gaige grits angrily.

I lean to him. Grabbing his chin I kiss him.

"Bet he's stopped eye fucking me now." I smile.

Gaige smiles against my mouth.

"You're trouble, you know that?"

"I don't know what you mean! I am a picture of innocence." I wink.

"Here's your usual. You doing another dance routine tonight?" Jack teases.

"Well you never know. I shall see how the night goes." I joke.

"You going to join me?" I ask.

"Esme, if you saw me dancing you wouldn't be asking me that question." He smiles and walks off.

I look at my wine and lick my lips. Gaige moves it away and I sulk and stick out my bottom lip.

"Sorry, I will get you a soda in a minute." He says drinking his beer and winking.

"Bastard." I mumble.

The band perform. There are a few looks my way; people obviously expect me to get up and dance.

"We are going to take a break but before we do, there is a young lady who would like to make an announcement to you all." The lead singer gestures for me to come up.

"Trust me." I whisper in Gaige's ear before walking up to the mic.

"Hey everyone." I wave lamely. I spot Tanner and his friends at the bar. Perfect.

"I just wanted to let you all know that I'm pregnant, and that it's Tanner's baby." I state.

I look over at Gaige who looks like he's about to exploded. I look at Tanner who's gone so pale he looks like he's about to pass out.

I laugh.

"I'm just fucking kidding! Of course Gaige is the father. I am eleven weeks pregnant. I got pregnant after one hot amazing night at Gaige's house. Not from a sixty second shag up in the woods with the guy crying out mommy as he orgasmed!" I state.

There are giggles and sniggers around the pub.

"So Tanner, I don't like you going around and telling everyone about something that's private and personal to me. I was nice. I didn't mock you, but Christ alive! You need to see a shrink because shouting shit like that is not normal! Unless there are any cougars in here tonight that are into that kind of freaky shit. If there are, there's your man. Tanner, this is me being nice. Spread shit like that again and I will tell your mommy." I smile sweetly and then go to walk off.

"Oh wait. Yay! Gaige and I are pregnant. Thank you." I cheer.

I smile at Gaige the whole way back to the table. The rest of the bar is silent apart from people muttering.

Tanner walks up to me and grabs my arm, halting me.

"You fucking bitch! How could you?" He seethes.

Gaige approaches me. I smile.

"Get your fucking hands off of her right now." He warns Tanner.

Tanner lets go of my arm and shoves me into Gaige.

"You're fucking welcome to her." Tanner spits.

Gaige moves me to the side.

"Jack, apologise now." Gaige yells.

"For what?" I ask, confused.

Gaige catches up to Tanner and grabs him by the scruff of his collar. He rears his fist back and punches him hard.

Tanner falls to the floor.

"If you fucking speak to her, if you lay a fucking finger on her again, I will make sure you never have kids. Am I clear?" Gaige states as Tanner's friends help him to his feet.

Tanner wipes his mouth and spits blood on

the ground.

"You can guarantee I will never be going near that again." He sneers.

He turns to leave.

"The kid will end up being a slag like it's mother." Tanner mutters under his breath.

"Right, that's it." Gaige grabs Tanner and beats the crap out of him.

Jack jumps in, holding Gaige back.

"That's enough Gaige. He's had enough." Jack warns Gaige.

"You get the fuck out of my bar and don't ever step foot in here again!" Jack orders Tanner.

"You're all fucking crazy, the lot of you!" Tanner whines as he leaves the bar.

I walk up to Gaige and he pulls me into his arms.

"You shouldn't have done that." I say checking his hands.

"I'm not going to let anyone speak like that about you or our child. Ever." He states.

He leans in and kisses me and then rests his forehead on mine. He moves his hand and caresses my stomach. I smile.

"Let's hear three cheers for Gaige and Esme!" Eloise yells.

The bar cheers and people come by to congratulate us throughout the night.

Chapter Twenty-Five

It has been an odd couple of weeks, in a good way. Nellie came by with knitted blankets for the baby and Eloise brought a cute teddy bear. A few of the older ladies that come by have knitted little hats. It's been surreal. It's something I never would have expected. It's only been a week since I announced I was pregnant. I guess Gaige is kind of a big deal to the town. It can't be me; I've only lived here a few months.

The bakery is quieter today and there's something I need to do.

"Amy are you okay minding the place while I pop out for an hour?" I ask.

"Sure. Where are you off to? Need to sit down?" She questions.

"I'm just going to talk to someone I haven't spoken to in a really long time." I answer.

I decide to jump in my truck rather than walk as it'll be quicker.

I pull up and walk along the dock and take a seat on the bench.

"Hi Jay. I'm sorry I haven't been to see you in a while or spoken to you. I'm moving on with my life like you asked me to. I've met this really great guy. I think you would have liked him. He treats me well and he's kind and protective." I smile and close my eyes as the sun beams down from behind a cloud.

"You always said you would watch over me, so you probably already know this, but I'm pregnant. Three months pregnant to be precise. It was a shock, believe me. I got mixed up with my implant dates. I'm sure I can hear you saying I told you so. You always did say I was bound to mix up the dates." I laugh.

I wipe away the few tears that have fallen.

"Anyway, I just wanted to come down and tell you. I felt that I had to, not that you would hear it from anyone else." I giggle.

I sit for a while longer, enjoying the feeling of the sun on my face. I feel someone sit next to me on the bench: Gaige.

He wraps his arm around me and pulls me to him. I rest my head on his shoulder.

"Have you been speaking to Jay?" He asks.

"Yeah, I told him about you and the baby." I smile.

"I hope he isn't too mad." He states.

"No, I don't think so. When I told him the sun shone brightly. He said in his letter that he wanted me to be happy and move on." I sigh.

Gaige kisses my head.

"How did you know where I was?" I look into his deep brown eyes.

"Amy said you'd gone to talk to someone you haven't spoken to in a long time. I guessed you'd come here to talk to Jay." He smiles.

I lean up and kiss him.

"Ready to head back?"

"Yeah."

Gaige walked down to find me so he drives my truck back.

"So Bob fired Tanner today." Gaige states.

"What?! You're joking?" I ask. I'm stunned.

"Nope. He heard what was said at the bar and he cares a lot about you. No way would he keep someone after that." Gaige points out.

We pull up at the bakery and walk in. Amy is dealing with a customer.

"I'm sorry sir, we don't have that." She apologies.

"It's okay Amy, I can deal with this. What can I help you with sir?" I say, looking up from tying my apron.

"Oh for god's sake! It's you!" I say exasperated.

"Well that is no way to treat a customer. I've come back to give you a second chance." He states while pushing his thick framed glasses up his nose.

"Everything alright?" Gaige asks, crossing his broad arms across his chest.

The man turns round and scrunches up his nose.

"Who's this? You brought in muscle to get rid of customers like me?" He asks.

"Sir, I don't need to bring in muscle to deal with customers like you, I am quite capable. Now, what can I get you?" I pause.

He goes to speak.

"Uh-uh. Just remember what happened last time." I warn.

"Do you have any gluten free, sugar free, vegan friendly cupcakes?" He ask.

I hold out my hand and Amy gives me a piping bag filled with strawberry buttercream frosting.

"Now don't start. I am well within my rights

to ask for such a cake." He says, holding up his hands,

"You want me to deal with him?" Gaige offers.

"Nope, I'm good." I say holding out my other hand.

Amy hands me a piping bag filled with chocolate frosting.

I have a bag tucked under each arm and I walk slowly around the counter. The guy steps back with his hands up in surrender.

"I can see that you don't seem to have updated your policies." He points out.

"No we haven't. I'm locked and loaded. What's your next move?" I ask, smiling. I make the noise as if I'm cocking a gun.

"It actually terrifies me how much she enjoys doing this." I hear Amy mutter to Gaige.

"Oh yeah, she would scare the shit out of most people." Gaige agrees.

"Well I have never been treated like this in any other bakery!" He fumes.

"Good, so piss off to them then!" I advise.

"You are one scary woman. I shall be complaining to the authorities about you." He threatens.

He keeps walking backwards and trips out

of the front step.

He stands up and brushes himself off.

"Well I'm out of your bakery now so you can just leave me alone."

I smile.

"Say hello to my little friends!" I yell in my best Al Pacino accent.

I fire off the piping nozzles and laugh.

The man runs away.

"You're crazy!"

Laughing I turn around to see Gaige leaning in the doorway with his arms crossed.

"You enjoying yourself there?" He asks, eyebrows raised.

"Yes, very much so thank you." I smile.

I walk to Gaige and he leans down to kiss me.

I turn the piping nozzle up and squeeze. I start laughing and run back into the bakery, leaving Gaige with chocolate frosting all over his chest and neck.

"You've got five seconds beautiful." He warns.

"Amy can you mind the bakery?" I ask breathlessly.

I take steps backwards toward the stairs, my eyes glued to Gaige.

"Three." He counts.

"Hey! What happened to four?" I ask.

"I whispered it." He smirks.

"Liar!" I accuse as I run up the stairs.

"Two!" He yells.

I squeal and stand on the other side on the bed, still holding the strawberry frosting. I'm aiming it at the doorway, ready and waiting for him.

"One!" He yells and I hear him barrelling up the stairs.

He comes into the bedroom and smiles.

"Time is up beautiful." He winks.

I squeal when he goes to move around the bed towards me. I climb onto the bed. Gaige moves quick and grabs both my ankles, making me land on the bed. He climbs over me.

"Hand over your weapon." He orders.

"No." I answer and bite my lip to stop me from laughing.

"I bet I can make you drop it." He threatens.

"Try all you like." I breathe.

He leans in, kissing me softly, teasingly. I whimper. He stops, smiles, and stands up, removing his clothes. I hold onto the piping bag tight, wondering if I could squeeze some of this frosting onto his delectable body so I could lick it off again.

He reaches forward and starts removing my clothes. I barely move, still keeping guard with my piping bag. I'm afraid that if I give in and place the bag down he will stop. I do not want him to stop.

He trails kisses along my leg and up the inside of my thigh. I moan as his mouth gets closer and closer.

Then he stops. I spring my eyes open.

"Gaige!" I growl.

"Give up the piping bag beautiful and I promise I won't stop again." He bargains.

I don't even think twice, I hand over the piping bag.

He laughs and shakes his head.

"I'm not stupid, do continue." I gesture.

He smiles, squeezes some of the frosting into his mouth, and hums in approval.

"Delicious."

I watch as he spreads my thighs apart. He then takes the piping bag and puts some frosting on my centre. I suck in a breath at the coldness. He doesn't give me much time to think about it before his mouth is on my clit, licking off every drop of the frosting.

"Oh fuck Gaige!" I moan.

He moans.

"Fucking divine."

He continues to lick me and every last drop of frosting. I can feel my orgasm starting to build.

"Gaige, fuck! I'm close." I moan.

He stops and quickly moves over me and places himself at my entrance.

"Gaige." I beg.

He glides all the way to the hilt. He pauses and I start trying to move my hips, desperate for friction.

"Gaige please." I moan.

He smiles and starts moving. I tilt my hips up to meet his thrust. It doesn't take me long; my orgasm hits.

"Oh god!" I scream.

Gaige continues, his pace not slowing or stopping.

"Come again for me beautiful." He demands circling his thumb over my clit.

I feel another orgasm building. My nails dig into his back and my legs start to twitch.

"Gaige." I whisper.

"I've got you beautiful, I feel you," He rasps.

He increases his speed and my orgasm explodes.

"Oh fuck Gaige!" I cry out.

"Fuck Esme." Gaige groans, finding his own orgasm.

We both lay back, calming our breaths.

"I don't think I will ever look at a piping bag the same way again after that." I laugh.

"Especially the strawberry frosting! I never knew it could taste so much better on you." Gaige says nipping my shoulder.

"Do you think they heard us downstairs?" I ask, concerned.

"No, we can't hear them so I'm sure we're good." Gaige reassures.

We get changed and head back downstairs. When we walk into the bakery Amy is fighting a smile and the customers, especially the elderly ladies, have a glint in their eyes.

One approaches Gaige and smiles.

"I could use some of what you gave her, it's been so long! But I must say, I never made sounds like that. I think I might hire a gigolo, clearly I missed out. Unless you want to treat an old lady some new tricks!" She winks at Gaige.

"Oh my god, you heard us?!" I screech.

Amy blushes and places her index finger and

thumb close together.

"Just a smidge." She says, holding back her laughter.

"Oh yes, we heard it all." Another lady says.

"June, you never made noises like that for me." A man says to his wife.

"Well, for a start, you don't look like him!" His wife retorts.

"Oh Christ." I say hiding in Gaige's chest. He wraps his arm around me.

"It's not funny Gaige! My customers heard us having sex!" I hiss.

"Oh now dear, that wasn't just sex, that was fucking." The old lady smiles.

Gaige chokes on his laughter.

"Right, anyone who's already brought their goods, please leave. Those who haven't, please buy what you need and leave." Amy orders.

They all groan and start shuffling out of the door.

"You coming back tomorrow?" The elderly lady asks another.

"If he's going to be here, most definitely!" She answers.

"June! I'm right here!" Her husband yells.

Soon the shop is empty and I feel the blush

slowly leave my cheeks.

"Changed your mind about moving in with me yet?" Gaige asks.

"I'm swaying towards a yes." I mutter.

"Um, Esme, if you do move in with Gaige, I have an idea to run past you." Amy says nervously.

"What's that?" I ask.

"What if you made upstairs into a café/seating area?" She states.

I pause for a moment and then smile.

"Do you know what? I think that's a great idea! There's a small kitchen upstairs that can house the coffee machines. I could take out the bath and have Bob split the bathroom into two separate toilets. Oh! I could have a few bookcases up there for people to sit and read a book if they chose!" I say excitedly.

"What do you think Gaige?" I ask.

"Does it mean you'll be moving in with me?" He asks.

"Yes, it means I'll be moving in with you." I smile.

"Then it's the best fucking idea." He laughs.

He cups my face and kisses me.

"I'm moving in with you." I whisper across his lips.

"Damn straight." He smiles.

Chapter Twenty-Six

Turns out that to Gaige moving in with him meant that night. We packed up most of my things. I told him I was coming back for my rocking chair because it would go in the baby's nursery.

Bob was happy to change the bathroom and bring upstairs to regulation for me. Luckily, I hadn't just paid out for a new bathroom suite.

I've just locked up the bakery for the day and I'm heading back home. I said I would swing by the grocery store on the way back so I walk down and pop into Nellie and Eric's.

I grab my groceries and head to the checkout.

"Hey there Esme." Eric greets.

"Hiya Eric." I smile.

"Congratulations on the pregnancy." He says kindly.

"Thank you." I answer.

"Your breasts giving you trouble yet? Nellie had terrible pains in her breasts; they grew so big she looked like she had a couple of soccer balls strapped to her chest." He laughs,

I just smile awkwardly.

"Oh and after she gave birth they just deflated! Now they look like a couple socks with tennis balls hanging in them. The kids sucked the life right out of them." He sighs as if he's mourning a dead pet.

"Oh and don't get me started on her piles. They were so painful for her." He tuts, shaking his head.

He leans and whispers.

"They were that bad that I used to have to strap them out the way when we were having S-E-X." He spells out.

"Otherwise they just hung there like a couple of balls. And, well, you know that after children it's never the same down there again. God, it's like chucking a sausage down the freeway." He sighs again. I try not to gag at the information he's just shared.

"I'm sure you'll be just fine though. The first pregnancy wasn't too bad, it was the fifth that tore her right through." He smiles.

I decide I'm having a caesarean.

"Well listen to me chatting on! That's twenty-five dollars please." He asks.

I hand over the cash and leave.

I try not to have a panic attack on the way home about what this child is going to do to me. What's my body going to look like afterwards?! Oh god, what if Gaige leaves me because I'm that much of a mess?!

I pull up outside the house and walk in. I'm completely zoned out.

"Esme?" Gaige asks looking concerned.

"I don't want empty tits." I blurt.

Gaige, a bit taken aback by my outburst, walks towards me. I hold up my hand to halt him.

"I don't want huge elephant piles and I don't want a bucket vagina." I whine.

"Okay. Where is this coming from?" He asks.

"Eric was telling me about Nellie's pregnancies and after birth." I shudder.

Gaige fights a smile.

"Okay. Well you know that doesn't mean it's

going to happen to you. Nellie and Eric have like five kids!" He states.

"I don't want you to leave me when I look like roadkill. What if I end up with monster piles? You're not going to find me sexy or attractive then." I sob.

Gaige smiles and wipes my tears.

"I will always find you sexy and attractive, no matter what, even with monster piles. I would even go as far as to strap a bunch of grapes to my ass just to make you feel better about it." He promises.

"Really? You'd do that for me?" I ask.

"Why wouldn't I do everything in my power to make sure you always feel loved and adored? There is nothing I wouldn't do to make you happy."

I sob.

"Why are you crying?" he asks.

"Because you're so lovely and sweet to me." I blubber.

"Okay beautiful, let's get you some dinner." He laughs and kisses me.

I get him to help me cook dinner and he manages to do it without setting the smoke alarm off or breaking anything this time.

We sit and eat our dinner. I kept it simple

with a stir fry. Gaige slides over a leaflet.

I put down my fork and pick it up, reading it.

"Antenatal classes?" I ask.

Gaige smiles shyly. I've never seen him be insecure about anything before.

"Yeah well, I went to the community hospital and asked some doctors if there were any classes or things I need to be doing." He shrugs.

"You did that for us? For the baby?" I ask stunned.

"It's no big deal." He shrugs.

I get up and walk to him and sit on his lap and wrap my arms around his neck.

"It's a very big deal; it means you care and love me and the baby a hell of a lot. I bet you most fathers-to-be wouldn't do that." I state and kiss him.

"I just feel like I need to do what I can to help in any way I can." He explains.

"I love you." I whisper.

He smiles and kisses me.

"I love you too." He replies.

Over the next few weeks we move all of my things into Gaige's place. I decide to leave my couch as I think it will be great for the café area.

I rang Sally and told her about me moving in with Gaige. She said she would be booking herself on a flight soon to get herself a decent Canadian man. I tried telling her that Gaige was American but she wasn't having any of it.

"You ready to go?" Gaige asks, leaning against the doorway.

"Do you always have to look all macho, alpha, and hot?" I sigh.

Gaige smirks.

"Beautiful, I'm just in jeans and t-shirt." He shrugs.

"I know but you have this aura to go with it. Like *I'm going to grab my woman, throw her over my shoulder, while I chop wood and rescue kittens from a burning building.* You know, that sort of thing." I say while doing my best deep voice.

Gaige laughs.

"Whatever you say. Now come on or we will be late."

"Okay I'm coming. I feel fat, nothing fits me anymore." I huff and stand, poking at my small round bump.

"Shut up woman. You're beautiful and pregnant, now get that ass moving or we will be late." He kisses me and starts pulling me out of the door.

"Don't tell me what to do Gaige Knox. I am a woman, I have my own mind." I warn.

"Don't I know it." Gaige mumbles quietly.

"What did you just say?" I snap.

"I said I love you! Now get into the truck." He winks, opening the door for me.

"Yeah that's what I thought you said."

Gaige slaps my behind as I climb into the truck.

"Bastard." I smile and shake my head. He winks at me as he rounds the truck.

We drive and park up at the hospital.

"Ready for this?" I ask.

"More than ready." He leans over and kisses me.

We are soon seen to. It's a different doctor today. She has a feel of my stomach and smiles.

"Well I think everything seems fine. You should start to feel little flutters, the baby moving, soon." She smiles.

"Really?" I ask, grinning.

"Yes, it will feel like trapped wind for a while until the stronger kicks happen." She answers, getting the machine ready.

"Now let's listen to baby's heartbeat." She says, placing the wand on my stomach.

The room fills with the whooshing sounds of the baby's heartbeat.

"Holy shit! Is that his heartbeat?" Gaige asks.

"Yes, all sounding good and healthy. Now according to your notes you will be back in a couple of weeks for your scan and the sexing of the baby. Do you have any questions you'd like to ask?"

"So we have to wait another four weeks until we can find out that it's a boy?" Gaige asks and I laugh.

"It might be a girl." I point out.

"It's a boy." He states.

"How would you know that?" I smile and shake my head.

"Because if it's a girl I'm bound to end up in jail. The universe can't be that cruel." He says with certainty.

"Want to place a bet?" I challenge.

"Sure, go for it." He accepts.

"If it's a girl, I get to name her. If its boy, you get to name him." I offer.

"Deal." Gaige smiles and shakes my hand.

"Um, did you still want me to answer the question?" The doc asks smiling.

"Oh shit sorry, yes please doc." Gaige.

"Yes is the answer. It gives us more chance to be sure that we have it correct. Depending on if it's a boy, you may spot his little ding-a-ling." She laughs.

"Oh we'll definitely be able to see it." Gaige winks.

I roll my eyes. What is it with men and penis size?! Mind you, if it is a boy I don't want him to have a tiny pecker and get the piss ripped out of him in school. Great, I'll add that to the other list of worries I have. It will slot in nicely in my worry file with 'I hope its not born with teeth' and 'I hope it's not born hairy'.

We thank the doctor and leave.

"Can we swing by Ted's hardware store on the way back?" I ask.

"Sure, what are you looking at getting? Need new bits for the bakery?" He asks.

"I was going to suggest we look at paint for the nursery?" I suggest nervously.

"You don't want to wait to find out the gender first?" He asks.

I shake my head.

"No. I was thinking about a nice light room with neutral colours. Unless you want to do something different?" I ask.

"That sounds great to me," Gaige states kissing my hand.

I'm standing in the paint isle and I can't choose between two colours. Biting my lip I turn and ask Gaige.

"Which one? Sandstone or Hazel Nut Cream?" I ask.

"They look exactly the same." I look at the shade on the front of the tin.

"No they don't. Hazel Nut Cream is slightly lighter." I point at it.

"Then go with the lighter one. Keep the room nice and light for the baby." He states.

I smile.

"Yup, you're right." I agree. Gaige takes the tin from me and we grab a few other bits for the bakery too.

"Want to swing by the baby store?" Gaige asks.

"Yes!" I clap excitedly.

"Wow! What does this do?!" I ask, holding up a weird contraption looking thing. "Oh look, it tickles." I say holding it on my face; it sucks my cheek. The sales assistant walks up with a disgusted look on her face.

"That's a breast pump." She points out.

I try to throw it off of my cheek but I must have accidentally knocked the settings, making the suction harder.

"Ow! Son of a bitch! Gaige, get this titty draining machine off of me!" I squeal, leaning over with the thing hanging off of my face.

Gaige tries but in his efforts he increases the settings.

"Ow! Oh my god! Gaige help me! Get this bloody face hugger off of my face!" I scream.

The twat assistant rolls her eyes and walks over and turns the switch, turning it off. The evil boob machine stops immediately and falls off of my face and lands on the floor, breaking.

"That was like some evil alien breast pump! Did the Alien movies inspire them?" I pant.

"Umm you're like, gonna have to pay for that." The assistant demands.

"What?! That thing attacked me! It attacked my face. Thank the lord it wasn't my breast because I fear I may have lost a nipple! Then how would I breast feed? With no nipples?! Huh? That thing is lethal! I have a mind to complain to the manager. In fact, I'm going to film it and post it all over social media about the face hugging killer breast pump!" I rant, pulling out my phone.

I don't look at Gaige but out of the corner of my eye I can see his shoulders shaking with his contained laughter.

The manager walks over, curious as to what's going on with the scene I'm causing.

"What on earth happened here?" He asks.

I tell him and show my face which I'm sure is either red or possibly covered in a huge hickey.

"We shall remove the product from the shelves immediately. Please accept our apology in the way of one-hundred dollars of store credit." He apologises.

"Well, that's appreciated. Thank you." I take the voucher and poke my tongue at the assistant as Gaige places his arms around my shoulders and guides me off to the other side of the store.

"Please tell me how you managed to get your face basically sucked off because you put the pump there and then come away with an apology and one-hundred dollars of credit?" Gaige asks.

"It's for damages! Do I have a giant hickey on my face?" I ask, turning my head for him to look.

"No, it's just a little red." He smiles.

"I wonder how many dads have shoved their dicks in that thing? I swear its suction is stronger than a vacuum cleaner!" I giggle.

Chapter Twenty-Seven

"Look at you! You're getting a proper little bump now." A customer rubs my belly.

Why do people think that it's okay to do that? I mean, men don't high five each other's dicks when they're congratulated on getting their girlfriend or wife pregnant! I know people are just being nice stroking my bump, but when it's people I hardly know or don't know at all, it's just annoying. I don't know where their hands have been! *That's it Karen, you give that arse of yours a good old scratch and then stroke my pregnant belly.*

"Esme." Amy calls.

"Huh?" I turn to her.

"You completely zoned out then. The poor lady stopped talking to you because you were just staring and growling." Amy points out.

"Sorry, baby brain." I sigh.

"What's up Esme?" Amy asks.

"Oh nothing, just tired I think. I will be more relaxed when upstairs is done and the interviews are over. What time are we starting those again?" I ask.

"Shutting the bakery at 4pm today. The first applicant is straight away and then we have four applicants after that." Amy states looking at the calendar.

"Right, I can't wait." I roll my eyes.

We finish off the day and clear up and close. I yawn. I'm feeling completely exhausted. I could murder a good strong cup of coffee, but apparently it's not good for the baby.

We set everything up to interview in the kitchen. I sit down and stuff an iced bun in my mouth. I can't have coffee to keep me awake so I will have to settle for sugar.

"Esme, this is Ambrosia." Amy introduces as she walks into the kitchen. The woman she is with has around twenty bangles on each arm, her hair is in dreadlocks, and she is wearing a long floral patterned sleeveless dress.

I quickly chew and swallow my iced bun.

"Hi, nice to meet you. I'm sorry, what's your name again?"

"It's Ambrosia." She shakes my hand and takes a seat.

"Like the custard?" I ask.

"What?" She asks.

"What?" I repeat back.

"Err....so Ambrosia, what experience have you got with working in a bakery?" Amy asks.

"Well I'm sure she can make a cracking custard tart." I snort to myself.

Ambrosia looks at me like I'm insane.

"I...well...don't have a lot. I worked in an herbalist shop for a while. You know you could use a lot of that in your baking. I make a mean brownie." She smiles.

"I bet you do." I mumble under my breath.

"So what other qualities can you bring to the job?" Amy asks.

I carry on eating my iced bun.

"Well, I have a very strong and powerful chakra." She answers.

"They have antibiotics for that." I retort.

Amy chokes on her drink.

Ambrosia either didn't hear my answer or had chosen to ignore it.

"I can feel that this place has a magnificent aura, it just exploded all over me as soon as I was near."

"That's what she said." I cough under my

breath.

Amy gives me a nudge with her elbow.

"Sorry." I whisper.

Ambrosia stands and holds her arms out wide.

"Yes, yes! I can feel the soul of this building. It's calling for my love, for my chakra." She sings and hugs a wall.

I turn to Amy and nod my head.

"Armpits!" I hiss.

Ambrosia has full under arm hair; she's like a really hairy man.

"Um Ambrosia, I hope you don't mind me commenting on it but I noticed your underarm hair." I point out.

"Oh yes, I don't ever shave or remove any hair. That is what mother nature intended. I don't use any products either, only water and my own musk." She beams.

I stand up.

"Well that's all for now Ambrosia, if you are lucky enough to get the position, we will be in touch." I say as I walk towards her and open the door. I get a whiff of her scent and it makes me gag.

"Oh lord, there's the musk." I say, gagging again.

"I do hope you'll give me the opportunity to work here. I have my own natural oils I could sell too, I made them from my body." She breathes, handing me a bottle of what I can only assume is piss.

"Right. I'm sorry, nope. This is not happening. We have a hygiene standard to upkeep here. On your bike chewy." I say pinching my nose and throwing the bottle out of the door.

She huffs and runs out after her bottle of piss. I slam the door and immediately go to wash my hands.

"So who's next?" I ask, walking back to the table and sitting down.

"Um, Mr Richard Stroker. He's forty-five and retired from the military." Amy says reading off his application.

There's a knock and Amy goes to great him as I pour a cup of tea.

"Esme, this is Mr Richard Stroker." Amy introduces.

"Hi, it's nice to meet you. Please take a seat." I gesture.

"Please call me dick." He says whilst sitting down.

I choke on my tea and start coughing and spluttering. Amy pats my back.

"You okay Esme?" She asks concerned.

"Yup, totally fine." I cough.

"Sorry, err, Dick Stroker. I swallowed it the wrong way." I cough and nearly combust with laughter.

"Don't apologise, it happens. Please just call me Dick, or Major Dick, if you prefer." He says smiling.

I can't contain it any longer; I burst into fits of giggles. I can see Amy fighting her laughter.

"Is she alright?" Dick asks.

"Oh yeah, she is um…just emotional, you know, being pregnant. Her hormones are all over the place." Amy states, clearing her throat and keeping a lid on her laughter.

"Ah I see, my wife was a bit emotional with ours. She said that holding her Dick tightly in her arms would always make her feel better." He smiles.

"Oh fuck! I can't! I'm so sorry, I can't." I giggle, holding my stomach.

Amy is now giggling with me.

"What on earth is with you two?" He asks.

"Seriously?! You don't hear it?" I ask wiping the tears from my face.

"No, clearly I don't." He snaps back.

"Major. Dick. Stroker." I state his name slowly back to him.

"What?" He asks. "You are clearly high. I'm leaving! Never in my life have I been interviewed in such unprofessional manner." He stands and leaves. Amy and I are roaring with laughter.

"Ahh Major Dick Stroker! I'm sorry but you need to lighten up! Don't be such a stiff!" I cry laughing. "Oh god I'm going to pee my pants." I giggle.

After we've calmed ourselves down we welcome the next applicant.

"I've got this Amy." I say, holding up my hand.

"Let's just cut to the chase. We've had the most surreal interviews and I just want to go home. So what's your name?" I ask.

The woman looks uncomfortable.

"Uh...Dawn Sullivan." She answers nervously.

"Good, now do you wash regularly and have good hygiene i.e. not bringing in your own bottle of piss as perfume?" I ask.

She looks even more baffled by this question.

"Err, yes I have good hygiene and no I don't carry around my urine in bottles." She answers.

"Great, you like cakes? Can carry a cup of coffee?" I ask.

"Yes." She nods.

"Great, the job is yours! Amy will fill you in on all of the necessary details. I'm off home." I say smiling.

"Welcome to the madhouse Dawn!" I yell over my should as I leave.

I tell Gaige about the interviews and he thinks I'm lying.

"I swear it's the truth! I don't even know if the other candidates turned up; I just had to leave to get out of there. I feel bad for leaving Amy to deal with it. I will give her some of her favourite cake as an apology tomorrow." I sigh as Gaige massages my feet.

"Oh god." I moan. "I'm exhausted."

"You need to start taking it easy. Oh and before you bite my head off, you need to look after yourself for the baby." He points out.

"I know, I know. I find it hard to step back what with the café opening. It's just I can't let it fall apart. I have to make sure that it all goes smoothly." I say, yawning.

"I know but today you've been on your feet

for fifteen hours. You need to slow it down. Promise me that after the opening you'll slow it down." He pleads.

"Fine. I promise after the opening I will slow it down." I promise.

Later that night before bed Amy texts. It turns out that Dawn was perfect for the job; she was a single parent of two and was desperate for the job. I smile to myself, at least one good thing came from those disastrous interviews.

Chapter Twenty-Eight

I walk around the upstairs of the bakery, my old apartment, and I cannot wipe the smile from my face. Bob has opened it all right up; he even put in a mini library and a reading nook for children. One wall is painted with chalk board paint so that the kids can draw and the adults can too if they wish. There is a couch, armchairs, coffee tables, and even some bean bags. The dark wood, open fireplace, and brightly coloured furniture makes it a warm and relaxed atmosphere.

"Bob you're a magician! This place looks amazing. I love it so much." I clap happily.

"There's a baby gate at the top of the stairs so the children don't run off. Each step up is not only a different colour but they different cake names painted on them. I also made sure there was a baby changing facility." He says and points to the bathroom.

I walk up to him and wrap my arms around

him and hug him tight. He awkwardly pats my back.

"Thank you so much Bob. It really is amazing." I sniff.

"Why is she crying?" Bob asks Gaige.

"Pregnancy hormones." Gaige smiles.

"Oh jeez." Bob groans.

I laugh and wipe my eyes.

"Don't do emotional women Bob?" I ask laughing.

"No, I can't handle women crying, I don't know what to do with myself." He mumbles, shoving his hands in his pockets.

I laugh.

"Well Bob, I shall try to keep my emotions in check when I'm around you."

Bob grunts and Gaige pulls me into his arms and kisses me.

"You ready to open tomorrow?" He asks.

"Oh yeah, more than ready." I smile excitedly.

The next morning I'm in full panic mode making sure that everything is ready to go.

"Will you stop worrying? Everything will be fine." Amy tries to calm me down.

"You're right, you're right." I sigh.

"Ooo there's a queue forming outside!" Dawn says excitedly.

"God my stomach is full of nerves! I don't know if I'm going to throw up or shit myself." I groan.

"Nice." Amy mutters.

"Where's Gaige?" Dawn asks.

"He ran to try and find me some non-alcoholic Champagne to celebrate." I smile.

"God, I remember those days. I don't know if I could go without wine now." Dawn sighs.

"Are you telling us that you're an alcoholic?" I laugh.

"No, but, well, you'll get it. When little one is a bit older that glass of wine at the end of the day is like a taste of heaven." She sighs, smiling.

"Right come on. Let's open up!" I sing excitedly.

"Three, two, one." I countdown and open the door.

"Welcome everyone. For those of you who want to sit with some coffee, tea, and cake, please follow the signs and head upstairs." I greet.

They file in one by one and most of them go straight upstairs. I stick my thumbs up to Amy and head upstairs to help Dawn.

She's already taking orders and starting to make coffees. She hands me a list of cake orders so I head downstairs to the kitchen to grab them and bring them up.

I do this for a while to help Dawn.

Being the clumsy nightmare I am I somehow manage to trip halfway down the stairs. Plates go flying and smash to the ground. I land on my back and tumble down the last few stairs.

Amy comes running over to me.

"Shit! Esme! I'm calling an ambulance." She panics.

My back and stomach hurt.

"The baby." I shout. I start panicking.

I hear Gaige come into the shop.

"What the hell happened here?"

"Esme fell. She's at the bottom of the stairs." I hear Amy tell him.

Gaige comes running to me with worry in his eyes.

"Gaige." I sob.

"Shhhh, it's okay. I'm going to take you to the hospital." He states, bending down and picking me up.

"Amy cancel the ambulance. I'm taking her

myself, it'll be quicker." He yells as we leave.

"The baby. Gaige." I sob as he seats me in his truck.

"It will be okay." He soothes and kisses my head before quickly shutting the door.

He drives fast, honking his horn and swerving around cars. My stomach keeps hurting and my back is throbbing. I bite my lip to cope with the pain.

He pulls up right outside and grabs a wheelchair. He runs, pushing me into the hospital.

"Help please! She's fallen down the stairs and she's pregnant." He yells.

Nurses come rushing over and wheel me off towards maternity. I grip hold of Gaige's hand the entire time.

I'm put on my back as they scan over my stomach. I see the baby come on the screen and the little blob that is his is heart pumping away.

"Oh thank god." I sob.

Gaige takes my hand and kisses my palm.

"Let's just have a listen of baby's heartbeat." She says and the room fills with the most glorious sound: a strong healthy heartbeat.

"Baby appears to be fine. It looks like the fall did cause some early contractions. Judging by what we've checked it's not enough to do anything and the machine is showing that they have stopped. We will allow you to go home but under strict instructions of bed rest for two weeks and you must only do mild exercise after that until baby is born I'm afraid. No stress or over doing it. I don't want anything to trigger early labour. You can take some paracetamol for the aches you'll probably feel but that's it. Rest is the key." She orders.

"Yes I promise. Um, can I ask, as I was due for my scan in three days is there any chance we can find out the sex of the baby?" I ask.

She smiles and nods and moves the wand over my stomach.

"I'm sorry, baby is playing hard ball. A real wriggler. I can't get a clear enough view." She apologises.

"Oh bugger." I blurt.

"I guess we will have to wait until I give birth." I mumble disappointed.

"I would like to see you back in fourteen days just to check that everything is okay. Other than that, please, if you feel any pain or twinges, ring us or come straight in. Now Dad, it's down to you to look after Mom. You've got to do the cooking and the cleaning. Make sure she doesn't lift a finger." The doctor orders.

"Of course." Gaige nods.

"Great. I'm going to either starve or get food poisoning." I complain. The doctor looks at me questioningly.

"He can't cook for shit." I clarify.

"Ah, well, in that case I suggest takeout or family." She smiles.

"Any other questions before you go?" She asks.

"Um, yes. Are we okay to have sex?" I ask.

The doctor looks a little surprised by my question.

"Wait a couple of days just to be sure. Then you're good to have sex. I don't normally have the moms asking me that question, it's normally the fathers." She states.

"He's a really great lay." I smile.

Gaige coughs a laugh.

"I bet." The doctor laughs.

"Come on, let's get you home to rest before you start telling the whole hospital about our sex life." Gaige teases as he helps me into the wheelchair.

"Don't be silly. Why would I tell everyone about our amazing sex life?!" I say loudly. I turn to the nurses and mouth the words 'huge' and accentuate with my hands.

"Woman I will spank that ass!" Gaige growls

in my ear.

I giggle.

"You can't do anything to my ass for a few days." I taunt.

"Countdown beautiful." He threatens.

"Promises, promises." I smile. All I can think about is how else can I tease him over the next few days.

We pull up outside the house and Gaige refuses to let me walk. He carries me upstairs to bed.

I get changed into my leggings and tank top and pile my hair on my head. I lay in bed flicking through the TV. Gaige is downstairs making lunch. I just hope he doesn't burn the house down in the process.

Frustrated there's nothing on I dump the remote and get up to grab my e-reader.

"What are you doing out of bed?" Gaige asks, carrying a tray in.

"I was just getting my e-reader." I say, holding my hands up in defence.

I climb back into bed and Gaige places the tray down. I smile.

"Sub rolls." I say grabbing one and taking a bite. "Hhmm, yum."

"Salami, ham, cheese, salad, mustard, and mayo." Gaige says taking a bite of his own roll.

"Okay, you can't cook but you can make a real good sandwich." I state.

I lean over and kiss him.

"You feeling okay beautiful?" He asks.

"I am now. I can't believe I tripped down the stairs like that. I'm such a clutts. I'm just glad little bean is okay." I say stroking my bump.

"Yeah me too." Gaige says. He moves the tray and lays down his head, resting near my stomach.

"Hey baby, kick once if you're a girl and twice if you're a boy." He says to my stomach.

"You're cute but I can't feel proper kicks yet, just flutters." I say to him.

Gaige kisses my round bump and then reaches up and kisses me.

"I love you so much." I whisper across his lips.

"I love you too beautiful." Gaige replies before kissing me again.

Chapter Twenty-Nine

I've been on bed rest for a week and I'm going insane. Earlier, when Gaige had to run to the grocery store for food, I snuck downstairs and started baking some flapjacks. I needed to bake something; I needed to do something. I was going out of my mind.

Of course he caught me in the act as I was spreading the melted chocolate on top. He thinks I didn't know how much he enjoyed them though. I could practically hear him moaning from upstairs.

"So is everything okay at the bakery?" I ask Amy.

"Yes! For the millionth time, everything is fine. The café side is going really well. No mishaps whatsoever." She states, trying to calm me.

"Okay good. Oh and Amy, I forgot to put the order through for the flour and food colouring, could you do that?" I ask.

"Already done. Stop worrying, it'll all be fine. Just you concentrate on getting better." She orders.

"Fine." I promise.

She disconnects because the bakery starts getting busy. I guess I should be happy that it's busy, but I miss being there.

I get up and walk downstairs to find Gaige. God I'm bored out of my mind and that's not to mention that I am beyond horny!

I find him outside in the garden. I say garden, it's more like a small field that backs onto woodland. I have no idea how much land actually comes with this house.

I lean on the railing on the decking, watching him with no shirt. He's only wearing his worn jeans and he's busy chopping wood. I watch as every muscle moves in his defined back. I bite my lip. I decide I've waited long enough.

Seeing Gaige hard at work like this makes me shiver. I have to have him or I may commit murder.

I walk towards him. I'm wearing one of his t-shirts with nothing else on underneath.

He hears me approach and turns. I swear to you, I feel like a lioness that's about to pounce on her pray. He notices the hungry look in my eyes and smirks. I know exactly how to wipe that smirk from his face.

I reach for the hem of the t-shirt and take it off before throwing it across the yard.

Gaige clenches his jaw and his eyes darken. That's what I want.

I stop just in front of him. We're toe to toe. His breath whispers across my cheek.

"Fuck me lumberjack, right here, right now." I whisper in his ear.

He doesn't need telling twice. He picks me up and I wrap my legs around his waist. I crash my mouth down on his, my tongue sweeping against his. I moan, needing more. Gaige slowly lowers me down onto the grass. He leans back and slides his jeans down, freeing his thick hard cock. He strokes himself.

"You want this beautiful? You want my cock deep inside you?" He asks. His voice is thick with arousal.

"Fuck yes." I moan.

Gaige positions himself at my entrance and slowly slides forward, filling me.

"Oh fuck, yes!" I groan.

"God you feel so good, I've fucking missed the feel of you." Gaige groans, kissing my neck.

Gaige moves slowly. He's taking his time. I

know he's being overly cautious.

"More Gaige, please." I beg.

"I don't want to hurt you." He breathes as he kisses me.

I push up and roll over so I'm on top. I start riding him hard and fast.

"Fuck Esme." Gaige moans.

He sits up and wraps his arms around me. I place my hands on his shoulders and grip tight. He takes my nipple in his mouth and sucks hard.

"Yes!" I cry.

I feel my walls begin to tighten as my orgasm builds. Gaige feels it too and he lets out a low throaty groan.

"Come for me beautiful." Gaige moans.

My orgasm hits me and my walls clamp tightly around Gaige. My pleasure takes hold of my whole body, making me shudder.

"Fuck!" Gaige roars his release.

We both sit back, panting. I kiss Gaige softly.

"Good job you don't have neighbours." I mumble.

"I do." He answers.

I sit up straight and look around.

"You know that no one else lives near here." He laughs.

"Bastard! Stop teasing me." I giggle. "I need to go and have a shower." I whisper in his ear.

I stand and sway my hips. Walking back to the house I stop next to the t-shirt and purposefully bend down to pick it up.

I hear him growl and jump up. I look over my shoulder and see him prowl towards me. I giggle and start running.

"Hello! I did knock but there was no answer! I Made you a beef casser..." Nellie pauses. She nearly drops the dish on the floor when her eyes take in the scene before her.

I quickly hold the t-shirt up in front of me.

"Shit." I mutter.

"Oh hey Nellie. Could you put that on the kitchen counter and shut the door behind you on the way out? That would be great thanks." Gaige says, walking in and doing his jeans up.

"I...err...yeah sure." She says. She looks stunned.

She turns back around and goes into the house. I quickly put the t-shirt back on.

"Oh my god! Gaige! She just saw me completely butt ass naked." I hiss, feeling my cheeks flame in embarrassment.

"I don't give a shit. She shouldn't just walk in. It could have been worse, she could have seen us fucking or my cock. Now get your fine naked ass upstairs and in that shower. I'm not finished with you yet." Gaige growls, spanking my behind.

I jump and giggle. He's right. I shrug to myself as I make my way upstairs. Gaige actually locks up the house so we can't be disturbed and thank god we weren't. I think I will be walking around Gaige naked a lot more often if that is what I get in return.

It has finally been two weeks. I had the check up and everything is as it should be. I'm measuring around twenty-three weeks now. I am allowed back at the bakery but I am to do no heavy lifting. I have to sit down as much as possible and I can't do anymore than a four hour working day. I'm fine with that as long as I get myself back into my bakery.

I'm on break and decide to give Sally a call as she's been seeing this guy. He was the model at the life drawing classes she's been taking. She's crap at art. She only goes to giggle like a schoolgirl and perv if the models are fit. Well, now she's pulled this model and I need the latest gossip.

"Hello my knocked up friend. Are you sat down resting?" She asks.

"Yes. Now come on, spill the beans, who is this guy?" I ask, taking a bite of an apple turnover.

"He's everything Esme. He's tall and almost surfer looking with his tanned skin. He's got blue eyes and messy blonde hair. Oh and fuck me! His cock is even prettier." She blurts.

I cough on my turnover.

"Jesus Christ Sally! Warn a girl before you say things like that! I nearly choked on a turnover." I cough.

"Sorry but it is! I think it may be the most beautifullest cock I ever did see." She sighs.

"How romantic." I snort.

"Oh shut up. It's not just that it's beautiful, it's what he can do with it too. It helps that he is hung like a horse." She giggles.

"I'm sure it does. You walking okay?" I laugh.

"Ha! Oh yeah. I'm a bit bow legged but other than that I'm great." Sally giggles.

"Well if it ends up being serious you'll have to come over and bring him with you. Tell him to keep his monster cock to himself though, I'm not sure the residents of Baddeck are ready for that yet." I snort.

"Oh no bitch is getting a look at my man's cock, that's for sure. I am going to look into flights soon though because, well, I miss you. Oh, and I still have to meet the tall dark and grumpy guy that knocked up my best friend." She points.

"Okay, keep me posted. Loves ya." I reply.

"Loves ya too." She says before disconnecting.

I finish my turnover and water and head back out to the bakery to help Amy out.

It's pretty busy but Amy orders me to sit down and relax. I don't mind so much. Seeing my bakery thriving from the side lines makes me feel really proud at what I've achieved. I know that Jay would be beyond proud.

I feel a sharp movement in my stomach. It catches me off guard.

"Woah." I panic. I place my hand on my stomach and I feel it again.

"Are you okay? What is it? Do you need me to call Gaige?" Amy asks, worry on her face.

I shake my head and smile.

"No, it's okay. I think I just felt the baby kick for the first time." I smile. I feel the baby kick again.

"Aww! My mom always said I was a slow kicker, slow walker too, but I was an early talker." Amy states.

"I can see that." I nod.

I sit calmly, waiting for the baby to kick again. I poke my belly but nothing happens; the baby must have got comfy and gone back to sleep.

I give up and serve some customers. They are all lovely and kind and offer well wishes. They say they're glad that me and the baby are okay.

Gaige walks in a while later to pick me up. He's not letting me drive at the moment either. In his words: he's not taking any risks.

"Hey beautiful." He greets, pulling me into his arms and kissing me.

"Hey yourself." I smile.

"See Mary! This is why it's the best bakery in town. Not only does she make a decent cake but you get a show with your purchase, and what a show it is!" An elderly customer sighs behind us.

"Seriously? Have you started an elderly club here or something because every time I come in here they are here, just waiting!" Gaige whispers. "It's like they're hunting me." He shudders.

I giggle. "Ladies, back off. You're starting to scare my man." I warn jokingly.

"Don't mind us. We live in a small town where there isn't much action. Since you've moved to town you've brought us plenty of action. Not to mention drawn our attention to this fine hunk of a man." She states.

"Woah, easy lady." Gaige jumps. "She just pinched my ass!" He says, clearly stunned.

"Right, that's it! No touching my man. He's not a piece of meat for you to ogle over. Go on, go home. Maybe watch some Netflix and watch 365 DNI. You might leave my man alone then." I laugh.

The elderly lady hands me her notebook and pen.

"Could you just write that down for me." She winks.

I laugh and shake my head. She is relentless!

I hand her back the notebook and she smile and gives Gaige a little wave over her shoulder as she leaves.

"What is it with the elderly ladies of this town?" Gaige asks. "They weren't like this before." He states.

"That was before the town saw you with Esme and before they heard about you in your yard." Amy mutters the last part under her breath.

"Oh my god. Nellie told the whole town we were shagging in the garden!" I screech.

"Well, she didn't tell us that." Amy points out.

"She just said you were naked and Gaige was shirtless and doing up his jeans. Doesn't mean you were shagging. You could have been doing some gardening or maybe sitting for a painting."

Amy adds.

I stare blankly at her.

"I'm going over there right now to give her a piece of my mind." I state. I storm out and walk down to the grocery store.

I storm in calling her name.

"Nellie!" I yell. "Nellie!" I call out again.

"Oh hello Esme. How are you feeling?" Eric asks.

"Great Eric, thanks. Nellie!" I yell again.

"Great, great. It's good that you're not letting go of the horizontal jog." Eric winks.

"Err, sorry, what are you saying Eric?" I ask.

"You know, bumping uglies, mattress dancing, threading the needle, marinating the loin, playing hide the cannoli..." Eric lists on.

I hold up my hand.

"Are you talking about sex Eric?" I ask bluntly.

"Yes." He nods.

"Ah, I'm not really sure what to say to that. Umm, thanks?" I try to answer but it's more like a question.

Finally Nellie appears. As soon as she sees me she starts to turn around.

"No you don't Nellie. I will drag your behind

back here if you take one more step." I threaten.

She sighs and turns back around to face me.

Gaige comes in behind me a moment later.

"Oh thank god. I was worried you'd be here throwing cake at her or something." He sighs.

I turn to him and raise an eyebrow in question.

"Why on earth would I be throwing cake at her?"

"It could be a sexual fantasy of his. It's quite common to fantasise over your loved one with food substances." Eric interjects.

We all turn and stare at Eric with a what-the-fuck expression on our faces.

"Nellie, why did you tell the whole town about what you saw in Gaige's garden?" I ask.

"I have no idea what you're talking about." She says, trying to play it coy.

"Like hell you do! Gaige has been molested by senior citizens because of you running your mouth off." I fume.

"Oh my god. Gaige, is this true?" Nellie asks.

"Well, I w…" I hold up my hand, halting Gaige.

"Yes it is. That elderly lady got a right good handful of his behind. If she had reached under any further she would have had more than just a handful of butt cheek!" I point out, crossing my arms over my chest.

"I...I am so sorry. I shouldn't gossip I know, but, well, I just was so shocked. It was shocking, walking in and seeing you both in that way." She apologises.

"Oh come on Nellie! What do you think this is? Immaculate conception?" I say, pointing to my bump.

"Now we know that's not true. You need the man to ejaculate his sperm to fertilize the egg to conceive a baby. Although some women claim they fell pregnant from swallowing the sperm." Eric snorts to himself.

"Jesus Christ." Gaige mutters.

"Just in future Nellie, if someone doesn't answer the door, don't just walk in. There's probably a good reason those people aren't opening the door. You also shouldn't go around the town telling everyone about our private life!" I finish on a huff.

"I'm sorry, it won't happen again." Nellie apologises.

"Thank you." I mutter. "That being said, your casserole was lovely and I will bring the dish back." I rush out before turning and storming out.

Gaige is hot on my heels trying to catch up

with me.

He opens the truck door.

"Esme, get in the truck." He points.

"I left my bag at the bakery." I point out.

He points to the back seat and there in the back is my bag.

"Fine." I huff.

Gaige gets in and starts the truck up.

"So is it just the pregnancy hormones or are you always this crazy?" He asks.

I look at him with a raised eyebrow, challenging him.

"Right, got it. Shut up Gaige. Do not poke the bear." He mumbles under his breath.

"This bear felt our baby kick properly for the first time today." I mutter.

Gaige breaks and pulls over.

"Esme! Why didn't you say sooner?" He asks, placing his hand on my bump.

"I got distracted by the old ladies and Eric with his weird sperm facts." I point out.

He sits for a moment, waiting for the baby to kick. Nothing happens.

"Baby is as stubborn as you are." Gaige complains.

As soon as the words have left his mouth the

baby kicks.

"Holy shit." Gaige smiles.

He leans down and kisses my bump. My heart swells at how sweet he can be.

Chapter Thirty

I'm not sure what happens but time just seems to fly by. The days just all go by in a blur. I once had this cute bump and now I feel like a weeble. I'm seven months pregnant. The kicks that were cute and gentle are now harder and they seem to be focused on kicking me in the rib or the bladder. Baby is not fussy on which.

I have decided to take a completely behind the scenes role at the bakery. I pop in to check the books, do the admin side, and sometimes I'll decorate some of the cakes. Then I always eat them because apparently no food is safe near me. I'm like a vacuum cleaner, inhaling any food I can.

It's getting cold again and everyone is preparing for snow. Gaige has ordered me to wear comfortable, safe shoes incase snow and ice come in. I purchased these cute boots with thick two inch heels. It probably wasn't what he had in mind but I like them and they're a low heel for me.

I'm sitting in my little office feeling absolutely exhausted. I decide a quick nap will not do me any harm. I lean forward and rest my head on my desk.

"Beautiful, wake up." I hear Gaige say softly.

"Uh?" I sit up with an invoice stuck to my face.

Gaige chuckles and removes it from my cheek.

"Oh shit." He fights back his laughter.

"What?" I ask yawning.

He points to my face and I frown in confusion. He hands me my compact mirror from my purse and bites his lip to stop himself from laughing.

I look in the mirror and gasp. There staring back at me are the words '**Heavy Load**'.

"Oh my god, I must have dribbled on the flour delivery receipt." I whine.

I try desperately to rub it off but it's not shifting.

"Come on!" I complain, licking my fingers and then rubbing my cheek harshly.

Gaige has lost control of holding in his

laughter now. He's laughing so hard that he is holding his stomach.

"Gaige this isn't funny!" I fume.

"Sorry but I disagree. Stop rubbing it so hard, you're making your cheek all red. Come on, I will take you home. There's got to be something at home you can use to get it off." He suggests.

"Good thinking." I grab my bag and coat and jump up. "Come on Gaige, let's go!" I yell.

He follows, chuckling beside me.

"Oh Esme before you go, can you sign off on the…" Amy pauses and looks at my face.

She squints and leans forward.

"Heavy load? Why have you written heavy load on your face? Is it a new health and safety guideline because you're heavily pregnant?" She asks.

"Oh fuck." Gaige laughs harder behind me.

"No, I fell asleep on the flour receipt and its print came off on my cheek. New bloody health and safety!" I say rolling my eyes and shaking my head in disbelief at what she just said.

I push forward.

"Excuse me!" I yell.

A customer turns and looks at me and then turns back around.

"Out of the way! Heavy load coming

through." She yells and then turns back to me. "There you go dear, all clear now."

"Jesus Christ I'm dying!" Gaige continues to laugh uncontrollably.

I roll my eyes and storm out to the truck.

Gaige drives me home, thankfully getting enough of a hold on his laughter to actually drive.

It took a face mask, cleanser, and toner to get the writing off of my face.

I'm sitting on the sofa watching the Gilmore Girls. Gaige walks in with a bowl of ice bream and hands it to me.

"I'm sorry for laughing so much back there but you have to admit it was funny." He smiles.

I smile and nod. "Yeah it was. Not so much at the time, but yeah. If it was anyone else I probably would have peed myself laughing."

"So um, my mother is coming to visit." Gaige blurts.

"What?!" I say, sitting up straight. "But I don't know how to talk to mothers!" I protest.

"You'll be fine. She is trying to make up for lost time and you're the most important thing in my life. She just wants to meet you." He states and kisses my hand.

"Smooth, very smooth." I smile.

"I try." He shrugs.

"So when is she arriving?" I ask, taking a mouthful of ice cream.

"Tomorrow morning." He replies.

"Oonemoro worning?!" I screech.

I hand him the bowl and jump up. Well, when I say jump up I really mean I shuffle to the edge of the sofa and do three rock back and forth motion. In my head I'm singing 'heave-ho!'. Then I make it to my feet.

"What are you doing?" Gaige asks.

"I'm going to put fresh sheets on the spare bed. Then I need to hoover the room. Oh! Clean towels! And what shopping do we have in? I need to bake!" I panic.

Gaige takes me by the shoulders and directs me back to the sofa and sits me down.

"God I love that you want to make things perfect for my mom, but you don't need to. The house is clean. There is enough food in and I can put clean sheets on the spare bed." He says handing me the bowl of ice cream.

"Okay." I relent.

He leans in and kisses me.

"Hhmm. Love you beautiful." He says across my lips.

"Love you too." I reply smiling.

He gets up and heads off to put clean sheets on the bed. I make a mental note to try and sneak out of bed early in the morning to bake some fresh cake and rolls. Nothing smells better than freshly baked goods.

∞∞∞

It's still dark outside when I wake. Luckily our bed is fairly high so I can roll out of bed easily without making any noise. Gaige doesn't even move. I quickly sneak out the room and go to the toilet. The baby seems to be using my bladder as a cushion.

I reach the kitchen and put on my apron and wash my hands. I lay out all of the ingredients and sigh happily.

I have red velvet cupcakes in the oven along with some cookies. I'm kneading dough when Gaige walks in. He's wearing his grey sweatpants which hang low on his hips and show off his toned body.

"Morning beautiful." He smirks, shaking his head.

He wraps his arms around me and caresses my bump.

"So what time did you get up to come down here and start baking this lot?" He asks over my shoulder.

"Umm 4ish I think." I answer. The timer beeps.

"Oo! Cookies are ready." I rush out as I make my way to the oven.

I place them on the cooling rack and go back to the dough.

"What time is she getting here?" I ask.

"Not sure, she just said morning." He answers, pinching a cooking.

"Oh shit! Gaige I just realised, I don't even know her name! All this time she's just been your mum." I panic.

"Stop panicking. Her name is Fiona." He answers, kissing my neck.

He reaches around and takes the dough from me.

"Hey!" I snap.

"Go upstairs, have a long shower, and go back to bed for a bit. I've got this." He states.

"Can I just wait until the cupcakes are done and then go and lie down? You can just leave that in a bowl to prove. Not that I don't trust you or anything." I say giving him the side glance.

"Yeah right. Fine, you have ten minutes." He

says kissing me.

I quickly pull the cupcakes from the oven and place them on the cooling rack. I cover the dough to let it prove and then head off to shower and nap.

"Esme, wake up. Mom will be here in twenty minutes." He whispers.

My eyes spring open.

"Twenty minutes!" I scream.

I look in the mirror. My hair is a mess. I went straight to sleep with wet hair and now I look like I have a hay bale on my head. I quickly chuck on my wrap dress and try and brush my hair out as best as I can.

"Esme, you looked beautiful as you were." He tries to calm me.

Giving up on my hair I chuck it up in a messy bun and head straight to the kitchen. I notice that a cupcake and two cookies are missing. He's like a kid sneaking treats. I place the dough in the oven and quickly grab the piping bag I prepared earlier. I quickly pipe the cupcakes with Gaige watching me.

"I love watching you decorate cakes." He says in awe.

I'm finishing the last cupcake when the doorbell rings.

"Holy shit!" I jump.

"Calm down." Gaige says and kisses the top of my head.

I walk with Gaige to answer the front door, trying to keep hold of my nerves. I have no idea how to speak to mothers. Mine was a bust and, well, Jay's mum was a bitch from hell.

"Mom!" Gaige greets and pulls her in for a hug.

I stand back and nibble my thumb anxiously.

"Mom, this is Esme." Gaige turns to introduce me to his mum.

She's a tall slim woman with dark hair and dark eyes. She reaches forward and pulls me in for a hug.

Taken aback I awkwardly pat her back.

"Err, nice to meet you Fiona." I stutter.

"It's nice to meet the girl that captured my son's heart." She smiles.

"And it's nice to meet err, you, his mum." I rush out, still feeling nervous.

Gaige holds the back of my neck, giving me a gentle squeeze and stroking his thumb in a soothing motion.

"Mom, let me take your bags. I'll put them in your room." Gaige says as he takes her bags.

I notice she's brought a lot of luggage. How long is she planning on staying?!

"I'd love a coffee, is there any in the pot?" Fiona asks.

"Oh yes! Sorry, baby brain. Let me get you a cup." I smile.

I pour her a cup of coffee and hand it to her.

"No cream?" She asks.

"We only have whipping cream. Gaige drinks his coffee black. We have milk?" I offer.

She sighs.

"That will have to do."

I hand her the milk. She scrunches up her nose as she takes her first sip of coffee.

I place the milk back in the fridge and grab the freshly baked cupcakes and cookies and place them on the side.

"Help yourself, I made them fresh this morning." I say, taking a bite of a cupcake.

"No thank you, I don't do carbs. I don't want to pile on the pounds." She states as her eyes sweep my body.

Did she just call me fat?! I swear I will shove this cupcake down her throat.

"I'm sorry, I didn't realise you were on a special diet." I respond politely, although I can feel my reserve close to snapping.

"I'm not. I hardly ever eat carbs and I if I do, it will only be the best." She smiles tightly.

She did not just insult my cupcakes! That's it, the bitch is getting a throat full of delicious cupcake.

I move to give her a piece of my mind when Gaige walks in.

I watch as Fiona picks up a cookie and takes a bite and smiles brightly at Gaige.

"She makes the best cakes and cookies mom." He says, kissing the top of my head and reaching for a cupcake.

"Oh sweetie, she really does." She beams falsely.

My jaw drops. Jesus Christ! Has this woman got split personality or is she an Oscar winning actress? I'm not sure what her game is but I know I'm going to be watching my back. I've got a feeling she will be ready to stab me in the back at any moment.

She acts all sickly sweet with Gaige all day. I don't get a second alone with Gaige to tell him what she said. Although seeing him so happy having his mum in his life I don't know if I should. She's been absent for so long and I don't want to ruin it for him.

It's getting late and I feel exhausted. Gaige

pulls me to him and I smile and snuggle into his side.

"Well, I best get to bed. Nothing like a good night's sleep to keep you looking young and youthful." She states. Again, that's aimed at me.

What she can't see is that I'm sticking my middle finger up at her that I have hidden in my sleeve. Take that you evil cow!

"Goodnight Fiona. Sleep well." I smile.

Me and Gaige lock up and head upstairs to bed. He pulls me into his arms and places his hand on my bump. We fall asleep like that every night.

I awake the next morning to find Gaige's side of the bed empty.

I frown and then I smell a waft of bacon coming up the stairs. I smile. She may be a bit of a bitch but if she's going to wake up and make breakfast each morning, I can live with that.

I get up and take care of business. Then I walk down the stairs and see Gaige sitting there eating his breakfast. He smiles when he sees me.

"Morning beautiful." He greets, pulling me in for a kiss.

"Hhmm bacon." I say licking my lower lip.

Gaige smiles and playfully nips my lip.

"Ahem." Fiona coughs.

We turn to her and she smiles tightly.

"Take a seat Esme, I've made you breakfast." She states.

I sit down next to Gaige and she places down a bowl of fruit, seeds, nuts, and what look like natural yogurt.

"Err, Fiona, I'm happy with just some bacon and eggs." I state.

"Well that's healthier for you." She points to the bowl.

Not bothering to argue with her I take a bite and scrunch up my nose in disgust.

"Sorry I slept in so late." I apologise.

"Don't apologise beautiful, you need your rest." Gaige says, kissing me.

"Yes don't apologise Esme, some of us need more beauty sleep than others." She smiles sweetly.

I swear I feel my eye twitch. I bite the inside of my cheek to stop myself chewing her out.

"Mom." Gaige warns.

"Oh no I didn't mean it to come out that way. I'm always mixing up my words." She laughs it off.

"Yeah Gaige, it's not your mum's fault. They say when a woman reaches a certain age they can get easily confused. I suppose you have to be careful and watch out for signs of Alzheimer's at your age." I smile sweetly back.

Take that you bitched face hag!

Gaige looks to his mum, questioning if she has early onset of Alzheimer's. I wish Sally was here she would be so proud of me right now.

"I'm fine. Had a full health check at the doctors just last month." Fiona smiles.

"Well, I can't sit around and eat…um…this. I have to get to the bakery." I stand to go get ready.

"Actually Esme, I have to do a quick job for Bob. I thought maybe you could take mom with you to the bakery. I'm sure she would love that." Gaige insists.

"Great." I fake enthusiasm.

I go upstairs to get ready, already dreading the day ahead. Maybe I can dump her with Amy and go to the Sunken Ship and eat poutine.

Once dressed I look in the mirror and smile. I have a black fitted bodycon long sleeved dress on. It's stretchy and comfy and it hugs my bump which I love. I know some women like to hide it and at first I did too. Let's face it, all women feel it when it's at the 'has she put on weight or is she pregnant' stage.

I walk downstairs and smile when Gaige does a sweep of my body, his eyes hungry. He reaches for me, grabbing a fistful of my hair, and takes my mouth.

"You look fucking stunning." He whispers as he kisses my neck.

"Mmm, we can be a few minutes late to the bakery." I moan.

Gaige smiles against my neck and bites playfully.

"I'm ready!" Fiona sings, walking down the stairs.

Just like that the moment is dead.

"Cock blocked." I mutter.

Gaige laughs.

"Later beautiful." He whispers in my ear.

"We better or you will have a moody pregnant women on your hands." I threaten.

On the car ride over Ice Cubes 'You can do it' comes on. I see Fiona scrunch up her nose so of course I turn it up.

I sing along and dance in my seat and flirt with Gaige. He laughs and shakes his head.

We pull up at the bakery and Gaige turns the music down.

"Hallelujah! I can hear again." Fiona sighs from the back seat.

I lean forward and kiss Gaige.

"Later beautiful." He smiles.

Walking into the bakery I smell the sweet smell of freshly baked cakes and bread.

"Hey Amy." I yell.

"I'm out the back!" She replies.

I walk to the kitchen with Fiona following behind me.

Amy is traying up cakes for the day. I walk-over and help her.

"Amy this is Fiona, Gaige's mom. Fiona this is Amy, my friend and the manager here." I introduce.

"Nice to meet you." Amy smiles.

"You pay someone to manage the place for you? It's not exactly very big." She snipes.

Amy looks to me and I shake my head.

"There is a café area upstairs too. We may not be very big but we are very busy and sell out most days." I smile, gritting my teeth.

"Well, we shall see." She huffs.

"We do. We are the best damn bakery in the whole town and the next town over." Amy defends.

I place my hand on Amy's arm and mouth 'don't worry about it' to her.

We finish loading up the cakes and take them to the shop front to display them. Fiona doesn't even offer to help, she just takes a seat and looks bored.

Josie arrives for her shift a little while later and we open the bakery.

It's a normal busy Saturday and it doesn't seem to stop. As I'm serving a customer I overhear Fiona talking to a gentlemen I've just served.

"If you like these cakes you must try Mama's home bakes online. They deliver to your door and their brownies aren't as dry as these. Oh and you'll save money too." She smiles.

"Esme." Amy says next to me.

"I know Amy. Piping bags, stat!" I demand.

"Do you think that's a good idea? I mean technically she's your mother-in-law." Amy says. Then she hands me the piping bags.

"She's crossed the line too many times. I don't care anymore." I fume.

I walk around the counter and the customers part like I'm Moses parting the Red Sea. They know what it means when I'm locked and loaded with my piping bags.

The gentlemen Fiona is chatting to spots me over her shoulder. His eyes go wide and he practically sprints out of the door.

"Why are you running?" Fiona asks.

I tap her shoulder she turns around and eyes the piping bags.

"What are you doing? Piping more cakes?" She asks.

"Get out of my bakery." I say calmly.

"What are you talking about? Silly girl." She huffs, waving me off.

"I said get out of my bloody bakery." I repeat, slowly losing my cool.

"I don't think so. We both know that would upset Gaige and he loves his mother. He wouldn't do that to me. You just wait, I will show him what you really are and you'll be out of the picture. You're just after his money." She spits angrily.

I laugh.

"What money?! I couldn't give a shit if he had millions in the bank! I have my own money, I don't need his. Now this is your last warning. Get out of my shop or I will be forced to fire." I threaten.

"You really have no idea about the money?" She asks.

It hits me then for a moment. I have no clue what she is on about regarding Gaige's money. I don't really care but she seems to know all about his money. She showed up with far too many suitcases to just be visiting.

"You're broke, aren't you?" I ask.

Her eyes flicker, confirming I'm right. "No of course not. Did you not hear? I'm a highly successful psychologist. I have my own books published and had my own show on the radio." She boasts.

"Yeah HAD being the operative word. You're penniless and you're here to milk Gaige for money." I state.

"This place never disappoints for drama." A customer mutters behind me.

"I'm not penniless! This is a designer suit!" She huffs.

"Yeah the leftover of what you had when you had money. Take your designer suit and sod off out of my bakery now or you will be wearing a one of a kind frosting as well." I threaten angrily.

"You wouldn't dare." She spits back.

"SHE WOULD." The entire bakery says back which makes me laugh.

Fiona starts stepping back, edging her way out of the bakery.

"You wait. Gaige will finish with you when I tell him about this." She threatens, tripping out of the step.

I smile and take aim and fire, covering her in

frosting. The entire bakery cheer and chant my name.

I laugh as Fiona wipes her face and stares down at her suit which is now covered in frosting.

"What the hell is going on?!" Gaige barks loudly as he jumps out of his truck.

My smile falls and I bite my lip nervously.

"Oh thank god you're here. Son, she's mad. She threatened me and attacked me with her piping bags. Just look at me! It was completely unprovoked, she's insane!" Fiona lies, acting as the perfect damsel in distress.

I roll my eyes.

"Esme?" Gaige asks.

"I'm sorry Gaige. I did threaten your mother, but only after I caught her telling my customers to shop elsewhere. And I'm sorry, but she's broke. She is only here for your money." I say softly.

"That's just not true! Gaige I swear it's not true." She pleads.

"IT IS!" All of the customers and staff have followed and are standing behind me, backing me. They all yell in union.

"Thanks guys." I whisper back to them.

Gaige looks at me. He knows that what I'm

saying is the truth. I have no reason to lie to him about the money situation and he knows me well enough to know that unless someone pissed me off I wouldn't be standing here, piping bags in hand, kicking someone out of the bakery.

"How broke are you mom?" He asks.

"I…well…I'm, err, $20,000 in debt." She sighs.

"You know if you had just asked me I would have helped you out and we wouldn't be in this situation now. I will give you the money." He pauses.

She smiles and looks up to him.

"But I don't want to see you ever again. You take the money and don't contact me. You're dead to me." He says coldly.

"But I'm your mother." She says softly.

"No you're not. You've been out of my life more than you've been in it. You stopped being a mother the day you stood by and let my father, your husband, beat the shit out of us. You could have run away with me but you chose him. I met with you and I have forgiven you for that. I gave you a second chance and yet you come here and insult my girlfriend. Actually, she's not just my girlfriend, but the woman carrying my child. Which, by the way, you haven't even acknowledged the fact she is pregnant! She's carrying your grandbaby. I will take you back to the house where you will pack up your shit and leave. I will give you the fucking money just to keep you out of my life!" Gaige roars.

Fiona skulks away and gets into Gaige's truck

The customers behind me cheer like they're watching a stage show.

I walk to Gaige and he welcomes me into his arms. He strokes the hair from my face.

"I'm sorry she was such a bitch to you Esme." He apologises.

"It wasn't anything I couldn't handle. Listen are you sure about this? I mean, she is your mum after all, bitch or not." I shrug.

Gaige smiles.

"You'd put up with her for me?" He asks.

"I'm not making any promises that I wouldn't try and kill her, but I think I could refrain from actual murder." I offer.

Gaige kisses me and smiles.

"No beautiful. I never had an actual mom in my life so I'm not going to miss her. She has always been selfish. It's better cutting her off completely. I'm more than happy with my life being filled by you and our baby." Gaige states before kissing me.

He drives off and I turn back around to go

into the bakery. All of the customers are smiling. I shake my head and smile.

"Free cookies for all. Then you can all bugger off home!" I yell.

"Woohoo!" They all cheer.

Chapter Thirty-One

We never heard from Fiona after that day. As the weeks passed I thought maybe we might hear something, especially with Christmas just a matter of days away, but there was nothing.

I've been shopping like crazy for Christmas. I'm extra excited because Sally and her donkey dick boyfriend are coming over to spend Christmas with us.

I would be lying if I said I wasn't a little nervous for Gaige to meet Sally, I mean, I barely have a filter but Sally's is non-existent.

"IT'S CHRISTMAS!" I shout as I enter the house.

I smile, taking in the decorations: the beautiful wreath up the banister including fairy lights. I chose a huge seven foot Christmas tree for the living area and I got us all stockings to hang on the fireplace. It's snowing so it's going to be a perfect white Christmas. The only downside is that I'm pure weeble. I could roll like an armadillo if I could tuck in properly. Everything about me is huge: my arse, my breasts, and I reckon the baby must weigh like twenty pounds. There will be no drinking for me this Christmas. At least I can eat, and boy am I good at that at the moment.

I find Gaige in the kitchen eating a Christmas cookie. He freezes like a naughty child caught with their hand in the cookie jar.

I laugh and walk over to him and kiss him. I do my best to try and perch on the stall but Gaige has to help lift me up after I struggle.

"So Gaige, there is something I want to ask you. Please don't feel like you have to answer though." I ask nibbling my thumb.

"Esme just ask me." He states.

"Your mum was here for your money. I know you do okay because, well, you have this place. I just didn't realise you had twenty grand in the bank to dispose of your mother. I'm not interested in having a penny of your money, I just, well, I'm intrigued because you don't exactly go around flashing it." I ask.

Gaige smiles.

"Esme what's mine is yours. I mean that. You're carrying my child. I had around two million in the bank the last time I checked." He states.

I swear my jaw hits the floor.

"Hold up there a minute lumberjack. You're hot, you have a magnificent dick and you certainly know what to do with it, and you're a millionaire?!" I screech excitedly.

Gaige laughs. God I love watching him laugh. I swear if I weren't pregnant I would be. His laughter alone enough to make me want to jump his bones. He is so bloody hot.

"Beautiful, it's the money that was left to me by Tom along with the lumber yard and this house. I've never spent it because I've never had a need to. I have everything I need." He says, cupping my face. He leans in and kisses me softly.

"God you really do have it all." I sigh.

"Yeah, I really do." He whispers across my lips, his deep chocolate eyes conveying the meaning of his words.

He kisses me and it starts getting heated. He nips at my neck and I moan. I move but my bump is in the way,

"God damn it." I complain.

Not deterred Gaige keeps kissing me, working his magic. He caresses my breasts.

"Yes." I moan.

"Err beautiful, your breasts are leaking." Gaige states.

"What?" I look down and sure enough there are the wet patches.

"Oh man, the doctor said the colostrum can come in before the baby is born. Jesus! I'm already like a cow with leaky udders." I cry.

"Esme, you're beautiful. Even four weeks away from your due date I want you." He says trying to reassure me.

"Now I hate to upset you but we have prenatal class in fifteen minutes." He informs me.

"Oh god! Damn you leaky boobs! We could have got away with it if you had kept yourselves contained!" I chastise my breasts as I walk up the stairs to change.

We walk into the room where all of the other expectant parents are ready and waiting.

"Hi, hi, oh hi!" I say falsely.

I hate these classes. The parents in them all think they are better than us just because they're married and we're not. Well also because I may have dropped the doll a couple of times when being taught how to hold the baby and how to bathe the baby. Effectively dolly drowned that day. I tried to perform C-P-R but it was no good, there was no life in her. I start giggling to myself at the memory.

"What's so funny?" Gaige whispers.

"Just remembering the day I drowned dolly." I giggle.

"Ahh, yeah. I don't think I've ever seen someone try C-P-R on a dolly before. It was so funny when you were doing compression on it and her arm popped off and hit the teacher in the face." Gaige laughs.

I snort at the memory. We were dismissed that day as the rest of the class looked on in horror.

"Good afternoon moms, dads, surrogates!" The teacher beams as she walks in.

I smile and wave. I swear I see her smile waiver. I think a little bit of her dies seeing us here.

"So today we are learning how to swaddle baby and ways to comfort baby if they're having a bad night and won't settle." She smiles as she informs the class.

"Piece of piss. We totally have this in the bag." I high five Gaige.

"So you have your babies, now you want to keep their arms down close to their bodies and wrap the blanket nice and snug around the baby. This helps to make the baby feel safe and secure." She instructs.

"A bit like the straight jackets in a mental institution." I comment.

All eyes come to me.

"What? It's true. Their arms are strapped down tight." I shrug.

I wrap the doll in the blanket and smile at my perfect job. I turn to the teacher.

"Stick that in your pipe and smoke it." I say cockily.

"Well done Esme. That's exactly how it should be." The teacher says with surprise.

She walks off to the couple on our right.

"Not quite Melanie, try this technique." The teacher advises. When Melanie's gaze turns to us I smile smugly and scratch my nose with my middle finger.

"Beautiful, if I had known you were this competitive I would've suggested a private class." Gaige laughs shaking his head.

"I'm not competitive. I just like taking down a snotty nosed cow every now and again." I smile.

The next part of the class is to try a different way to calm a baby. This time though, because the dolls don't actually cry, our partners are asked to pretend to be babies.

Some really go for it, even kicking their legs. I mean really, someone get these guys an Oscar.

Next up it's our turn. Gaige rolls his eyes at me and pretends to scream, putting very little effort into it. I have the giggles watching him which of course makes Gaige laugh.

"Now come on, what would you do to calm the baby?!" The teacher says, getting ratty with us.

"You really want us to play out how I would calm the baby?" I ask.

"Yes, that is the whole point in this exercise." She huffs.

"Fine."

Gaige pretends to cry. I pat his back as if winding the baby, pretend to check his bum, and then finally I pull aside my top and press Gaige's face to my bra covered boob.

The whole class is silent.

"What? Burp it, change it, feed it." I state.

"To be fair, I'm with babies on this one. This calms me right down." Gaige smiles, snuggling into my breast. I roll my eyes and smile.

"For goodness sake! What are you doing?!" The teacher exclaims.

"Pretending to breast feed. I have a bra on because I'm not about to actually breastfeed my boyfriend, that's sick." I state disgusted.

"I said to practice calming the baby." She sighs.

"Listen lady, I don't know about you but I'm

following your guidelines here. I'm not about to try and pick him up because that would be bloody stupid. If you want me to shove my nipple in his mouth and pretend to breast feed him then you are all sick mother effers that need to get a reality check." I snap.

Gaige helps me off of the floor.

"You can all go and kiss my fat pregnant behind. We are raising our baby the American and British way. Wing it all the way and always make sure the fridge is stocked with beer and wine." I state as we head towards the door.

"That sounds about right. Parents like that raise those little shits who will end up on the world's most wanted list." Melanie tuts.

I turn around and face her.

"Kiss my arse Melanie. Oh, and your husband has been shagging the teacher, I heard them in the closet." I smile and walk off, flipping them off as I go.

"You ever take me to a class like that again and I will never give you head again." I threaten.

"Now that's a threat I need to be scared of." Gaige smirks.

We head straight to the airport to pick up Sally. We will arrive early but can grab some lunch while we're there.

I smile to myself and think back to the moment I met Gaige. God I thought he was such a dick when in reality he is anything but that.

At the airport we head to a pizza place and sit and eat. It's so strange watching the people rush by to catch their flights, the people waiting at arrivals for their loved ones, family members hugging each other goodbye. It's full of the best and worst emotions.

"You enjoying yourself people watching?" Gaige smiles.

"Sorry I completely zoned out. I love people watching, especially in an airport. I mean look at this family for example." I say pointing to a large family hugging their young son goodbye.

"What about them?" Gaige shrugs.

"Look at the emotion pouring from his mother. It's killing her that he is leaving, even the father looks like he wants to grab his son and never let him go. They are scared and worried for him but they are trying to stay positive for his sake." I observe.

"How in the hell did you get all of that just by looking at them?" He asks.

I point to the son's large duffel bag that has the Canadian armed forces logo on it.

"He's leaving to go back to the army. All parents are proud of their children if they join the military but they're also petrified because they just want to keep them safe." I state smiling and stroking my huge bump.

Gaige places his hand on my bump and the baby kicks.

"Woah! I guess he knows his dad is here." He smirks.

"She certainly does." I quip.

An announcement over the speakers lets us know that Sally's flight has landed. I clap excitedly.

"Come on, I want to be ready for when she arrives. Do you have the sign I made?" I ask.

"Yes I have the sign ready. Why do you need this exactly?" He asks, looking at it.

"Because it's funny. She would have done it to me. Now come on or we will be late and it won't have the full effect." I say dragging him by the hand.

We stand and wait at arrivals. I hold the sign up and people laugh and point to it.

The sign reads: **Welcome home from rehab Sally, glad they removed the anal beads. #sexisarealaddiction #saveourprostitutes #thinkbeforesinkintothestink**

"What the hell have I let myself in for?" Gaige sighs.

I turn and smile at him.

"You're in for a hell but it will be fun, I promise. Just be thankful I can't drink." I wink.

The doors open and people from the flight start filtering through.

"Ahhh she's nearly here." I screech excitedly.

I spot her in the distance walking with a handsome guy who is pushing a trolly with their suitcases.

"There she is!" I yell.

As they get closer her head comes up. Her eyes squint as she reads the sign. I watch her as she bursts out laughing and then points, showing her boyfriend it. She doesn't give him a chance to comment because she starts running towards me and screaming like a loon.

When she reaches me she hugs me tight.

"Oh my god Esme! I've missed you so bloody much." She sobs.

"I've missed you too." I sob.

We break our hug as her bloke finally catches up. I wipe my eyes.

"Esme, this is Flynn." Sally introduces.

"Hi Flynn, nice to meet you. I've, um, heard a lot about you." I smile.

"It's good to meet you too." He replies with a thick Australian accent.

"You're Australian?" I ask.

"Yeah. I guess that's one bit of information Sally left out hey." He smiles.

He's a good looking guy. He's the hot blonde surfer type.

Gaige and Flynn shake hands and greet each other.

"Gaige, this is my bestest friend in the whole world, Sally." I state.

"Well knock me down with a dildo! You're even hotter in person than on video call." She laughs and pulls him in for a hug.

She turns back to Flynn,

"Of course he's no match for you. You two are like polar opposites, dark and light, day and night." She shrugs.

She leans forward and cups her hands around her mouth and presses against my pregnant bump.

"Hello my gorgeous child! Auntie Sally here, just to say I'm here for all the non-parenting fun. You know, booze and late night parties. You can call me anytime." She stands and winks

"Now that introductions are done, let's go. I want to see this bakery and I haven't had one of your buns in forever. Also, nice work on the sign! You totally nailed it." Sally states, linking arms with me as we walk ahead to the truck.

Chapter Thirty-Two

Gaige drops us off at the bakery and him and Flynn take the bags back and go and grab some beers and whatever else they want.

As we walk in Sally smiles wide.

"Holy fucking Christ! You have done it Esme, it's beyond amazing." She praises.

The customers look at her in shock because of what has just come out of her mouth.

"God there's another one worse than her! If she's staying here permanently I'm coming every day just to watch the drama unfold." A customer mutters behind me.

"Amy this is Sally, my best friend visiting form England." I introduce.

"Hi Sally, it's good to meet you." Amy says politely.

"Hey Amy, good to meet you. Esme I'm jet

lagged and hungry, are you going to feed me some cake or what?" Sally complains.

I smile and shake my head, getting us some cakes and buns.

"I will be out the back if you need me." I yell over my shoulder to Amy.

We sit out the back in my makeshift office. Sally dives into an iced bun and moans.

"God I've missed this."

"So it's going well between you and Flynn then? I'm glad you introduced him by his name, I nearly called him donkey dick." I laugh.

"Donkey dick would have been perfectly acceptable. I even joked with him about paying for another seat on the plane just for his enormous member." Sally snorts.

"Well, it's good to see you happy and able to walk so well considering you have a dose of the donkey dick." I giggle.

"Ha-ha, yeah. I am really happy. We joined the mile high club on the flight here you know." Sally winks.

"Oh good god, you didn't?!" I choke on my iced bun.

"Yup, ticked that one right off my bucket list and it was fast and intense, highly recommend." Sally says proudly.

"Well I think we will wait to try that one. Can't really see Gaige fitting in the aeroplane toilet with me at the moment." I point out, rubbing my bump.

Sally smiles and strokes my bump.

"I can't believe you're pregnant! You always wanted a family. You look so happy and it's amazing seeing you like this. I never said anything but I was terrified for you when you came here. You were so broken and a shell of the person you were/are. I was worried that if things didn't work out here for you, that you would do something silly and I would lose you." Sally admits.

I lean over and grab her hand in mine.

"Sally, I never knew you felt that way. I was broken, completely broken, I can't deny that dark thoughts crossed my mind. What saved me was coming here. Gaige saved me in so many ways, even when he was being an arse that spark, that feeling, brought me back to life a little bit more each time." I smile.

We hug each other tight. I needed this, I needed my best friend.

"Come on. Let's finish these and then I will show you upstairs." I say wiping away the tears.

"Christ, look at us sat here bloody crying! I'm having a stiff drink when we get back to yours and I will have an extra one for you." Sally smiles and wipes her tears.

"He would be so happy seeing you like this you know? This is what he wanted for you." Sally sighs.

"I know. I still miss him every day, even though I'm with Gaige who I love beyond words. I just wish he could have seen all this." I smile.

"He can. He is always looking down on you Esme. Well, maybe there are certain times he's not. If you know what I mean." Sally winks and smiles sadly.

I laugh and shake my head.

"Come on. Let me show you the rest of the place." I stand up and hold out my hand.

It's late by the time we're home and Sally and Flynn are exhausted. They decide to get to bed and get some sleep. I lay with Gaige on the sofa watching a series about serial killers.

"I would love to meet him, wouldn't you? He would be fascinating and terrifying. God, can you imagine the stuff he would tell you?" I ask, completely enthralled by the show.

"Err is there something you want to tell me?" Gaige laughs.

I look up at him and laugh.

"No, but come on. These guys get to go

around and interview the most prolific serial killers. I mean wow, just wow. Take Edmund Kemper for example. He was a highly intelligent man! He was kind and cautious and would sit nicely and talk to you." I state.

"Yeah and he also killed women, cut off their heads, and had sex with their dead bodies. Something tells me he isn't a true gent." Gaige laughs.

"Fair point." I admit.

"I do find serial killers interesting though." I state.

"Good to know. Remind me never to piss you off." Gaige laughs.

"Come on, enough serial killers for one night, let's get to bed." Gaige switches off the TV and we can hear noises.

"What's that?" I ask.

Gaige helps me off of the couch and we walk to the bottom of the stairs.

The sounds become clearer. They are coming from upstairs. I start giggling.

"Are they doing what I think they're doing?" Gaige asks.

"Umm yes, it appears so. Jet lag my arse!" I giggle.

"Want to finish watching serial killers for a minute?" I ask, still laughing.

"Yeah I think that's a good idea." He agrees.

We both fall asleep on the couch.

"Pssst. Esme, wake up." Sally calls.

I open my eyes and Sally smiles.

"What?" I mumble.

"I came down to get a drink. Why have you guys stayed up so late?" She asks.

I rub my face, trying to wake myself up a little.

"Because someone was shagging too loudly for us to go to bed." I state.

"Oh shit, you guys heard that?" Sally asks while looking embarrassed.

"Yes. The whole of Canada heard you." I say moving to sit up.

Gaige groans and opens his eyes.

"So the fuck bunnies have stopped then?" He asks.

I snort with laughter as Sally turns bright red.

"I am so sorry Gaige. We didn't mean to, um, make so much noise." Sally apologises.

"No worries." Gaige says stretching.

"Come on, let's get to bed." I say to Gaige.

"Night." Sally calls after us as we walk up the

stairs to bed.

"Night Miss Shagalot!" I yell over my shoulder.

The next day Sally and I bake ready for Christmas. I've closed the bakery to let the girls spend a good few days off with their families. We have the Christmas tunes turned up loud and are dancing and singing around the kitchen.

"Jesus, it's like Christmas threw up in here!" Gaige states walking in and taking a cookie.

"It's the eve of Christmas Eve! It is Christmas!" I say excitedly.

Gaige smiles and walks to me. He takes my finger which has some chocolate on it. I'm currently making Christmas truffles. He places my finger in his mouth and licks the chocolate off. I bite my lip and smile.

"Oh Christmas cracker that's hot!" Sally says whilst fanning herself.

Gaige kisses me.

"Love you beautiful." He says across my lips.

"Love you too." I reply smiling.

He grabs two more beers for him and Flynn and leaves the kitchen. I'm smiling like a complete goofball and Sally is still fanning herself with a baking tray.

"Seriously, you guys together are beyond perfect. I swear I nearly sat down with a bag of popcorn to enjoy the show!" Sally laughs.

We spend the rest of the day baking various things and don't stop laughing and joking around the entire time.

Christmas Eve is spent pretty much the same way. We are all sitting in the living room and Sally hands us each a gift.

"Sally it's not Christmas until tomorrow." I point out.

"I know but these are for tonight really." She shrugs smiling.

We all rip open our presents. They are all the same. A pair of pyjamas with lots of little images all over it.

"Oh my god Sally where did you get these?" I laugh looking at the images.

One of the images is Mrs Claus bent over next to a Christmas tree with the words: *fucking around the Christmas tree.* Then there's another image of Santa clearly getting a blow job from Mrs Claus with the words: *I'm dreaming of a white Christmas.*

"Aren't they brilliant?! They are all matching for us to wear tonight ready for Christmas morning." Sally claps excitedly.

"Bloody brilliant." I agree.

Too excited and wanting to get to Christmas day we decide to get to bed around 11pm. I am so excited to give Gaige his presents. Gaige is about to learn that I go all out at Christmas.

Chapter Thirty-Three

"IT'S CHRISTMAS!!!" I yell at eight in the morning. Yes, I am that person.

I may have already been up for two hours excitedly filling the stockings. I have put the coffee pot on ready and the fire is burning. Christmas songs are full blast on the TV.

"Jesus Christ! You did not warn me that you were like this at Christmas." Gaige complains yawning.

"Last Christmas I wasn't me. This year I'm happy and back to being myself which means I'm more hyper on Christmas than Buddy the Elf!" I smile.

Sally opens her door and dances out into the hallway.

"I wish it could be Christmas every day!" Sally sings excitedly.

Smiling but still sleepy Flynn follows her out of the room.

"Come on! Let's see if Santa has been!" I wink.

I go to move but Gaige grabs my hand and pulls me to him.

"Merry Christmas beautiful." He smiles before kissing me.

"Hhmm Merry Christmas." I smile.

We get in the lounge and Sally and Flynn are sitting with their coffees and stockings in front of them.

"Wow, what time did you get up this morning?" Gaige asks.

"Um around six." I shrug.

I hand Gaige his stocking and take a seat with mine in my hands.

"You filled your own stocking?" Gaige asks.

"No! Santa did." I smile.

I sit and watch them open their stockings.

"Lumberjack the soundtrack?" Gaige laughs.

"Santa knows all." I laugh.

"Oh wow! Santa got me the new lube I wanted to try." Sally squeals excitedly and Flynn looks quite excited by that gift as well.

"Beautiful, open yours." Gaige states.

"It's okay. I love watching people open their presents. Plus I know what Santa got me." I say happily.

"Beautiful, open your stocking." Gaige insists.

I roll my eyes and pull out one of my presents. I open it and it's not what I expected. It's a baby grow that says 'mommy will you marry daddy' on it.

I look up to see Gaige drop to one knee in front of me. He's holding a small box in his hand with a beautiful sapphire princess cut ring.

"Oh my god." I whisper.

"Esme, you came crashing into my life and you completely turned my world upside down. You're the most relentless, passionate, and fucking beautiful woman I've ever met. I love you with all of my heart and soul. Make me happy for all eternity and marry me? What do you say, do you fancy becoming Mrs Knox?" Gaige asks, his eyes full of love and anxiety.

I look to the ring and the baby grow again with tears running down my face.

"Yes." I whisper.

"Is that a yes?" Gaige asks.

"Yes Gaige Knox, I will marry you!" I shout.

Gaige slides the ring on my finger and takes

my face in his hands and kisses me passionately.

"I love you so fucking much." Gaige says across my lips.

"I love you Gaige. Heart and soul." I say repeating his words back to him.

"Yes!!!!" Sally claps.

She pulls out a bottle of champagne from behind the cushion and pops the cork.

She pours us all a drink and Gaige hands me mine.

"I can't drink." I state.

"Oh shush, you've just got engaged! There's only like two sips in there anyway." Sally shrugs.

I shrug. She's right. I neck the tiny bit of champagne and it tastes heavenly.

"Jesus! Wait for the toast." Sally mocks.

"Whoops. I got a bit excited about having a proper drink." I apologise.

"Anyway, as the best friend I feel it's only right I should make a toast at this very special time." Sally smiles.

"As you know, we have been friends since school. I have been with Esme every step of the way. She has been through hell and I am so happy to see her come out the other side of it. She's happy, contented, and madly in love. So let's raise our glasses, some with actual champagne in." Sally pauses, giving me the eye.

"To Gaige and Esme! May you have many years of love, happiness, and hot sex! Cheers!" Sally yells and raises her glass.

I smile. I'm absolutely bursting with love and happiness.

"Umm, Esme. FYI, I am choosing my own bridesmaid dress. You ain't putting me in no poofy pink coloured candy floss dress." She states adamantly.

"Who says I'm having you as bridesmaid?" I throw back.

Sally raises her eyebrow, calling me out.

"Fair enough. You're right. Of course you'll be my bridesmaid." I relent.

I look down at my engagement ring and sigh happily. Gaige takes my hand in his and kisses my ring.

"You've made me the happiest man alive today. Merry Christmas beautiful." He whispers leaning in to kiss me.

"Merry Christmas Gaige." I whisper back and then his lips are on mine, kissing me sweet and tenderly.

"Alright you two, enough of the show. Let's finish opening the presents and get the day started, which of course means eating and drinking too much until we fall asleep on the sofa later." Sally orders, clapping her hands.

We finish opening our presents. Sally got loads of baby things for us and a very large packet of incontinence pads for me.

"Sally! I will not be incontinent after having this baby!" I protest.

"Honey I have friends that have had kids. They can no longer go on a trampoline. They can't even sneeze without pure fear that they will piss themselves! Don't even get me started on coughing. It's a real thing, You need to do the pelvic floor exercises from that book I got you or your whole uterus will just fall out and your muscles will be no more. You'll be walking around hearing clapping and it won't be applause, it'll be your saggy vagina lips slapping about all over the place." Sally insists.

I roll my eyes but inside I panic a little. No woman wants a saggy overstretched vagina!

"On that note I'm off to stuff the turkey." I announce.

I prepare the turkey and put it into the oven, set the timer, and then head to the shower.

Once out of the shower I take a seat in the bedroom and pull out my phone. I call Frank.

"Hello?" He answers.

"Frank, it's Esme."

"Oh hello Esme, how are you? Oh and Merry

Christmas." He asks happily.

"I'm good actually Frank. There is something I need to tell you. Well, I thought I should tell you." I state nervously.

"You've met someone." He states.

"Yes I have but there's more. I'm pregnant and he proposed to me today and I said yes." I inform him.

He goes quiet.

"Frank?" I ask.

"Sorry dear, I'm in a bit of a shock. Good shock though. Don't concern yourself with worry. I am extremely delighted for you! Thank you for telling me although you know you didn't have too. I appreciate it all the same." He says politely.

"Well I thought it was important that you should know because, um, well, I want to ask you if you would walk me down the aisle?" I ask nervously.

The line goes quiet.

"Look Frank, it's completely fine if you don't want to. It's just, well, I never had a father and apart from Sally I don't really have any family. I thought maybe it would be nice having you there. But I see that it's silly and I get it…"

Frank interrupts.

"I would be honoured to walk you down the aisle. I am just shocked that you see me that way."

"I, well, we have stayed in contact all this time and you're a good person Frank. Jay loved you. A father giving away his daughter on her wedding day is her moving forward with her life, moving on to the next stage in her life. That's not too different from what I'm doing." I say honestly.

"I am beyond honoured that you asked me. As soon as you have things booked you tell me the dates and I will be there." He promises.

I sigh with relief.

"So you're pregnant?" He asks.

"Yes. I'm sorry I kept it from you, I wasn't sure how to tell you. I'm actually due in a few weeks." I admit, feeling guilty for not telling him.

"I understand. I'm glad you are happy Esme. That is all Jay would have wanted. I'm also glad that you continue to include me in your new life. It makes me feel closer to Jay in some way." He admits honestly.

I sniffle back my tears, smile and nod.

"Yeah. It feels the same for me too."

"Well it's a pleasure as always to hear from

you. I will speak to you soon. Take care of yourself and the baby. I look forward to hearing from you about the birth of your little one. Much love to you Esme." Frank says with affection in his voice.

"And you Frank, take care." I say before disconnecting

I wipe my eyes and take a deep breath. I stand up to head downstairs and jump when I see Gaige in the doorway, leaning with his hands in his pockets.

"Jay's father?" He asks.

I give him a small smile and nod.

"I'm sorry. I know I should have spoken to you first about him giving me away but I just felt compelled to call him to ask him to do it." I explain.

Gaige walks towards me and tucks my hair behind my ear.

"Esme, you don't need to ask or even explain why you want Frank there to give you away. I understand completely and it's your decision. Him and Sally are the only family you have, of course you want them there." Gaige states.

I smile. When did I become so lucky in finding this amazing man?

"Now come on. Sally is pulling out the board games and I'm scared if she doesn't win she will kill me in my sleep." Gaige states, feigning fear.

"Oh she definitely would kill you! What game has she pulled out?" I ask as we walk downstairs.

"Monopoly." Gaige answers.

"God help us all." I mutter.

∞∞∞

"Pay up sucker!" Sally gloats, holding out her hand.

"Seriously, how did you manage to own all of the expensive streets and then put bloody hotels on them? You have to be cheating." Gaige complains, handing over his last bit of board game money.

My eyes go wide and I shake my head vigorously at him in warning. He has just crossed a line and Sally is likely to snap. I've seen her make a seven foot three-hundred pound man cry before. That was because he accused her of cheating at trivial pursuit.

"Gaige, you're new to this, new to me. I will be as polite as I can. I never cheat, I am quiet simply the board game master. I am relentless and ruthless in taking out my opponents. I show no mercy. I have never been beaten and I don't intend that to change. Call me a cheater again and

I will grab your balls so tightly and twist them until your screams can be heard in the depths of hell. Capiche?" Sally warns.

"Did you just add an Italian mafia accent to the end of that threat?" I ask, fighting back my laughter.

"I did. I am one quarter Italian. Who knows what connections I may have!" Sally brags.

I snort my laughter and shake my head.

"Okay Al Capone of boardgames. You've made yourself very clear. I don't want to sleep with the fishes." Gaige mocks.

"I'm a kind person. I'm kind to everyone, but if you are unkind to me, then kindness is not what you'll remember me for." Sally threatens in a thick Italian mobster accent.

"Oh Christ I'm dying! Did you just quote Al Capone?" I burst out laughing.

"I'm just emphasising my point." Sally huffs.

We are all laughing apart from Sally who is taking this all very seriously. I swear whoever invented the board game, well, someone needs to go back and eradicate them from history. They only ever bring misery to families. I've seen operation tear a family apart. Board games are no joke.

"Okay, who is up for a game of Pictionary?" Flynn asks.

"No!" I cry.

All eyes come to me. Well, all except for Sally's.

"Pictionary must never be played. Sally took an oath to never touch the game again after the incident of 98." I say solemnly.

"Why? What happened in 98?" Flynn asks, looking back and forth between us.

"It was a dark day in the world of board games." Sally starts.

"No. Sally don't. You don't have to tell him." I plead.

"It's okay Esme. He has a right to know, we are in a relationship after all." Sally sighs.

I see Gaige fight a smile. Just wait, I think to myself. You will not be smiling at the end of this.

"It was a Saturday in autumn. It was beautiful, orange and red leaves had fallen to the ground." Sally says dramatically, standing next to the fireplace.

"We were in pairs playing and I was with Elliott. I had a crush on him and I couldn't have been happier to be paired with him." Sally smiles.

"My mistake was thinking that it was a good pairing. He was awful at it. His drawing were sub-par at best. I mean, I've seen a toddler draw better. His pencil was blunt. He was too busy thinking he was funny and just wouldn't focus on the game." Sally sighs and shakes her head.

Gaige's shoulder are shaking with silent laughter and so are Flynn's.

"I was, of course, on top form. It wasn't enough. We were losing. I kept on top of my game. My pencil was razor sharp, making sure I had clear and precise lines. Then it happened. Elliot was up and if we got this we would take the lead." She draws in a long breath.

"But I couldn't tell what Elliot was drawing. It was a mess. Was it a hissing snake, a stick, a lasso? I just couldn't guess. All of the other kids were laughing. Of course I knew what it looked like, but I also knew this was child Pictionary and not the R-rated version. In pure frustration and anger at being mocked, I threw my pencil at Elliot. I threw it hard." Sally admits.

Gaige and Flynn wipe the tears that are falling down their faces.

"So what happened next?" Gaige asks.

"I swear, I swear that I didn't mean to hurt him in any way. I swear. But the pencil was deadly sharp. When I threw it, it acted like a javelin soaring and landing with speed and force." Sally states sadly.

I wince.

"Oh god."

Gaige and Flynn look to me and back to Sally.

"Where did it land?" Flynn and Gaige ask, their laughter ceasing.

"It landed like a harpoon straight in his penis." Sally sighs, shaking her head.

"Ooooh shit!" Both Flynn and Gaige cry, cupping their crotch.

"Yeah, he had to go to hospital to have it removed. Poor Elliot." Sally sighs.

"That's not all of it. He was ridiculed for it throughout the rest of school and college. He was never called Elliot again." Sally adds.

"What was he called?" Flynn asks.

Sally pauses and looks at me.

"Pencil Dick. PD for short." Sally answers.

Gaige and Flynn burst out laughing. I bite my lip to stop myself from laughing.

"That's it, laugh it up. That poor kid was known as pencil dick for the rest of his life because of my actions during Pictionary. I'm a monster. He could never get laid in college because not everyone knew the story. Most girls genuinely thought he had a pencil dick!" Sally exclaims.

Flynn reaches for Sally and pulls her onto his

lap, still laughing.

"Well you may be a monster but you're my monster. Just remind me never to make you mad when you have stationary in your hand." Flynn smirks.

Sally is about to fly off of the handle at him but he moves quickly, kissing her to shut her up.

"Do I need to be aware of any crazy side of you?" Gaige asks cautiously.

"Don't worry, you've seen my crazy with the piping bags, remember?" I remind him.

"How could I forget." Gaige laughs.

Chapter Thirty-Four

Throughout the rest of Christmas day and Boxing day we shared a lot of laughter and eating and they did a lot of drinking too. It's time for Sally and Flynn to fly home and I'm gutted. They've only been with us a week but Sally has to get back to work and Flynn's family are doing a new year celebration because he wasn't with them for Christmas.

After a long drive to the airport we say our goodbyes. I can't hold back the tears. Having my oldest and dearest friend with me after not seeing her for so long just made me realise how much I missed her.

"God I'm going to miss you so much." I sniffle.

Sally smiles and wipes her tears.

"I'm going to miss you too but I will be back. I need to visit this little one and of course when you guys set a date I will be there for your wedding too. So don't worry, you'll be sick of the sight of me soon enough." Sally says, trying to make me feel better.

"I suppose at least we can both get ridiculously drunk the next time we are together. There's always that." I shrug.

"Can't wait for that." Gaige mumbles under his breath.

We hug again and Sally and Flynn make their way to departures. Gaige pulls me into his arms and comforts me while I cry and wave off my best friend.

On the drive back Gaige holds my hand nearly the entire time, comforting me.

"Can you drop me at the dock for a minute? I want to tell Jay." I ask.

Gaige kisses the back of my hand.

"Of course beautiful. Do you want me to come with you or shall I wait in the car?" He asks.

"I kinda want to be on my own for a moment. Is that okay?" I ask.

Gaige smiles and shakes his head as he pulls up by the docks.

"Go. I will wait here. Please be careful out there."

I smile and kiss him.

I walk steadily along the dock, being extra careful not to slip on ice or fall into the sea like I did last time. I find my bench and take a seat.

"Hi Jay. As you can see I'm close to popping. I weigh about the same as a whale at the moment, but yet have a bladder the size of a walnut apparently. I spoke to your Dad on Christmas. He's doing well. I rang him because Gaige asked me to marry him and I said yes. I want your Dad to give me away, it'll be sort of like having you there I suppose. I wanted to tell you and let you know that Gaige is a really good guy. When your Dad flies over here I will bring him here so he can see how beautiful it is. I will come back soon, take care. I love you forever and always." I whisper the last part and stand to go back to the car.

Gaige is standing behind me, watching me.

"I came to help you walk back up to the truck. I don't want you falling and hurting yourself or the baby." He states.

"Thank you. Umm, you know I love you right? Just because I say that to Jay that doesn't mean I don't love you." I say, worried that he will get upset by what I said to Jay.

Gaige stops and turns to me, the freezing, bitter wind bites at my cheeks.

"Esme, I know you will always love Jay. I'm

not stupid in thinking just because I love you or that you love me that your love for him will die. I am not worried or jealous of Jay, I have your love now, I know that." Gaige states, kissing me softly.

I smile up at him and shiver.

"Come on before we both end up getting frost bite." Gaige states.

Over the next few days the snow continues to come thick and fast. It's new years eve and The Sunken Ship is holding a party but Gaige and I have decided to stay in. I'm permanently exhausted and with the snow fall I just want to be curled up in the warm.

That's not to mention that being a Brit I am still not used to seeing this amount of snowfall. Back in the UK we would be excited and also probably panic as it would bring the country to a standstill. Our small island is not prepared for any form of snow.

Gaige dropped me to the bakery while he delivered some lumber. We were open but closing up early for new years eve and also due to the fact that the snowfall was getting just a little too heavy.

"Right so everything is packed away. I'm not planning on opening until the 3rd of January. So go crazy tonight! Get drunk because you have two days to recover." I smile to Amy, Dawn, and

Josie.

"Err, Esme, I'm sixteen." Josie reminds me.

"Oh yeah. Well don't get drunk in front of your parents then, maybe try to avoid a hangover." I laugh.

"Dawn, turn the sign on the door would you? No more customers today." I sing.

I head into the kitchen and make sure again that everything is off and that things are sealed and packed away.

"Sir you need to leave. We are closed for new year now. Please leave." I hear Dawn argue with a customer.

I sigh and roll my eyes. I stomp through to the front of the shop. Well, it's more like a slow and loud waddle but I make my point. I'm pissed and not in the mood to be messed with.

When I see who is causing the issue I groan.

"Why are you back here?" I ask.

"Well I wanted to buy a cake of course. Why else would I be back here?" He answers back.

"One, we are closed. Two, we still do not serve vegan, gluten, and sugar free cakes!" I yell.

"I guessed that might be your response. I have recently changed my diet. I am now just vegan and gluten free." He states.

"So let me get this straight, you are now allowing yourself sugar but the rest is a no, no? And you expect a small town bakery to have plenty of those sort of cakes lying around just in case someone with special dietary requirements needs them? Am I correct?" I ask.

He smiles.

"Yes!"

"Here, I have the perfect thing for you." I hand him a box of sugar cubes.

"Sugar cubes, is this a joke?" He asks.

"No it's not. What's a joke is you coming in here each time demanding ridiculous cakes just so I can say what I've said before and what feels like a million times! We tell our customers that if they have a special dietary requirement, they are to contact us with notice so we can take the proper precautionary measures to make the bloody cake!" I yell.

As I yell I swear I feel a pop and a gush.

"Oh crap Esme! I think your waters just broke, that or you peed yourself. I can't tell which." Amy points out.

A cramp in my lower stomach makes me hold my stomach.

"Owww." I groan.

"Holy shit! Esme is in labour." Dawn points out.

"Someone call Gaige!" I yell panicked.

"I'm on it." Josie volunteers and runs upstairs. I think she saw her escape and ran.

Another contraction hits me and this time it hurts a lot more.

"Mother fucker." I complain.

"I would appreciate if you didn't use language like that around me please." The customer states.

I look to him and I swear my look alone makes him retreat a couple of steps.

"Why are you still here?! Get out!" I yell.

He turns to leave but pauses.

"Err, I don't think any of us will be going anywhere." He states, staring out of the window.

I look up and see the craziest snowstorm I've ever seen. You can barely see through it.

Gaige.

Josie!" I yell.

I hear her come running down the stairs.

"What?" She asks.

"Did you get hold of Gaige? Is he alright?" I ask.

"Yeah. He's stuck at Bob's delivering. He said he will get here as soon as he can." Josie answers nervously.

"Ohh fuck!" I pant. "Sweet mother of pearl! How do women do this for hours? I've been doing it for five minutes and I've already had enough." I complain.

"Deep breaths and keep calm, all will be okay. Women give birth everyday. You are fine." Dawn reassures me.

"Hoo-hee, hoo-hee." I pant.

"She's right of course. You see, the world's species give birth all the time and you don't see them complaining about it. Take my dog Tootsie for instance, when she gave birth to her puppies it lasted hours. I think she only howled once. She panted a lot but never made a fuss. You only have one to push out so you have it easy." The customer states.

I pant and Amy, Dawn, Josie and I look at him with murder in our eyes.

"I'm going to kill him." I growl.

"No don't be silly. You have to concentrate on yourself and the baby, ignore the idiot man over there." Dawn says walking in front of me, intentionally blocking me off from murdering the customer.

"I can kill him and give birth. I'm a woman, I can multitask. I will plead that I didn't know what I was doing, that I was delusional from the pain." I threaten and the guy looks scared.

"Actually that's a myth, women can't multi-task. No human can. You've also just preempted your plans to murder me, therefore under the criminal act of sub 2.0 sub section 14d you would be tried for murder since you planned it." He points out.

"Seriously dude, you are not making this easy for yourself." Dawn warns him.

"Owww! Son of a bitch!" I moan.

"Here, try leaning on the counter and rocking your hips from side to side. I will rub your lower back. It worked for me." Dawn advises.

I do as she says. At the end of the day she has had kids so she's been through this hell.

"Um, any chance of a tea?" The gentleman asks.

"Oh just fuck off!" I growl.

"I'll take that as a no then." He sighs, sitting down.

I breath, pant, rock my hips and Dawn, Amy, and Josie take it in turns to rub my back.

"Ahhhh, god. They're getting stronger. Where the hell is Gaige?!" I cry out in pain.

Josie place down her phone and puts it on speaker. It starts ringing and eventually Gaige answers.

"Hello?"

"Gaige!!!" I cry.

"Shit Esme, is that you?" He asks.

"No it's Princess fucking Diana from beyond the grave. Who the fuck else would it be?" I snap.

"Christ, okay. How are you doing?" He asks.

"Did you just ask how I'm doing?! Really Gaige?! My whole stomach, back, and bloody vagina are contracting to get this little human out of me and to top it all off I'm stuck here with a gluten free fucking vegan!" I yell.

"I have a name you know." The guy huffs.

"Sorry, is this moment about you right now? Are you the one that's going to have to push a human the size of a melon through a pea sized hole?! No?! I didn't think so."

"How many minutes apart are your contractions?" Gaige asks.

"I don't bloody know! We don't have a stopwatch!" I complain. "Ooow hooooo!" I cry out in pain as one hits.

Amy holds up her phone showing there's a stopwatch on it.

"I'm on my way beautiful, I promise. Stay strong. Has anyone rang Doc?" Gaige asks.

"On it!" Dawn yells.

"Does anyone want my opinion?" The customers asks.

"No!" We all yell.

"Well, you're getting it. They are currently four minutes apart. She could have the baby in the next hour or it could last hours. Who knows?" The customer shrugs.

"What's your name?" I ask, panting through the contraction.

"Norman." He states.

"Norman, how in the hell do you know so much about it?" I ask.

"I have birthed three litters from my dogs, two calves, and a litter of kittens." He states proudly.

"Sweet Jesus! Dawn are you there? Any word from Doc?" Gaige asks over the phone.

"Yeah he's on the way. He'll be about forty-five minutes though due to conditions out there." Dawn informs.

"Great. Can you hold on for Doc Esme?" Gaige asks.

"I want you here Gaige." I complain.

"I know. I am trying to get there as fast as I can." He promises.

"Oh god, here comes another one." I moan.

"That's three minutes. They're getting closer." Norman sings.

"Shit, I'm going. I will be there soon." Gaige disconnects.

I breath through it as best I can. The pain is like nothing else I've ever experienced in my life. Amy and Josie run around gathering towels, table cloths, and cushions from upstairs to make me as comfortable as possible.

I lay down and the contractions are coming thick and fast.

"You know most women find it more comfortable to give birth on all fours like cattle do." Norman points out.

"Oh my god! Someone shut him up!" I cry.

"Esme I need to pull off your underwear, tights, and boots. Don't worry I will make sure you're covered." Dawn states.

"Ha! I wonder what environmental health would say about this." Norman snorts.

"Okay that's enough from you. One more word and I am throwing you out." Amy threatens.

"Alright, only making a point." He says holding up his hands in defence.

"Where's my piping bag? I'm going to frost him. Ahhh!" I cry out.

"I think you have more pressing matters right now sweetie." Amy states.

"Okay Esme. Tell me if you feel like pushing. I'm not a doctor but I've been where you are now. Until Doc gets his ass here we are just going to have to make do." Dawn states.

"Are you not going to check how dilated she is? She could get the desire to push at eight centimetres but she needs to be ten or she will tear." Norman states.

"Tear?! I don't want to tear! I'm not pushing. Uh-uh, no way. Baby can just stay up in there. I shall just cross my legs...annndd fuuuuck!" I scream as another contraction cripples me.

"One minute and thirty-five seconds apart." Norman informs us.

"Jesus Christ will you either shut up or actually do something to help?!" Dawn yells at him.

Amy places a cold damp cloth on my forehead and tries to comfort me.

"Where the hell is Doc? Where is Gaige?!" I shout, making Josie jump.

"I will call them for an update." Josie says scurrying off.

"OH god this hurts a fucking lot! I need drugs. Does anyone have any drugs? Cannabis, cocaine, heroin. I'm open to suggestions?!" I beg.

"Um no sorry sweetie. I have Paracetamol." Amy offers.

"Paracetamol! Paracetamol! I don't have a fucking headache! I have a great big bastard baby trying to come out of my vagina!" I yell. I'm panting.

Josie comes running in.

"Doc is here! He's just parked up." Josie says with relief.

"Oh thank god!" I cry.

There's a knock on the door and Norman opens it. Doc comes rushing in from the blizzard.

"Patient is contracting every minute and a half. I think she's probably close to ten centimetres right now. Coping well with pain. No meds given." Norman says to Doc.

"Who are you?" Doc asks.

"Oh my god will you just shut up! Doc please hurry, I have a baby torturing me." I cry out as another contraction hits.

"Okay step aside please. Let me take a look." Doc crouches down and looks under the blanket.

He reaches for his bag and put on some gloves.

"Okay Esme, I can see the head. You'll probably get the urge to push and when you do, with each contraction, I want you to bare down and push with everything you've got." Doc orders.

"But Gaige." I wail.

"He will get here when he gets here. Right now your baby is ready to come. Mother nature waits for no one." Doc smiles.

"Oh god I need to push. Do I push? What if I shit myself?" I cry.

"You won't." Doc reassures.

The urge to push gets stronger and stronger. I try to fight it because I want Gaige here. I don't want him to miss it. The urge is too strong, I start pushing.

Chapter Thirty-Five

"That's it, keep pushing!" Doc orders.

I stop. I've been pushing for thirty-five minutes now and I'm exhausted.

"I can't keep pushing. I'm so tired. Maybe this is a false alarm, clearly the baby doesn't want to come out." I sigh, flopping back onto the cushions.

"Someone call Gaige, Esme needs to hear his voice. He'll help encourage her." Doc asks.

Josie dials Gaige and he answers immediately. I can hear the strong wind whistling down the phone.

"Esme?!" He yells.

I immediately start worrying. Why is he out in this awful and deadly weather?

"Gaige?!" I yell

"I'm on my way. I've had to walk. The roads were too dangerous to drive down here. I'm close, I promise." Gaige says and disconnects.

I look to the others who are also clearly worried. I don't have too much time to focus on that as another contraction hits. I start pushing.

"That's it Esme, well done! Keep going, the head is coming." Doc coaches.

I push with everything I have until I can't anymore.

"Ow-ow-ow! holy god that burns! Ow-ow-ow!" I cry out.

"The head is out. Now just a few more pushes and you will have your baby Esme." Doc smiles.

I smile.

"You can do it Esme." Dawn squeezes my shoulder and Amy squeezes my hand.

I'm about to start pushing when Gaige practically breaks through the door with a bluster of snow following him. He looks like a yeti with the snow all stuck to his clothes and face.

"Gaige!" I cry out.

Amy and Dawn move and Gaige runs to me. He takes my face in his hands and kisses me.

"I'm here. I'm here beautiful." He whispers across my lips.

I sniffle and smile. I scrunch up my face in pain. Mother nature is clearly not letting us have a moment.

"Esme, come on now. Push." Doc coaxes.

I bare down and grunt. Just imagine if the Hulk played tennis, it sounds like that. I push for what feels like forever. It honestly feels like someone is ripping me apart.

"That's it, keep going and going." Doc cheers.

I flop back down exhausted and the room is suddenly filled with the sounds of a screaming baby.

"Esme you did it!" Gaige says with emotion thick in his voice.

"Eh?" I say exhausted. It takes a moment for my brain to catch up.

"Congratulations Esme and Gaige on the birth of your baby boy!" Doc states, laying him on my stomach.

"A boy?!" I ask, my throat clogging with tears.

Doc nods and smiles.

I look down into his eyes. They are open and staring at me. I stroke his little fingers and toes, his light dusting of dark hair.

"Hey beautiful boy." I whisper, tears falling freely down my cheeks.

I turn to look up at Gaige.

"We have a son." I smile.

Gaige kisses me.

"I'm so fucking proud of you." He whispers against my lips.

"Hey, son." Gaige says, gently running his finger over his little cheeks.

"You know what this means beautiful?" Gaige states.

"What?" I ask.

"It means I get to name him." He smiles.

"You are seriously going to hold me to that? I just pushed him out of me, surely I get a say?" I argue.

"Nope. A deal is a deal." Gaige smiles,

"Sorry to interrupt you two but I have cut and clamped the cord. Gaige, if you could hold your son while Esme delivers the placenta." Doc interrupts.

"What?!" I ask.

"The placenta. If you were in hospital they would've probably given you an injection and it would've just came right out, usually with a tug on the cord. Unfortunately you're here so you have to birth it." Doc informs me.

"Well you don't see this in the movies." I state as Gaige carefully takes the baby with him wrapped in a sheet. Dawn, Josie, and Amy all coo over him. Even Norman, the customer from hell, is smiling.

I birth the placenta which is the most bizarre feeling. It's like passing a blancmange. I shudder at the thought of it.

Amy and Dawn help me prop myself up so I can sit and feed the baby while Doc clears away.

"So come on then, what are you naming our son? Just promise it isn't some bizarre crap that I can't even spell." I plead.

Gaige smiles and kisses me.

"Okay everyone, I would like you to meet Colton Jay Knox." Gaige announces.

My heart lurches and my bottom lip wobbles.

"You've given him Jay's name?" I sob.

Gaige smiles.

"Why not? From what I've heard of him he was a great guy, one of the best. Plus he loved you." Gaige states.

I sob and smile. Gaige kisses me.

"Thank you. I love the name so much. It's even macho and manly like yours. It fits perfectly." I beam.

Gaige rolls his eyes and I laugh.

"Now what? We are stuck here until the snowstorm eases." I ask.

"We will just have to wait it out. It's too dangerous to take a newborn out in this. I have rung the hospital and informed them. As soon as it eases I can drive you both to the hospital so you and baby Colton can be checked over." Doc states.

I sigh. I wish I still had my apartment, I could at least then have a bath. Amy makes everyone a coffee and makes some quick cookies for everyone.

I soon fall asleep curled up with Gaige and Colton in my arms.

I'm not sure how long we are asleep for but I wake when I feel someone tap my shoulder repeatedly. I open my eyes and see Norman right up in my face. It makes me jump.

"Hello." He smiles.

"Um, the snowstorm has stopped." He points to the window.

I focus my sleepy eyes and look out of the window. Sure enough the snowstorm has stopped.

I look to Gaige and smile. Colton is laid on his chest. All of us are wrapped up in tablecloths because that was all we had.

"Gaige." I whisper.

"Hhmm," He mumbles sleepily.

He slowly opens his eyes and smiles, looking down at Colton and then to me.

"It has stopped." I point.

He looks and then hands me Colton who stirs and stretches his little arms.

Everyone wakes up and heads home. We go to the hospital for a check up and all is fine. Colton weighs a healthy 7lb 9 ounces. Doc informed us that Colton was born at 11:25pm that night. He was a new years eve baby.

We settled in fairly easily once we got home. We weren't used to the sleepless nights but Gaige was helpful where he could be and often tried to give me a break.

One week after Colton's birth I ask Gaige to take me down the docks to speak with Jay.

Gaige parks up.

"I will wait here for you and Colton." He smiles.

"No, I want you to come with me." I state.

"You sure?" He asks.

I nod.

We walk down with Colton wrapped up in his pram to the bench. We take a seat and shiver in the cold winters breeze. Before I can speak Gaige does.

"Hey Jay, there is someone I would like you

to meet, our son Colton Jay Knox. I chose his name because of you. That way Esme will always have a piece of you with her. You still mean a lot to her and it's important that you are around in some way." Gaige smiles.

He turns to me and kisses me.

"I'm going to leave you for a minute. I will wait up here while you talk to him." Gaige says, kissing me briefly before walking off a little.

"So you've met Colton Jay. Gaige named him and he's perfect in every way. I will tell him all about you, all of our fun times, although maybe not every detail. I would like to avoid giving my son the encouragement to be underage drinking or stealing traffic cones." I laugh.

"I can't tell you how happy I am. I suppose I have you to thank for it for making me come here. I did what you asked. The only tears I cry now are happy tears. I'm not sad anymore Jay. Gaige has made me feel complete and I can't explain the love I feel for Colton, it's beyond any words."

"You ready beautiful? The temperature has really started to drop." Gaige asks shivering.

"Just one second." I yell.

"I have to get going. I miss you and I'll love you forever and always." I sniff back my tears.

It's amazing how when we are younger we plan out our lives. Sometimes they go to plan but the majority do not. I suppose it's all about what we make of the plans that go wrong and don't work out how we had expected. It's about whether we let the bad take over our lives or we choose to learn and enjoy life again. Life is the most unpredictable force. You just have to hold on tight to the good that you have. Cherish every moment and don't waste too much time crying over things that you cannot control.

Live for what makes you happy. Live for those moments that make you cry those tears of joy.

The End

Epilogue

"I can't believe you wouldn't let me throw you a hen party! Since you've become a mother you're very boring you know." Sally huffs. She's sitting in her dressing gown having her hair styled.

I roll my eyes. She hasn't stopped bitching about it. Today is my wedding day. I didn't want to wait around to get married. I still wanted there to be some snow on the ground. It's April and it's a mixture of spring and snow.

"Ow!" Sally yelps.

"I'm sorry." The stylist apologises.

I'm currently having my hair styled too whilst breast feeding Colton. It's the main reason I didn't have a hen night. With the amount of alcohol Sally would have made me drink Colton here would end up admitting himself to the Betty Ford clinic.

"Sally stop moaning! It's my wedding day. There is plenty of time for us to get shitfaced. I'm only breast feeding Colton for a couple more months and then we can get trashed." I promise her.

She sighs and smiles.

"Okay maybe I can arrange a summer trip over to visit just for that. Plus I don't want little lumberjack here forgetting his aunt Sally." She says tickling his little feet. "Also I'm just saying, you're a total cow-bag for losing your baby weight so bloody quickly! I mean, I expect when I eventually have kids the child bearing hips will remain child bearing. I shall have to get 'wide load' tattooed on my back and maybe install one of those speakers that say '*beep! Large vehicle reversing! Beep!*' I'm telling you, it's in the family genes." Sally states.

I laugh as do the stylists.

"Wow that kid is really going to town huh?" Sally laughs, pointing to Colton who has been feeding for over thirty minutes. As if he hears her he tenses and a makes sound I've become all too familiar with.

"Oh sweet god! Did he just fill his nappy?!" Sally gags.

"Yup and if you saw it you would never eat korma again." I laugh.

"Oh god I think I'm going to throw up." Sally gags.

There's a knock at the door and Dawn sticks her head in. How is it going? Nearly ready? You're getting married in forty-five minutes." She says excitedly.

"Oh crap ladies, hurry up please." I beg. "Dawn, I hate to ask, but would you be able to change Colton's nappy?" I ask.

"Sure." She answers happily. I hand him over and she takes him off to change him.

"She must have a stomach of steel! She didn't gag once." Sally says in awe.

"Dawn has kids, she's used to it." I answer.

"Ahh that makes sense." Sally nods.

"Okay ladies, we are all done." The stylist announces.

I look at Sally with her low, pinned bun. Stands of hair hang beautifully, surrounding her face.

I look in the mirror and see my hair in loose curls, pinned to one side with a beautiful crystal pin holding it. I had both of our make-up kept subtle; I didn't want anything too overpowering.

"Thank you ladies so so much. I really appreciate it. Our hair looks amazing." I say, honestly loving how special I feel.

"It's time." Sally smiles.

I nod and get up to put my dress on. It's a simple ivory fitted dress with lace overlay. Its V-neckline is wide to the edge of the shoulders. It is buttoned all the way down my back to the floor where there is a small train. I smile to myself; I don't think I've ever felt more elegant and pretty in all of my life.

"Wow, you look smoking hot." Sally says whistling.

"I know!" I clap excitedly.

"Oh wow Sally, you look gorgeous. Hottest maid of honour ever!" I compliment.

Her long satin deep red spaghetti strapped dress hugs her every curve. She looks stunning.

"I fucking know Flynn is going to be sitting through your wedding with a boner the entire time." She giggle.

"Wow, nice thought for me to have while I say my vows." I answer sarcastically.

Dawn comes back in with Colton in his special wedding day onesie. It has a illusion that he's in a little suit. He looks adorable. Each day he looks more and more like Gaige with his dark hair and chocolate eyes. I fear that I may have to beat the girls off of him with a stick when he's older.

We make our way down to the dock near The Sunken Ship where we had our first date. It's also where we are having our reception. They decorated the outside in fairy lights and it looks beautiful.

Frank greets us from the car and smiles.

"Esme you look stunning." Frank states, kissing my cheek.

"Thank you." I beam up at him.

"Oh crap! My flowers! I forgot them, I…"

"Here." Amy hands them to me. "I knew you would forget them. It's an odd bunch of flowers to be having altogether." Amy states.

I smile looking down at my bouquet of red roses, white lilies, and daisies.

"They are just my favourite flowers." I shrug.

Dawn and Amy take Colton and take their seats.

"Ready to sat goodbye to Mrs Tucker and hello to Mrs Knox?" Frank asks, holding out his arm and smiling.

"I'm ready, but there will always be a part of me that is Mrs Tucker." I smile.

The music starts. Clare de lune.

"This is it sister!" Sally says excitedly, squeezing my hand.

She turns and walks off down the aisle. I take a deep breath as we follow her. Gaige turns when Bob nudges him.

His eyes land on mine and he smiles. His eyes lazily sweep down my body appreciatively. I bite my bottom lip, knowing what that look means.

Once we reach him Frank kisses my cheek and takes a seat. Gaige pulls me into his arms and kisses me.

"Erm, that is for the end of the ceremony." The vicar coughs.

Gaige pulls back slightly and whispers across my lips.

"You look unbelievably stunning."

We exchange our vows and people cheer. Gaige takes Colton from Dawn and holding my hand we walk back down the isle. Everyone throws confetti.

Half way through the reception I go outside for some air. I wrap a shawl around my shoulders and sigh, looking up at the night sky.

"You okay beautiful?" Gaige asks. Coming up behind me he wraps his arms around my waist and kisses my neck.

"I'm more than okay." I say honestly.

"Ready for some super cheesy shit?" I ask.

"Hit me with it." Gaige laughs.

"You've made me the happiest woman on the planet. I honestly didn't think I would ever get to feel happiness like this ever again. I can't tell you how much or even try to explain how I feel, there aren't enough words that describe it." I say with emotion.

"Can I hit you back with some cheesiness?" Gaige asks.

"Sure." I laugh and turn to face him in his arms.

"You don't need to tell me or try and find the right words because I feel it too. There is nothing that can describe what we feel or what we have." Gaige states, stroking my cheek.

"I love you tall dark and grumpy." I smile and lean into his hand.

"I love you beautiful." Gaige smiles before kissing me.

I lived through hell. I had to watch my loved one suffer and pass away. I had a gaping hole in my heart that I thought could never be repaired. I was wrong. Gaige helped me heal, he helped me to rebuild my heart and my soul.

Life is too short. Love hard, love without fear, love with your whole heart and love unconditionally. Forever and always.

Eternally Grateful

Thank You For Reading My First Standalone Novel. I Hope You Enjoyed It.

If You Are New To My Books You Can Find The Rocke Series On Amazon. Also Avaliable On Kindle Unlimited.

Upcoming Releases Satan's Outlaws Series.

Follow Me On Facebook, Instagram, Twitter, And Goodreads For All Of My Latest Releases, News, And Giveaways.

Printed in Poland
by Amazon Fulfillment
Poland Sp. z o.o., Wrocław